Picking Up BREADCRUMBS

A JOURNEY OF UNCOVERING FAMILY SECRETS

URSULA HUGHES

ISBN 978-1-7379178-0-9 Paperback
ISBN 978-1-7379178-1-6 Hardcover

Library of Congress Control Number: 2022906941

San Jose, California

For Sid, Darren & Melissa, with my deepest love.

&

In memory of Johnny

During the Great Migration of the 1900s, millions of Black families fled the Jim Crow south seeking a better life in major cities across the U.S.

Their secrets traveled with them — into the next generation…

CHAPTER 1

April 7, 2010, Los Viento, California...
I'm a mom whose life was shattered on April 7th,
but vengeance came through a detective...

My internal clock welcomes me without the alarm buzzing. Most mornings I'm awakened by a single gray stream of light peeking through the shutters. This pale stream, however, initially has me puzzled. The peaceful drip of the falling rain adds to the serenity. A drop glides down the window, catches another, and moves with effortless motion down the glass.

Adding to the bliss is Quentin's shallow breathing, lying on his side and dozing peacefully. Watching the motion of his back rise, then wane, is pure bliss. Moving closer, my chest against his back, I rest my cheek against the hollow of his spine and wrap my arms around him. He stirs, exhales, and resumes his quiet slumber. I don't want to move.

I'll snuggle in for a few more moments of shut-eye.

Beep. Beep. Beep. Beep. Beep. Beep.

Dang. Maybe just a few more minutes.

"Babe, you'd better get going. You know how long it takes you," he whispers while tapping my thigh with his fingertips.

Quentin's groggy murmur is enough to motivate me. Always purposeful and devoted, he's the quintessential man's man. Middle-aged stability is who he is and what I'd envisioned he'd become when we started dating in college.

Somehow the rain has thrown off my vibe. My brain feels like it's in a fog. I'd better get a move on before Robbie wakes up. I had promised to make banana pancakes for him this morning. Tossing the covers off, I sit up and begin making mental notes of the course of the day.

Staggering into the bathroom, the cold tile prompts the quickening of my steps. The grogginess starts to wear off as I step into the shower. I'm welcomed by the lavender scent as shower gel in my palm mixes with the mist and glides across my skin. Pulsating bursts of water beckon me into a new day along with the scent of the dried eucalyptus leaves hanging from the showerhead. I think I'm awake and coming to my senses.

Outside my bedroom, I can hear Robbie's movements in the other bathroom, as the sound of water swishes in the sink. I'm glad he's up and moving, without me having to wake him. He's been sleeping like a ton of bricks. When I'd done his laundry last week, there was the strangest thing. There was the usual stuff of an eight-year old boy—some pants grungier than others—but I couldn't get over his polo shirts. Every one of his uniform shirts looks like they've been through the wringer. The collars look like a puppy has chewed on them. I keep buying new ones, and before long he does the same thing. I can't figure out why he has started that again. He's been so solemn lately. A few weeks ago, his pediatrician said nothing was physically wrong. I just don't understand it. And the psychologist said he was just adjusting to a new environment. He's been somewhat listless.

Last week I'd noticed he wasn't interested in playing video games, like he usually is.

As I head down the stairs, I can't help but worry. For some strange reason, he seems as though he's not as mature as the other third graders. I'm probably imagining it, but when I was watching the kids line up for class the other day, he suddenly seemed smaller than the other boys. I know my imagination can surely go sideways.

Robbie adjusts the stool against the counter just as I slide the empty plastic bowl of batter across the granite counter and into the sink of sudsy water. On the range, the pancakes take shape as the bubbles form small craters on their tops. The last one forms a brown crust around the edges right before I scoop it onto the plate.

I know. I'm just a worrier. Quentin says so all the time.

"Mom? Mom?"

"Huh? What, sweetie?"

"You forgot to put the bananas on top."

"Oh."

At least his appetite is good. Whew.

I smile as I watch syrup gather in the corner of his mouth. That's my baby boy. He's got the cutest grin, especially with those two front teeth missing. He's growing up so fast, but at other times he seems like he's stuck back in kindergarten. Is it insecurity? A new school would make anyone nervous.

I'm beyond thrilled that Bethel Academy had a third grade opening. We'd been on the waiting list for weeks. And now he's finally in. He's still adjusting, but Robbie's going to be so happy in this new environment. Lakeview Elementary was OK, but Bethel offers so much. The curriculum is outstanding.

"Good morning, big guy! How's my man doing?"

"Fine."

Quentin walks around the kitchen island, to the counter, where the platter of pancakes lie.

"Mom's pancakes are the best, huh?"

"Mmm-hmm."

Quentin pulls the stool up to the counter next to Robbie to enjoy the few moments before we all have to head off in different directions. He'll be gone for a few days on a business trip to a client's site. Owning his own construction company has been all he's ever dreamed of—having known from the time he was a boy that he wanted to be in business for himself. He's worked so hard.

Quentin Shields. A man who positively dances to the beat of his own drum. Self-assured and focused. Those were some of the characteristics I saw when we met in college. I knew that Quentin would chase his dreams with all the gusto he could muster. I felt somewhat intimidated at the time by his determination and focus. Now through tons of sweat and God's blessing, he's realized his dream—Shields Construction & Design Services.

Quentin leans over, gripping the back of Robbie's head with his large palm before he kisses the top of his head.

"Bye, man. I'll see you in a few days. Love you."

"Okay, Dad. Meet me on the field after school on Friday, okay?"

"All right, son."

Quentin stands and reaches over, tenderly kissing me on the forehead. I already feel sadness washing over me, knowing that he'll be gone for a few days. I gather the dishes, swish the water over them, then put the plates in the dishwasher.

"OK, big boy, let's go." I reach for my keys on the hook at the kitchen entry.

With Robbie a few paces behind me, we head toward the front door. His backpack is just where he left it last night—by the console table in the entry. He slings it over his shoulder, opens the door, and heads down the steps and across the circular driveway to the car.

As we whisk through the morning traffic, I can't help but notice Robbie's distant gaze as he peers out the window. He's quiet, almost detached, like he's been for the past few weeks. Not his previous chatty self.

He's changing so fast right in front of my eyes. I find myself studying him more than usual. I wonder what's so intriguing that he's fixated on. My eyes follow his gaze out the window and upon the ordinary scenes of our route to school—same streets, same neighborhood; nothing new. I guess he's just deep in thought and observation.

I turn from the main thoroughfare and onto the side street of the old established neighborhood. Neatly trimmed hedges nestle against the front windows of the small homes. School zone signs along the way signal the changing pace ahead.

The energy of the bustling traffic transfers to the rhythmic pace of children, making their way from parents' cars in the school parking lot to the brick building sheltered in the center of the block. This morning's volunteer crossing guard appears to be some student's mother, who cheerfully moves the children along and gestures to drivers to be cautious.

Bless her. It's all I can do to get us out of the door on time, let alone put in the required volunteer hours. She motions, directing me to turn left into the parking lot. As I do, Robbie unfastens his seatbelt and lifts his backpack off the floor.

"Have a good day, sweetie."

"Kay. Bye Mom."

His feet hit the pavement before he turns and closes the car door. Classmates and older kids hop from their parents' cars, collectively migrating to the school building. Robbie's pace merges with the other children's, as I watch through the rearview mirror. It strikes me how somber he looks as he walks in the direction of his classroom.

With little effort my car makes its way in the direction of the freeway for the thirty minute commute. As if it's on autopilot, my thoughts shift gears to work-related projects and goings-on in the office. Being the editor-in-chief at *Dynamic Parent* is beyond challenging. Always a new layout or design approval is needed. There's the constant overseeing and drawing up of budget proposals. Not to mention the new series we're doing on Stranger Danger. Never ending, but it's quite fulfilling.

As I enter the building, I see that the usual hustle and bustle is in full swing. My heels click on the tiled marble floor as I make my way onto the elevator. Never a dull moment. Always a new project calling, as the elevator travels to the tenth floor where the design team sits. As I enter my office, I glance at my nameplate—Darby Coleman-Shields. Before Quentin and I got married, I mentioned to him how I thought that Coleman hyphenated with Shields would have a nice ring. A bit more pizzazz than a simple last name—not that anything was wrong with the simpler name, Darby Shields. He'd commented that he thought it was a bit over the top, but that it was my name to live with.

These days I feel like I'm swimming upstream. Between editing upcoming issues and listening to writers pitch their stories as, "the next big fish you want to catch," it's all I can do to keep afloat. Sometimes I feel exhausted just trying to make it through dinner in the evening.

Truth be told, I amazed myself by exceeding all of my metrics. But last year's success is a thing of the past. In terms of performance goals, the publisher's prevailing mindset is always "What have you done for me lately?"

My mobile phone on the desk vibrates. *Wonder who that is?*

Hmm, the caller ID says Bethel Christian.

"This is Darby Shields."

"Hello, Mrs. Shields. This is Principal Donnelly over at Bethel. Robbie is fine, but I wonder if you can come by my office within the next hour. I have something I'd like to discuss with you, along with his teacher, Ms. Garcia."

"Oh, okay."

"Mrs. Shields, please drive carefully. I can assure you that Robbie is fine. He's here in my office right now, and I don't want you to be alarmed."

"Okay. I'll be there shortly."

I wonder what's going on?

My mind begins to race as to what the concern could possibly be. Several weeks ago Robbie had to stay in detention because he wouldn't stay in his seat during class time. Ms. Garcia said he had been agitated and disruptive after repeated warnings. She also mentioned that he was not his usual self that day.

I scurry out of the office and tap on Vince's partially open door. His head is buried in some documents as he talks on the phone. He looks up, smiles, and motions for me to come in. I'm thrilled to be on his team. Micromanaging is not his style.

"Hey, Vince, Better Baby had to cancel today, but they're still on the hook. I'm heading out for an early lunch. I'll sync up with you this afternoon."

"All right, Darby. Good job bringing in those other advertisers."

As I head down the elevator, I'm bewildered.

What the heck is going on with Robbie?

I pull up to the school and enter the front office, trying not to appear frantic. Entering the brick building, I walk as calmly as I can to the front office. Behind the counter, the steady rhythm of the copy machine hums through the office. At a nearby side table, a trio of junior high girls form an assembly line, stuffing envelopes with precision. I'm greeted by a fortyish secretary, with a friendly demeanor. Before she can ask me my name, the woman seated at the desk behind her rises.

"Oh hello, Mrs. Shields. Principal Donnelly is expecting you. Please follow me."

I follow on the heels of Ms. Donnelly's assistant. The clickety-clack of her footsteps on the shiny linoleum is doing nothing to soothe my raw nerves. The lively corridor stretches to Ms. Donnelly's office at the end of the hall. Pictures of previous years' middle school graduates line the walls and cast shadows of youthful exuberance. As I approach the open door, I see Robbie seated in a chair against the wall, next to Ms. Garcia. Principal Donnelly is seated at her desk, facing her door. Principal Donnelly rises from her desk as she sees her assistant and I approaching. She escorts me in and closes the door.

I'm confused. There's a sudden shift in the atmosphere. I sense that Robbie's not in trouble, yet the heaviness clogs the air like an impending fate.

"Hello, Mrs. Shields. I'm so glad you could come right over. Please have a seat." She offers a sullen smile as she extends her arm towards the empty chair directly across from Robbie and Mrs. Garcia.

"Thank you." I acknowledge her gesture, but my gaze is on Robbie. "Hi, honey."

"Hi, Mom."

Circular beads of moisture rest on his brow. His eyes widen as if he's just bolted from a bad dream. The front collar of his polo shirt looks like it's been through a grinder. I can tell he's been chewing it since he left home this morning—some kind of nervous habit he's recently formed, which I had pointed out to his psychologist. The left collar is still damp. Just above the buttons. *What's this anxiety all about? What the hell is going on?*

Ms. Garcia speaks softly. "Mrs. Shields, Robbie has something he wants to tell you." The thickness of the silence cannot lift the heaviness.

"What is it, hon?"

Robbie's legs stick out in front of him. His hands slide up and down both arms of the chair. I reach over to him, bending down at eye level, while I wrap both hands around his waist. His head drops, as the tears pour from his eyes, down his face, and onto his shirt.

I'm terrified, and I look over to Ms. Garcia.

"It's okay, Robbie," she softly whispers.

"Mom … Mom…"

"Yes, sweetie, tell me what's wrong?" I ask as I return my gaze to him.

Softly he whimpers, "Mommy, Pa … Pa … Papa George hurt me."

My gut tightens. The wind rushes out of me. "Wha…Where did he hurt you?"

Robbie's voice is hardly audible. "He… he hurt my bottom."

Darkness overtakes me and swallows me whole.

CHAPTER 2

My head throbs as if it's being ruptured by a seismic shift. Both my heart and head are confused. Where do they exist in my body? Are they actually *in* my body?

The rupture begins from my head, tearing down my anatomy and causing unimaginable bursts along the way. I can't stop the feeling as the pain I'm experiencing moves from my cranium to my spine and legs, and pierces throughout my total existence.

I'm not in my body. This is not me. Not Robbie. This room is not real.

I'm being transfixed above my body. Suspended in the air, looking from above. Seeing Robbie trembling and peering back at me. Is that my little boy?

Is the woman in the chair me? She can't be me, because *this* is not happening.

This. Is. Not. Real.

My muscles throb and scream, confirming that I'm in a conscious nightmare. I need air.

Whose voice is that?

That sounds like a primal scream? A wicked force is pounding on my chest, beating me! Looking down as the scene is displayed through a foggy lens, Robbie's uncontrollable sobs grab my attention, causing me to come back and grasp this agonizing moment as it really is.

My baby boy? *Oh God, no! Oh God, please tell me this is a mistake.*

Somewhat still suspended, I'm being lowered—just a bit—as childhood scenes display in fast-forward motion before me. The scenes are moving swiftly, like dominoes falling one after the other. My mind travels through the mist, lingering from time to time, upon particular scenes. I'm viewing each scene as though peering through a clear window. Every frame is transparent.

Yes, *this is real.*

And I'm in every one of the scenes, as the light passes through the transparency of my childhood.

It's as if I'm in two places simultaneously. One, reaching to hold Robbie. He stands, his little head lowered, an arm's length in front of me. In the second place, my eyes are open, fixated and gazing at my dysfunctional family history playing out before me. Slowly, my mind reaches out and takes hold of each bewildering childhood incident in motion. My consciousness slowly touches the truth, in a painful attempt at uncovering its purpose. In my hands I hold each scene, imaginary—yet real—which adds meaning to the horrifying magnitude of it all. I can vividly see my two older sisters in each of the distant scenes of my youth. The image of me opening Gloria's door, to find her lying in bed as Papa George lunges toward her. Her arms swing violently at him. They both look horrified when they see me standing there. He suddenly leaves her alone and runs out of the room.

Every muscle in my body aches.

It's real. This is real. In the slicing of seconds, some of those scenes now make sense.

Oh my God. He molested each of them too.
Oh Jesus.

Except for the loud ticking of the clock, which sits on the credenza, the room remains silent. Only moments ago I stepped into Ms. Donnelly's office. And in three horrific minutes, my world has been shattered into a million pieces.

The dark motion that was once in my mind has gathered its spirit, left me, and drifted out the door, into the light.

The spring breeze from Principal Donnelly's window allows me to inhale. I have to. My baby boy is alive, yet he's not really alive.

If I don't breathe, he can't breathe.

He looks quite different than when I dropped him off only a few hours ago. His eight-year old body suddenly looks as though it's four.

How could I have missed this?

Ohhh, Jesus. Why? How? Oh please, God.

I have to come back. For Robbie.

My primal scream has given way to a murmur which is barely audible.

"Oh, my baby. Oh, God! Robbie!

He stares at me without any expression.

"I'm so, so sorry." My whispers do nothing to bring his gaze to me.

Can he hear me? He looks like he's here, but somehow I know …

He's somewhere else.

"Robbie? Robbie?"

Only seconds have passed since he muttered the terrifying words. My arms are gripped around him as he clutches my waist. The glimpses of childhood scenes lasted for nanoseconds although the lapse in time feels like I've traveled backwards for hours.

I rub my hand against his clammy forehead. His body trembles against my chest.

"Let me get you both some water," Ms. Garcia says as she leaves the room. The opening of the office door infuses new oxygen into the room.

"We'll leave you two alone for a while." Principal Donnelly follows Ms. Garcia.

I hold Robbie's head and rub his back. "Babe, I'm so, so sorry. You did nothing wrong and you are so brave for telling me this. No one is going to hurt you anymore."

I hand him a tissue. He nods and dabs his eyes.

⸻

Later back at home, Robbie turns in his sleep as I rise from his bed to answer my buzzing phone. We managed to eat dinner and afterward, all I could do was hold him in his bed until he fell asleep. I step into the hallway to take the call.

"I'm so sorry, Mrs. Shields," Ms. Donnelly says. "I'm sorry to disturb you this evening." I can sense her uneasiness. "I just wanted to call you and let you know that we have followed protocol and have already notified CPS."

"Of course."

"We are here for Robbie, so please let us know whatever he needs."

"Thanks, Ms. Donnelly."

"Um, Mrs. Shields?"

"Yes."

"This…This is extremely hard, but I feel you should know. Robbie said it happened more than once."

"OK. Thanks, Mrs. Donnelly."

I'm numb. I tap the phone off before peeking inside Robbie's door. In light of what my father has done to him, I'm amazed at how peaceful he looks. Moments later I receive a return call from Robbie's psychologist.

"How in the hell did you miss this! You're the expert on childhood abuse and trauma!"

"Mrs. Shields, I'm so sorry. When I heard your voicemail…my heart goes out to Robbie. Sometimes the signs are not evident. Please bring him in tomorrow."

I tap the phone off and stand against the wall in the darkness.

The load is with me as I try to sleep—holding me like the clenched teeth of a beast with his prey. I feel as though I'm trying to escape from a horror movie. The damp pillow reinforces the anguish of the news. I think about Ms. Donnelly's call after Robbie and I arrived home. How she said that Robbie said it happened more than once.

I can't help but replay the scenes over and over in my mind. Like moisture, they seep through my consciousness—drenching my reasoning, causing me to confront the chilling reality. How Papa George has always doted on Robbie. He often picks Robbie up on Fridays to take him to an afternoon movie. Mom would beg for him to spend the night so that Quentin and I could have a date night. My mind then goes back to the days when Robbie was first born. How special he was. Their first grandchild.

Both my dad and my mom were ecstatic when he was born. He and my mother were uncharacteristically giddy. Something wildly beyond my imagination. How they doted on him was nothing short of unbelievable. It was because of Robbie that the rest of us began calling my father Papa George, since Robbie called him that and it had quickly become a term of endearment.

And now to think that *my* father could do such a thing? The man that everyone thinks is solid and nothing short of a man of high integrity. He's even a deacon in his church.

The scenes play on. And on. This doesn't make sense.

But somehow it does.

How could evil be so close to *me*? I always thought of evil as something *out there*, certainly not among *something*, or *someone*, so familiar to me. Not the ones I love and have trusted.

Who the hell is this person?!

Papa George. My Dad, who beams when he introduces me.

"This is my youngest daughter, Darby."

I'm torn. I can't move. I feel as though my father is embracing me with a smile, yet shoving a knife in me, at the same time. My neck is throbbing.

There's no question that Robbie is telling the truth. It all makes sense now. He's deeply broken and torn. His wounds are not visible. I can't believe we've been so stupid.

God, I literally don't want to think it's true. But that small voice keeps telling me to lean into the truth, no matter the pain. I wish I could erase the memories which seemed trivial at the time. Now the images and events have begun to gnaw and torment me.

The signs were there. How did we miss them?

God. I want to wake up. This is a very bad dream.

Please tell me it's a mistake. *My father molested my son!*

Help. Me. Pleaseeeeee.

How will I tell Quentin? He's had to travel for business a lot lately. He obviously detected something in my voice yesterday when he called to say goodnight. I think about our conversation last night as I drag my body from the bed.

"What's wrong, babe? You sound really tired."

"Oh, it's just been a long day."

I heard the magnitude of concern in his voice. How in the world is he going to take this?

He's normally calm and steady--always the voice of reason. His moods and reactions don't swing too high, nor too low.

"How's the project going?" I asked.

"Really good. We're actually ahead of schedule, so I'll be home tomorrow, early evening. How's Robbie?"

"Oh, uh, he's had a rough day, and he went to bed shortly after dinner."

"Oh. Give him a kiss for me, and I'll see you guys tomorrow evening."

"OK, Love you."

"Love you too."

Still dazed, I had clicked the off button on the phone with the slight motion of an involuntary reflex and remembered…My mind drifted to one of the first times he and my dad traveled out of town for a contractor's convention.

"Hey, Pop!" Quentin is full of excitement as he opens the front door.

"Morning, Quentin." Papa George eagerly steps inside. I watch from the kitchen as the two embrace. "I know I'm early, but I can't wait to get on the road with you—thanks for inviting me. A bathroom convention is a thing I've never seen—let alone dreamed about. Shoot! This ole country boy could never have imagined such a thing. Growing up, all I ever knew was an outhouse. I was almost ready to leave home before we had an indoor toilet."

As the two walk from the entrance, into the kitchen, they chuckle at my dad's boyhood memory.

"Well, Pop, I'm happy to see you so jazzed about a bathroom convention." Quentin laughs.

"Morning, Baby." My father leans over the kitchen island and kisses my cheek. "Where's that grandson of mine?"

"He's in his room. He should be out in a minute. Want some coffee?"

"Nah, thanks."

After several minutes Robbie comes squealing down the hall. Clearly, he's heard his grandfather's voice. My father scoops him up and tickles him under his armpit, leaving Robbie laughing all the more.

"All right, son, have a good day. I'll pick you up tomorrow from Pre-K." Quentin leans down and hugs Robbie, then turns and kisses me.

"You guys have a good time and drive carefully."

"Bye, Daddy."

As I remember this scene and how Quentin and my father got along so well, I wonder, how I will tell Quentin about Robbie? There's no way I'll let Robbie go through the pain of repeating himself. I don't know how to navigate this. My life has changed forever.

CHAPTER 3

Yesterday's nightmare is still with me, and reminds me of the present reality. The dull throb in my head lingers, like a menace who's threatening to stay. The minutes on the clock roll to ten after seven, as I drag myself from the bed.

When I open Robbie's door, the stream of gray light stretches from his window and into the hallway. Its lurking shadow taunts me about yesterday's revelation. Amazingly, he's sound asleep.

I'll let him sleep as long as he wants to—even if he's late for school. Heading back into my room, I debate whether I should get back into the tousled bed or head for the shower. My muscles ache as if I've been punched all over.

I wish Quentin was here.

I feel as though I'm in a fog. Moments after drying off, I try going through the motions of my regular routine. But there's nothing typical about what has happened to Robbie. And there's no mistaking the explosion that's moving inside me. It's oozing through my pores and grows hotter by the minute, looking for its escape.

I take slacks and a blouse from the closet before reaching for my laptop bag above the clothes. Instead, a monogrammed dust bag falls from the shelf. I grab it as it comes down, and immediately remember that inside is the purse Quentin bought me several years ago. He'd been at a convention in New York and surprised me with it. I'd forgotten all about it, because I only use it occasionally.

I haven't carried this purse in a while. Maybe I'll use it today.

I pull out the stuffed tissue wrapping inside the purse and gasp when I see what lies at the bottom.

⁓

"Love you. Don't forget that when I pick you up, you have an appointment to talk with Dr. Gardner."

"Okay."

I watch Robbie as he gets out of the car and merges with the other children. Outwardly, he looks unscathed. Unharmed. But appearances are deceiving. Internally is a very wounded little boy with a bleeding soul.

He waits on the sidewalk with the other children, until the crossing guard blows his whistle and motions for them to cross. When he's no longer in sight, I pull into the street and turn my car in the direction of Denton, to pay my father a visit.

During the thirty mile drive, I can think of nothing other than holding him accountable for violating Robbie. He won't get to speak. I won't stand for some snarky denial. Just like that, it'll be over. Nothing else. The end.

Along the highway the California poppies have sprouted, signaling signs of spring. The season of renewal. A sign that all is well. Yes, soon it *will* be. I take my sunglasses from the console and take in the warmth of the sun beaming through the windshield. Everything will be just fine.

Up ahead I see that there is roadwork and repaving going on. My fingers tremble as they grip the wheel. Maybe I'll have to take an indirect route, which will be longer. I wonder if there will be a detour. The traffic creeps along for what seems like an eternity. Along the way, workers repave the highway, while a few others motion to keep the flow going. I'm relieved when the mild congestion ends, and the movement picks up.

The suburban street is noticeably quiet when I turn onto his lane. The mature foliage of the neighborhood tells the story of a place where children once played, but have now left the nest. The eastern sun has settled on the dew-kissed lawns, leaving sidewalks dampened from its moisture. A neighborhood cat who has been sunbathing against the garage door scrambles away at the sound of my car pulling against the curb.

Yes, finally I'm here. I find Papa George in his front yard tending to his award-winning roses which line the window. He's got on his usual baseball cap that he's never without, along with his oversized gardening shirt. Although he's almost 70, he could easily pass for a man in his late 50s. He attributes his youthful appearance to the amount of melanin in his skin. Whenever he gets the opportunity, he loves to chant, "the blacker the berry, the sweeter the juice," before breaking into deep laughter. With his back towards me, his tall, lanky frame is in full view.

He steps back, admires his rose bushes, then bends over to pull a stray weed that has sprouted from the ground beneath them.

Perfect.

I reach for my purse on the seat beside me and step out of the car. He hears the car door closing, and turns around with a pleasant, though puzzled, look of surprise.

This is even better.

"Hi Darby, didn't you go to work today?"

I don't acknowledge him.

Instead, I take the pistol from my purse, and aim directly at his chest. My throat is dry. My bottom lip shakes, yet my hand is steady.

He drops the garden glove he's been holding. His mouth opens. His body stiffens as he stares at the pistol pointed directly at his chest.

I squeeze the trigger. It makes a clicking sound. I squeeze it again, but it doesn't fire.

And that's when I realize, there are no bullets inside.

CHAPTER 4

Robbie stares at his plate as he moves the salad around with his fork.

"How'd it go with the wagon project we carved for social studies?" Quentin's eyes scan Robbie with a look of concern.

"Oh, it was okay. I got a B on it," Robbie's disheartened voice trails along faintly.

Quentin's chewing stops, but his stunned expression stays. The dismal atmosphere hovers like a smoke-filled room that's been vacated by its offenders. Robbie's glance at me is his signal that he wants to disappear.

"Honey, why don't you go on and finish your homework. I'll be there shortly to check it, okay?"

Without further prompting, he heads down the hall. The sound of his bedroom door shutting follows. My throat feels as though it's closing. Running my fingers around the edge of the placemat, I quietly begin the conversation with Quentin.

"Why don't we go sit outside on the deck. I want to talk with you about something," I gently prompt. "I know what's been going on with Robbie and why he's been struggling.

Standing in front of the kitchen sink, Quentin stares silently out the window. Slowly he turns around and follows me from the dining room and onto the deck.

The creases between his brows have deepened. Gone are the playful lines which usually lay on the outside corners of his eyes. Without saying a word, his piercing brown eyes convey that he has my full attention. He stands outside, next to the patio table and waits for me to begin. "I got a call from Principal Donnelly yesterday morning. She asked me to come to her office because she had something to discuss with me."

"Okay?"

"When I got there, she and Ms. Garcia were in her office with Robbie." My throat tightens as I try to hold back the tears. "Once I was seated, she told me that Robbie had something to tell me."

Listening intently, his bewildered look speaks for itself. I can almost hear his thoughts. *What's going on? Cut to the chase.*

With trepidation, I press on. "After some prompting, Robbie told me that something awful happened to him." I then proceed with the unimaginable. "He told me...he told me that Papa George molested him."

Seconds pass. Quentin's lips, already pressed together, now stiffen. His eyes squint closely together, then diverge from mine.

"What'd you say?"

"My dad molested Robbie." My matter-of-fact statement, which I've said over and over in my head, now spills from my lips.

There. I've said it out loud.

The shock of the silence is like dying again. I can no longer hold it together. I've done it all day. The stream of tears spill down my neck and settle onto my blouse.

Quentin's jaws tighten. The muted air feels suffocating.

He lowers his head into the palms of his hands, as the seconds give way to minutes, which seem eternal. His lips tremble.

"Did…Did he say anything else? Wha… what else did he say?"

"His exact language was that 'Papa George hurt my bottom.' It was pretty clear with all the distress he was in, what he meant." Reaching for a napkin to wipe my eyes, I shake my head. "I called Dr. Johnson. He'll examine him tomorrow morning." My throat has tightened. The fountain of tears flow into my napkin.

"Darby, this is unimaginable. Papa George is my friend. I've respected him—loved him like he was my *own* father. This is unreal—that he would do this to our son!" Quentin's voice rises while he tries to make sense of what is imperceivable. His pulsating anger grows louder as I notice the veins on his neck, just beneath his skin.

Pushing himself violently from the table, Quentin stands and begins to pace the deck. "Honey, please don't let Robbie hear you. He's been through so much."

Usually composed and levelheaded, the magnitude of the news I've just delivered moves intensely across Quentin's face. His eyes grow dark and his face changes into an expression that I don't recognize. He swiftly turns and treks back into the house. With deliberate steps, he heads for the laundry room.

Instinctively, I dart behind him, trying to keep pace.

Grabbing his keys off the hook on the wall, he turns to find me standing between him and the door leading to the garage.

"Where are you going?"

He ignores my question, looks past me and focuses on the door behind me. With a forced cadence, he responds, "I. Need. You. To. Move. Out. Of. My. Way."

"Not until you tell me where you're going," I say, hoping my intonation mirrors his.

It's a standoff. After what feels like an eternity, his tone softens. "Move, Babe." His weight shifts from one leg to the other. His response has become ingratiating, though telling, as I interpret frustration simmering just beneath his rage.

"Tell me where. Please."

"I've got to head back to the showroom to pick up something." He looks directly from the door and knowingly into my eyes. He declares coldly, "Then I'm going to have a come-to-Jesus with your father."

My thoughts race to his gun. The one he keeps at his showroom.

"Noooo!! Please, Quentin. Don't! What good would it do if *you* end up dead?" My appeal is overtaken by my sobs, causing my legs to give way and end in a squatted position against the wall. As the words leave me, I'm overwhelmed by the sense of an undercurrent that wants Quentin, targeting him as an unsuspecting victim who's about to be engulfed in its surge of destruction.

"I'm not the one who's gonna end up dead!" he yells.

"No! No! Please don't go. I already did!"

"Huh?"

"I came across the gun you gave me a few years ago. Robbie was a little guy. He had started walking and was into everything. All I could think about was accidental deaths in the home from children who find guns."

"Yeah?" Quentin is growing impatient.

"It was in a handbag on my top shelf. I got it out and went to my father's house."

"And?" The tension in his voice rises as he waits for me to finish.

"He was in the yard, I pulled the trigger, but the gun didn't fire. I remembered later that I had stored the bullets in the closet in the spare bedroom."

He closes his eyes and exhales intently through his mouth-- clearly relieved.

The release of his breath steadies me, as I proceed in a deliberate fashion. "And even though we're in a lot of pain, killing my father is not the way."

He turns to leave the laundry room, then in a move that seems unsure of what to do, he brushes past me and slams the door. Next, I hear the sound of heavy blows repeatedly striking the garage wall.

After some time, he comes back, winded and dripping with sweat.

"What the hell am I *supposed* to do? If he thinks he's gonna get away with this he's got another thought coming." His wails reach a crescendo as he paces the small laundry room. "He was more than *your* father. I treated him as if he were *my* father!" Quentin's screams have turned into convulsions, interrupted only when he pauses to question himself. "I took him to conventions with me! A few times he went with me and Robbie to baseball games!"

"He's *my* father!" I wail. Let *me* handle it!

His eyes grow wide as he processes the admiration that Papa George displayed for him. "He used to tell me that I was the son he wish he'd had!" Then he whimpers, "How did I miss this? How?" With his hands covering his eyes and his back against the washer, Quentin breaks down onto the floor beside me and sobs. "I'm supposed to protect our family. I'm so, so-o-orry."

My spirit is overwhelmed by the forceful energy of this sinister intruder. He has brazenly pulled up a chair, made himself comfortable, and sat down to dinner. With the clear intention of taking up permanent residency, I can sense his depraved personality—beyond wicked.

The automatic timer shuts off the ceiling light as we both weep in the darkness.

This monstrosity is larger than life.

CHAPTER 5

April 13, 2010 Los Viento, California...

My phone buzzes as I step into the lobby while heading toward the elevator and the fifth floor of Vanguard Publishing. The display indicates that the number is blocked, but my curiosity has the best of me, so I tap to answer the call.

"Hello?"

"Hello, this is Investigator Jim Simpson, Los Viento Police Department. Is this Darby Shields?"

"Yes."

"I'm calling about Robbie Shields and an allegation of sexual assault by George Coleman." The forcefulness in his voice sounds as if it could kick down a door.

"Yes," I answer, ready to hear what the next steps will be.

"I want to let you know that a case has been opened and an investigation will begin. Is this a good time for you to talk?"

"I can't speak right now. I'm about to walk into work, but I'll be happy to talk to you after four thirty."

"Okay, I'll give you a call back then."

"Thank you."

Yeah, I hope they lock his ass up.

⌣⟶

Hours later, I remove the last glass from the table, and put it in the dishwasher. I pick up the remote from the kitchen counter, point it to the TV mounted on the wall next to the cabinet, and start channel surfing. Looking for no particular program, I stop surfing now that I've found the evening news. A commercial comes on, displaying a man standing in front of his bathroom mirror applying shaving cream to his beard.

I forgot about shaving cream. I didn't know men still use that funky smelling stuff. I'm glad Quentin uses a razor.

My thoughts drift to childhood and Papa George's shaving ritual. He'd strut shirtless around the house in all his bravado, with his chin covered with that stinky smelling shaving cream. The odor would penetrate the hallway and announce prematurely his entrance into the living room, where the family would be watching TV in the evening. Sometimes he would head to the kitchen, adjacent to the living room, open the cabinet above the stove and reach for his bottle of Jack Daniels. After taking a swig, he'd pat his belly, roar like a bear, and head back down the hallway to his bathroom.

Yuck.

As I remain fixated on the shaving cream commercial, my thoughts wander to a specific incident when I must have been around ten years old.

I was not particularly fond of my body at this stage of my life. Friends and classmates were developing breasts and womanly curves at what appeared to be an astonishing rate. Needless to say, my waif-like body felt forever stuck, as though it would never mature beyond puberty.

Taking leisurely bubble baths was one of my favorite things to do. The welcome ritual offered the solitude I craved, where no one was calling me for some mundane reason or another. It had become quite an annoyance to hear the enunciated syllables DAR-bee in harsh volumes throughout the house. As if a cowbell had been rung, the expectation was that I would respond to any one of the four family members, upon their calling. The family pecking order was in full swing. No one was about to upset the hierarchy. And the message was clear—I was at the bottom.

Early one particular evening, there was that odor of shaving cream looming throughout the house. For some unknown reason, no one else was at home—or so I thought.

No earsplitting DAR-bee piercing the air and messing up my vibe. I had created my own private spa, and had locked the bathroom door.

Through the boombox on the tile counter, the sounds of my favorite R&B group, The O'Jays, serenaded me as I stepped into the warm water. The rhythm and harmony had me singing along.

I was careful not to mess up my do, because my hair had just been straightened. I adjusted the shower cap and dealt with the annoyance of its elastic pinching my ears.

My spine leaned onto the cool enamel backing of the tub. A new bottle of liquid soap sat on the ledge by the faucet. I took a whiff of the vanilla musk scent, then squeezed the liquid down my bony arms.

The song faded, and I was left to create my own melody. Then I heard a creaking sound. I looked over to the bathroom door, to the right of the tub and a few feet back. That awful smelling shaving cream made its entrance—way before the door began to fully open. I thought I was home alone.

"Don't come in!"

The door opened wider. I said it again, louder.

"I *said*, don't come in!"

After a few seconds, the door gradually opens. I gasped, now seeing Papa George stepping in with his chin splattered with that foul-smelling shaving cream. His eyes traveled up and down my body while I sat horrified in the bathtub. With a quick reflex, I instinctively crossed my arms and covered my chest.

I yelled with what I was sure was a face so contorted and a scream so visceral that I wondered where it had come from.

"I. Said. Don't. Come. In!"

"Uh … uh … Oh, I didn't know anyone was in here." In an instant, my dad sheepishly turned on his heels and closed the door.

What the hell? He had his own bathroom in his bedroom. He didn't need to come into this bathroom to shave. He had to have *heard* me say not to come in a couple of times before he came in. He had time to close the door after hearing me yell. I was sure of it!

Why? Why had he opened the door?

As unsettling as the bathtub incident was, I couldn't have imagined that things would get even more bizarre. Days passed as I replayed the disturbing scene in my ten-year-old mind.

Who could I tell?

Gloria was designated as the big sister to watch over me because she was three years older and fell in the middle of Maxine and me. My mom had this weird joke that she had given me to Gloria when I was born. And Gloria often fed off the story, so she teased me that I was adopted. Totally weird.

Gloria was tall and athletic. Not to mention, she was well endowed and loved to tease me about my undeveloped body. Her not so subtle message made its point—clearly something was wrong with *me*, scrawniness, and all.

No, I knew I couldn't tell Gloria about the bathroom intrusion.

I finally decided to tell my mother, and was happy to find her alone in her bedroom one evening, while the rest of the family watched TV in the family room.

I peeked through her door, which was partially open. She was seated on the edge of her bed, sewing a brown button onto a tweed jacket. The room was calm as she masterfully wove the needle through the thick fabric, into the buttonhole, and out the other end.

With one movement after the other, her sense of purpose was evident. She was physically there, seated on her bed, although it seemed as if she were somewhere else, far away. The amber glow from the bedside lamp cast a billowy shadow on the lace curtains. The entire room had the distinct aura of distance surrounding it.

I hesitated in the doorway, yet managed to gather the courage.

"Mom, I need to tell you something."

"Okay. Come in."

I took a few steps into the dimly lit room and quietly approached her.

She kept on with her task and never looked my way. I sat down next to her on the side of her bed. A few seconds passed. Softly I blurted out the details of the eerie bathtub event, like rapid-fire bullets.

"Mom, I was taking a bath the other night. I thought the door was locked, but I guess it wasn't. Daddy came in, even after I told him not to. He just kept coming. I know he heard me say not to, but he came in anyway. After I screamed at him, he ran out."

I waited for her to speak. She didn't.

More seconds passed. I softly inquired, "Mom? Did you hear what I said?"

The needle and thread glided through the air, as the singular movement made a sound of its own. I wondered if she had anything to say. Surely there was *something* more she wanted to ask or say about this incident.

Nothing.

I gazed at her and felt confused that I didn't see any sign of emotion coming from her.

Again, nothing. No surprise.

Her focus was the repetitive motion of the needle through the button's hole. After what seemed like several minutes, she finally spoke. "Okay. I'll talk to your dad."

Her nonchalant attitude mystified me. I was stunned.

"I *said* I'll talk to your dad."

Her stiff, forceful response was my cue. There was nothing else to say. I was free to go.

As I exited the room, I felt relieved of the burden I'd been carrying, knowing that my mother would speak to my dad about his behavior.

I'm brought back to the present when I hear the TV commercial's final announcement: "For a shave so close, you'll think you visited the barber."

Oh, my God! The commercial has triggered a memory I'd forgotten all about.

CHAPTER 6

"Just listen to your body. *Yes-s-s*. Breathe and flow. Think about your core."

It's prime time—8:00 a.m., and the upper floor of the gym is packed. As I enter the studio, the soothing voice of the Pilates instructor encourages both novice and advanced students. She walks among the group, guiding their stretching movements. After a while, she looks up and notices me with a pleasant greeting.

"Well, hello, Darby. So good to see you again."

"Hi, Cari."

She buzzes around the class, squatting to correct alignments and straighten postures. Her brunette ponytail freely tosses back and forth. I'm glad to be back after having missed the last couple of classes. I really need to loosen up and relieve this tension in my neck.

Slipping off my flip-flops and rolling out my mat, my body relaxes as my bare feet touch the wood floor and I proceed with double-leg stretches. I really need to get back to my center. Trying to take each day one at a time is the best I can do. My mind, however, is tormented by the awful things that Robbie has endured.

After a few minutes, Paige bounces in, as always with a dose of enthusiasm. She scans the room to find me. Her kinky curls are knotted into a high bun on top of her head. Without the aesthetics of makeup, her cinnamon-colored complexion is aglow which makes her look younger than her thirty-seven years.

She scurries to grab the available spot next to me. Of my closest friends, I can always count on Paige with her wise counsel. She's still as solid as when I first met her in college during our freshmen year. As in her younger years, her beauty radiates from the inside, and reflects on the outside.

Through the years, we became distant physically, living in separate parts of the country, but we stayed in touch and our friendship has stood the test of time. Paige met her husband, James, in Chicago, and his job later transferred him to Los Viento. Paige and Glen were ecstatic when we asked them to be Robbie's godparents.

"Hi, Darby."

I smile at her between deliberate breaths as my legs extend one after the other. "Hey, Paige."

The heaviness I've been carrying already seems lighter simply because she's here.

We continue with our squats and planks through the next fifty minutes. "This was just what I needed," I say as I rise to the tree position. I begin rolling up my mat and gulp the last of my water, as the class comes to an end.

"Yeah, me too." Paige pauses. Between wiping her moist face and neck with her towel, I can tell that she's studying me. With a concerned expression, she asks, "How's Robbie doing?"

Steadying my voice and pushing down the quiver in my throat, I respond, "He seems to be making a little progress."

Paige was the first person I had confided in. When I shared the horrifying news of Robbie being molested, she sobbed with disbelief. Since then, she has mourned with me through the agonizing details of Robbie's pain.

As the class comes to an end, she reaches over and hugs me. I feel like a rag doll, standing limp though trying not to feel lost, with my folded mat and empty water bottle.

"Let's go across the street and get some coffee."

"Okay."

The heavy aroma of coffee fills the air as we enter the BeanScene Coffeehouse. The two of us approach the counter while customers ahead order their brew of choice. One by one, each advances to the counter along the wall, filled with condiments. The sound of old school jazz flows through the morning air—a welcome change from the Pilates background music of moments ago.

"I'll have a tall iced mocha."

"And I'll have a tall Americano."

The barista busies himself with our orders while we grab a coveted booth along the front window.

Perched in my seat, I stare out the window, looking onto the street. Crimson leaves on the trees have overtaken the lush greenery of summer. The lingering, sweltering days of the season's end have dissipated along with the humidity. Steady temperatures in the low '70s nestle with the balmy breeze.

"Tall iced mocha. Tall Americano!"

Within seconds after it's called, Paige jumps up to grab our order from the pickup counter. She hands me the cup and softly inquires, "And what's going on with you?"

As the plastic cup approaches my lips, the ice cubes rumble, a delicate accompaniment to the soothing sweetness of chocolate mixed with coffee.

Without the formality of a preliminary discussion, my thoughts release, penetrating the fragrant atmosphere. "I'm struggling, but somehow I'm managing to churn through this."

"Really, Darby? You don't seem like you're doing that great." Paige then adds, "I know Robbie's in counseling, but have *you* spoken to a professional?"

"Not yet, Quentin's spoken to Bishop Jefferson. I'll probably see a therapist at some point. I'm just glad that I've managed to get out of my lounge chair. For weeks I literally couldn't get off the deck in the backyard."

"Mmmm," Paige murmurs sympathetically.

"When I tried to get up and walk, my feet wouldn't move. I just lay there in the sun, crying most of the day, after Quentin took Robbie to school. That's when I realized I was in a depression. Thank God I had several weeks of vacation on the books, so I took a few weeks off. I'm feeling better now. But..."

"But what?" Paige puts her cup down.

"I came across a pistol in a purse that I'd forgotten I'd put away. And I went to my father's house the morning after Robbie told me that my father molested him."

Paige says nothing, although her eyes signal disbelief.

I take a sip of my drink and put the cup down slowly. "I feel so, so ashamed. I can't believe I was so focused."

"What happened?" Her comforting voice leads me to finish the story.

"The morning was like a perfect setup. He was in the front yard. I wasn't even thinking. I pointed the gun at him."

"Oh-h-h, Darby. Oh my God."

"It didn't fire. There were no bullets inside."

The hush between us hangs like an unnoticed cobweb.

"It was like I was in a trance. I still can't believe what I did." I take a gulp of coffee before continuing. "This may not make sense to you, Paige, but I realized that I needed to be calm and controlled when I approached him. You see, in the family that I grew up in, if I had an issue and tried to hold the person accountable, I couldn't win. I'd lose immediately if I became upset and out of control."

Paige speaks between her fingers, which are slightly covering her mouth. "Mmm, many families probably function that way."

"There was no responsibility taken for a violation or offense that I may have had an issue with. The situation usually ended unresolved, with a retort about how emotional I was; therefore, something was wrong with *me*. When I think about it, the dynamics were pretty sinister." My eyelids are fluttering, and the tears start again. I feel so helpless.

"Whoa, Darby. That sounds so... hopeless and futile. And unhealthy. This has boggled my mind, because, of course, I've known your family for so many years. I'm crushed to think this about your father. It's just heartbreaking. But I guess it's a testament to the saying that you don't know what goes on behind closed doors."

"Funny that you should say that, Paige. When I was growing up, Papa George used to always say, 'What goes on in this house, *stays* in this house.' This was something that he routinely said, for no apparent reason. He could be standing in the kitchen, maybe pouring himself a cup of coffee, and out of the blue he would go into a tirade and pronounce this mantra. I understand now that it was part of the conditioning. To keep the family under his control. And for him to do whatever he wanted."

My unexpected purge feels satisfying, as I reflect on my family's dynamics. The images of my past are connecting and are beginning to make sense.

"You were there to get a glimpse, Paige. Only a glimpse during our college years, because you hung out at my parents' house during so many school breaks." I take a sip of my drink before giving her an update. "They interviewed Quentin and me separately from Robbie. They should have interviewed my father by now. I'm not sure what their next step is, but I hope Papa George gets what's coming to him."

"Darby, I know you're looking out for Robbie. But please, promise me you'll get some counseling too. Okay?"

"Yes, I will. Thanks."

CHAPTER 7

April 28, 2010, Denton, California...

The items travel down the belt while I maneuver through the express line. The cashier rings up the tortillas, cilantro, and other items for tonight's dinner. After scanning the items, she looks up momentarily at the growing line that has formed behind me.

"Did you find everything you were looking for today, ma'am?" she inquires while placing the last of the groceries in my shopping bag.

"I did. Thanks."

I'll be home in no time to whip up Quentin and Robbie's favorite—chicken enchiladas with extra cheese. Spanish rice and refried beans on the side.

At the checkout the vibrating sound of my phone buzzes from my purse. I fumble through its contents, digging through to the bottom. Seeing the caller ID on the display causes a primal stirring within me.

I don't want anything to do with any of my family. My suspicions tell me that somebody in the family has known that Robbie was being molested.

It's all going to come out somehow.

The back of my neck immediately stiffens. My adrenaline heightens, causing blood to increase its flow to every limb and muscle in my body. Any pleasant thoughts that previously ran through my mind now fade and prepare for combat. Seconds pass and I succeed in tapping the button before the call goes into voicemail.

I bluntly answer, "Hey, Maxine."

She begins describing the scenario in a single swoosh of breath. Clearly, she is in her finest hour of self-importance, esteemed to be the bearer of the latest sequence of events having to do with the Coleman family.

"I'm just calling to tell you that Mom has been having those episodes again—you know, those dizzy spells? I had dropped by earlier this afternoon to visit her and Dad, when she said she wasn't feeling well. Anyway, after a while, I decided to take her to the emergency room. Didn't want to take any chances. She stayed there for several hours while they checked her out. I just left her house after talking with her doctor. He admitted her to Lakeside Rehab for bedrest for the rest of the week. He'll keep evaluating her during that time. I just thought you'd want to *know*-o-o-o," she says in that annoying singsong chant.

"Well thanks for the call, Maxine."

Another dizzy spell. Mm-hmm. Surely my father told the family that I pulled a gun on him in the front yard. So now they're rounding up the wagons.

The thought doesn't escape me that my mother has to be an accomplice. Seems to me that a perpetrator always needs one... or two.

Robbie had spent a couple of days during spring break with my parents. For the love of me, I can't believe the lengths my mother goes through to do Robbie's laundry. She insists on not only washing his laundry, but she starches and irons each piece, then folds them neatly before putting them in his overnight bag. I don't remember my mom being that meticulous about *my* laundry when I was growing up. She says she doesn't mind and that she feels bad because he had an accident while visiting them. So she ended up doing laundry more often. That's so weird. Robbie doesn't have accidents. I know that kids will sometimes misgauge their timing—being intent on playing and then get to the bathroom too late. Robbie doesn't do that, though.

And now, it makes sense as to why she was adamant about doing Robbie's laundry. She was cleaning up after my father's evil mess. Literally.

The secret allowed Papa George to abuse the next generation. I'm convinced they're all conniving thieves—even if I don't have the evidence to prove it. Yet. But if I'm right, Robbie is paying the price for their deception.

This is way too big.

I redirect my thoughts back to the issue at hand as I tap the phone on Quentin's number.

He picks up after the first ring. "Hey, babe."

"Hi, hon. Hey, listen, I just got off the phone with Maxine. My mother had one of her dizzy spells. I'm going to drive over to Denton to see what's going on."

His concern speaks through the silence. "Do you want me to go with you?"

"No. I'm okay. You stay with Robbie.

He hesitates before warning, "Don't let yourself be put in a situation where you're outnumbered. You get me?"

"Yeah, It's okay. I won't be long."

Our goodbyes are shadowed by wondering, as my thoughts gather intensity. I'm not in the mood for Maxine's posturing and the usual alignment with she and Gloria. The hell with the family pecking order. I'm done! No need for me to receive secondhand information. I'll go check on my mom for myself. I'm sure she'll be surprised to see me, given that I haven't spoken to her or returned her calls in several weeks.

She's no doubt panicking, knowing that I'm on to their sick charade of pretense and coverup.

All the other times that mom became ill, I would rush to the emergency room in a frenzy. Her dizzy spells are nothing new. You can bet that there would be something she'd worked herself up about, and sure enough her body would respond. When I'd ask my sisters or my father what had set the "episode" in motion, Papa George would burst into his usual script. "You know how emotional your ma is!"

This had been our normal routine—until now.

While I'm driving the thirty minute distance from my home to the senior rehab in Denton, I feel like I'm running a routine errand. A calm peace has come over me.

Given Quentin's current aversion to my family, it's best that he's not with me. He's had all he can take from the Colemans. I'll navigate this charade by myself.

Mom's had "episodes" for as long as I can remember, starting when I was a little girl. She's always had a way of tolerating my father's verbal and emotional abuse. This time I guess she's found a way to check out and get some relief by having a respite at the rehabilitation place.

I feel as though I'm on a mission as I enter the rehab center, although I'm not sure what I'm searching for. The antiseptic odor overtakes me—like the smell of a coverup.

How fitting.

Maybe an elderly person soiled their pants. Maybe someone's stomach churned uncontrollably and spilled the contents on the corridor floor. The mess surely had to be mopped up, but the desperate attempt at covering physical evidence only adds to the stench of wickedness that cannot be contained.

Kind of like the Colemans.

Boy, I really need to get ahold of myself. There's no telling what condition I'll actually find my mother in. I need to find out what's really going on with her health. Even though there have been times where she's used her failing health to be manipulative, this might be the time that she's not crying wolf. But I feel conflicted. I don't want to have any regrets about the kind of daughter I've been.

The receptionist looks up from her monitor with a questioning, yet annoying, expression. No words needed. Her demeanor conveys that verbal communication is not necessary.

"Hello, I'm looking for Louvenia Coleman, please?"

Without an utterance, her attention returns to the computer. The click of her keystrokes on the keyboard transmits more than her words can. Finally she responds while nodding in the direction of the thick logbook on the counter to her left.

"You need to sign in and note your relationship." She pauses while typing again on the keyboard. "Louvenia Coleman. Let's see, that's 12B. Go all the way down the corridor, then turn right at the end." Her upper body motions in the direction of the bleak hallway.

I begin my stride down the hall, passing one room after the other. I can't help but glance at patients through open doors of the rooms as I pass along the way. A feeble resident with long gray strands of disheveled hair looks upward at a television mounted on the wall. Looks like she's immersed in *Wheel of Fortune*. On the screen, anxious contestants smile at the camera. Blaring sounds of the audience's applause spill from the TV and into the hallway.

Continuing down the corridor, I arrive at room 12. As I enter, I pass the foot of a bed where a helpless soul sleeps soundly. 12A. Her light snore flutters upward to the ceiling. A vinyl curtain separates the two beds.

Without sliding the curtain along the ceiling rod, I poke my head on the other side of the drape while still standing at the foot of the roommate's bed. On the other side in 12B, I see my mother sitting up with her back nestled against several pillows. Her arms are clasped behind her head while watching the same game show as the resident down the hall. She cackles loudly to no one. Appearing quite content, she smacks her chewing gum while immersed in the TV show.

Knowing that she doesn't realize I'm standing there, I seize the moment to study her. Yeah, she looks pretty pleased. Her presence soaks in long enough for me to conclude that she's pretty much placed herself on a mini-vacation for a few days—her way of taking respite from Papa George and his ill temper and abuse.

"Hi, Mom."

Startled, her attention abruptly turns from the TV and now rests upon me. She beams and cheerfully responds, "Oh, Dar-bee!"

In the same instance, she catches herself. Her back slithers down into the cocoon of pillows surrounding her. Her posture now lies horizontally, like a sly fox lodged in a burrow.

"How are you feeling?" I ask. "And tell me what happened."

Her animated response is suddenly replaced with a frail, weakened tone. "Oh, just another dizzy spell, honey. It's a good thing Maxine was there with me. Your Dad wasn't home, so Maxi drove me to the doctor."

Her frailty becomes more pronounced with each word.

The caution I'd received from Quentin filters past my ear. It occurs to me that I may be looking at an indirect route for confrontation with Papa George. Heck, this may be even better. Papa George, with all of his arrogance and indignation, would never admit to molesting Robbie.

Yeah, I'll take the next best thing. His accomplice.

"Watch the behaviors of the ones who are invested in the secret," Quentin had advised. "There's a story in their behaviors." The behaviors from the others may convey deeper issues that are hidden below the surface. With the entanglement of dysfunction, their responses could be like movements on a chessboard.

Maybe.

The best way to confront Papa George might be to take an indirect route. Yes, this could be it.

Cautiously, I begin.

"Mom, you know how I've been telling you about all the difficulties Robbie's been having? How drastically his moods have changed and the trouble he's been having at school?"

"Uh...yeah?"

"Well, now I understand why."

"Really? Why?"

Geeze. She really seems like she doesn't have a clue that I pulled a gun on my father. This is sinister.

Softly I cut to the chase.

"Dad molested him."

Like the queen protecting the king on a chessboard, she immediately moves into position. In the spur of a moment, she sits straight up in bed. Stunned. Her back is firm. Her sharp eyes squint at me as she begins to howl, "Who told you that?! Who told you? I *know* Robbie didn't tell you that."

There it is. All the little games she played with him—whispering in his ear, "Don't tell." I used to think they played the cutest games together. But I can see clearly now, what I hadn't before.

She was so sure he'd keep the secret.

Now she's outright hysterical. I'm captivated by her rage as I sit by her bedside, listening and watching her display. It's very telling.

She's shocked and furious all rolled into one, as her arms flail, landing blows on the mattress.

Her southern dialect kicks in. "You done gone crazy. Yo daddy did no such thing! No such! You done got the devil in you, girl! You sho nuff crazy! Why do you say such a thing? Tell me!" Her demand persists. "I said, *Why*?" Her fists tremble on the mattress as she glares at me, pressing for an answer.

Thoughts of the family dynamics drift over me again. The layers of dysfunction begin to shred right in front of me, revealing what would never be spoken. So many times I had been the one to lose self-control when bringing up some injustice, in an attempt for accountability within the Coleman family. It never worked because the person who became emotional was the one who would be pronounced crazy. This was Papa George's way of keeping control over the family. Instill fear of being labeled crazy. Then everyone else would line up and pile on with the goal of giving you a new name. Cuhrazy,

This has always been the Coleman way.

My mother's agitation persists. "You crazy. I want to know *where* you got this from?"

There it is. Get it off of yourself by being first to tag the other with a derogatory trait. Foolery at its finest. I've never been able to master this insanity. I'm determined to remain calm. This is the opening I've been hoping for.

"Mom, let me tell you something that I remember from child-hood. I only thought about it recently."

Her weight shifts to one side as she leans in toward me. Her body is stiff with anticipation.

"When I was little and we lived at Fort Costera, I remember taking a bath one day. It had been quiet one afternoon in the house, and I thought no one else was home. The bathroom door began creeping open slowly as I sat in the tub. I was surprised and yelled for the person not to come in."

She sits still, eyes wide open like a flytrap. Totally aware of wanting the fullest effect, I release my words in a deliberate manner. "The door still wasn't fully open yet it kept moving. I yelled again, but the door kept opening—gradually. Then Dad poked his head in. He came all the way into the bathroom and acted surprised—like he hadn't known I was taking a bath. He stood there and looked me up and down. I screamed at him and he ran out."

Her eyes expand before she manages to formulate her question. "Did... did... did anything else ever happen after that?" She awaits my answer, now sitting petrified in her perch.

Well, *yea-ah* that's a strange question. I wonder what else she was expecting would—ever happen after that? As disgusted as I am, I can only offer a solemn and detached reply. "No, Mom."

Without realizing it, she lets out a huge sigh of relief. She slumps back into the shelter of her pillows with a satisfied smile. Her attention is once again turned to the game show on the television, head turned upward, eyes averted from me. I know this familial stance all too well. Now that she has the answer to what she wanted to know—did anything ever happen?—she's tuning me out. I'm being dismissed.

The confirming reality creeps over me like celestial droplets trickling from the sky. The anger begins to ooze through my pores once again. My sisters were molested. They kept quiet. And the evil effects extended to Robbie. The wicked secrets thrived like a bad virus. The silence birthed the Coleman curse.

Her scornful behavior and posturing has me sensing that there may be other secrets.

Checkmate.

CHAPTER 8

My phone vibrates in my purse as I rush to pick up the call before it goes to voicemail. Maxine's face illuminates the screen.

"Hey, Maxine," I answer solemnly.

"Hi, Darby, just wanted to let you know that I'm stuck in traffic."

"OK. No problem. I'll see you soon."

"All right, see you soon. Bye."

It's not as though we hang out regularly. I wonder what she wants. Given my visit with my mother earlier this week, I know there must be a connection. I hope she gets here soon. I've got stuff to do.

Ice touching my lips calms my throat as I casually swallow the smooth latte. The sun casts its mid-morning shadow against the cafe window. One coffee lover after another goes inside the bistro and exits with a refreshing beverage heaped with whipped cream. Scrolling through my phone, I see that there are no urgent emails or texts.

The green umbrellas hovering over the tables provide a welcome shade from the sunshine. My anxiety from the past few days lifts a bit along with the balmy breeze. But only a bit, as

I think about Robbie and how he's still withdrawn and having nightmares. Quentin and I rushed to his room the other night to wake him from the torment he'd been screaming through.

Meeting Maxine at Cafe Noir is not what I had initially planned, but because of her prompting earlier this week, I agreed. She insisted that we don't see each other nearly enough. I don't feel the same. I've realized that I tolerated her for the sake of "getting along." You can never win with Maxine. It's always pure drama—and always her way or no way.

Where is she?

And I've only recently resolved my inner conflict—having a sister doesn't automatically make a friend. Somehow, I felt guilty once I embraced the realization, because it's totally against the way I was raised.

Within moments, her blue Toyota swerves into the parking lot, going up and down the aisles, looking for a space. She appears frantic. Silently, I'm enjoying watching her in a frenzied state.

After several minutes she does the waiting game in the aisle, as a car, previously unseen, emerges from a spot. Her sedan pulls into the spot almost as suddenly as the driver backs out.

Closing her door, she scans the parking lot before eyeing me on the patio, under the table's green umbrella. Signaling that her frenzy is dissipating, her face lights up, as she advances across the parking lot. I notice her gait—very purposeful, like she's on a mission. As she approaches me, her smile widens.

"Ohhh, Darby." She leans in for an air kiss.

"Hi, Maxine. How ya doin?"

"Oh I'm so glad you made the time for us to get together. I feel like I haven't seen you in forever. What's new with you?"

Oh, so this is how she's gonna play it—like she doesn't know. Okay.

I don't acknowledge her 'what's new with you.' "Do you want a drink?"

Her singsong chant heats up. "I'm gonna hold off for now. I've got my water, so I'll just hydrate, hydrate."

She removes the water bottle from her tote bag, and takes a gulp. After a few seconds, I decide to get the ball rolling.

"I got a call from Robbie's school several weeks ago. He was having trouble settling down in the classroom. So I left work and…"

She looks away, and shifts the conversation to herself, sounding somewhat giddy in the process.

"Oh. I can't wait until the next couple of months. We're planning on going to either St. Barts again or somewhere else. I'm not sure. It's gotta be a tropical place, though. Somewhere in the Caribbean. I can't wait to get away. It's been a rough year with fifth graders. Oh my God, they just seem to be getting worse and worse—the unruly things." She pauses after realizing that I'm giving her a blank stare. "Oh, did you say something about Robbie?"

Boy, she can flip a switch and go into diversion mode before anyone can see it coming. The girl's got game. She obviously could care less about Robbie. Why had I never seen this before?

I know mom must have told her that I said dad molested Robbie.

"I was saying that I got to the principal's office. Robbie was there with his teacher." My voice begins to shake before I finally come unglued. "Dad molested Robbie!" I blurt out.

Her face shows no trace of astonishment, She shuts the lid closed on her water bottle, then turns to ensure that I'm in full view of her. A slow grimace forms across her face.

Like the clicking of a stove's burner, igniting a flame, she flips again. "Dad would do no such thing!"

"How in the hell would you know what he did! And why are you defending him?"

She ignores my question and goes all in. "You and Quentin are just bad parents. There. The cat's out of the bag now. It's just bad parenting, and now you all have made up a lie because Robbie's having problems!"

Feeling like I've been sucker punched, my head manages to shake off the dizziness.

"Robbie did not make this up! And I'm not going to sit here and let you…"

She cuts me off, delighted that she's thrown me for a loop. "It's just bad parenting. That's what's wrong with him. You and your precious little Robbie!" Her spewing of venom elevates even further. "You and your perfect little family!"

The poison grows more potent with every word she ejects. In full viper mode, she presses on, determined for every bite to cut deeper.

She sneers. "You've been found out, uh-huh! We *all* see it. Mom. Gloria. Dad. Your perfect little family's not so perfect after all!"

What did I just hear?

So, this is what's been going on behind my back? And they've all piled on. The idea sends shockwaves through my body, leaving my stomach quivering. As usual, she's all about the drama, and has been unleashed as the pit bull.

Her pitch grows louder. At this point I tune her out.

Car doors in the parking lot gape open as people turn their heads in our direction to see what the commotion is all about. Nonetheless, she goes all in.

Her brows are so pronounced that I swear they have formed into a single line of hair enmeshed with the natural frown lines of her forehead.

She's thrown me in an emotional loop. I know I can't compete with her tirade. My instincts tell me to throw her off with the opposite tone. I gently interrupt. "Did he molest *you,* Maxine?"

Her reaction is as if I've slapped her. She ignores my question, gets her second wind, and starts up again.

"And if you've got anything else to say to Mom and Dad, you've got to go through *me.*"

There it is. Yep, Mom told her.

I turn toward the empty chair next to me where I've placed my purse. I can't help but notice the jacaranda trees along the perimeter of the patio. Their blossoms had been gently swaying, but now it seems as if they are standing still, angling their branches for a clear vantage point of the turmoil happening below them. As if they've missed some hidden insight, their blossoms seem to be wondering how and why this fiasco has come about.

My apparent uneasiness at the public chaos she's making only seems to fuel her even more. All I can manage is to shake my bag to find my keys at the bottom of my purse.

And now I see it. Their collective silence formed an alliance. A conspiracy of secrecy.

Feeling like stalked prey, I gather my sunglasses that are lying on the table. Not able to push my chair out fast enough from the table, I fumble. Although Maxine is clearly agitated, my inner voice keeps repeating, "stay calm." Without making eye contact, I rise from the table, certain that I'm fleeing from a rabid animal.

My nonverbal responsiveness has apparently thrown her for a loop, as she realizes that I'm not being baited by her crazy antics.

What a freaking lunatic.

One step down the walkway. Two stairs down the landing of the bistro's patio.

Keep walking.

Now that she's worked herself into a frenzy even more, her shrill escalates. I've managed to move several yards from her. She stands on the landing, with her hands on her hips, watching me head to my car.

"And if your man walks off and leaves you, then you've got to deal with *me*!"

Whoa. Her marriage must be in more trouble than I thought.

There it is. Her usual attempt at deflecting her situation from herself and onto someone else. She just had to throw that last stab in my back.

Stopping in my tracks, I turn around, now standing a few feet from her. Delivered with all the icy coldness I can muster, I even surprise myself.

"No, I won't, cause I really don't like you."

Her pupils dilate. Her face contorts with deep contempt.

Don't look back.

The stench of her poison follows me to my car. I'm done with this toxic family.

⤳

Feeling shaken from the incident at Cafe Noir, I tell Quentin about it that afternoon.

"Babe, I kept wondering when you'd see it. I've always looked at your relationship with your sisters, and how you tried so hard to be their friend. I saw it when we were dating in college. They simply weren't interested. I was baffled too." He pauses before adding, "And, well, Maxine's always been a little strange, what can I say?" He delicately adds, "They were only interested in a relationship on *their* terms. I knew you couldn't see it. But I also knew that there would come a day when you'd see it for yourself." Quentin's intolerance for Maxine has been longstanding. His patience at this point may have worn thin.

Quentin's solemn truth burns my soul, like peroxide into a fresh wound. The sobering jolt has me trying to gain my footing.

"They knew about it. They all knew." Speaking my truth out loud doesn't lessen the sting, but propels me into a new space.

Pulling my knees into the plush cushioning in the oversized chair allows me some comfort. Leaning back, I raise my neck in the direction of the ceiling to stretch the kinks out. The gloominess inside me tells me that I've been on a long ride, with Maxine driving the wheel. Somehow it feels like the whole family's been in the car with everyone headed for an unknown destination. I was just an accessory inside the vehicle.

I feel like a fool. Somehow I'm consoled by running my fingers against my jumpsuit's soft cotton sleeve.

Quentin comes behind me, places my cheeks in his palms, and kisses me on the forehead. His words offer the reassurance I need. "You're gonna be all right. This is a big blow you didn't see coming, but you're going to be okay, Robbie's going to be okay, and we're somehow going to get through this." He glides one finger across my cheek, and presses his lips against my nose. Speaking softer than before, he repeats, "Robbie's going to be okay, and the three of us are going to make it through this."

After a couple of hours, the afternoon sun glistens through the open shutters. Lying in the chaise lounge for hours has helped to center me. The smooth jazz floats through the speakers on the kitchen counter, offering soothing melodies which help me lick my wounds. I'd better snap out of it and get to the errands I need to run. I can only sulk for so long.

In the slit pocket of my jumpsuit, my phone vibrates.

"Hi, Mom."

"Hi."

"I was just headed out the door. What's up?"

"Maxie told me how bad you've been treating her."

"What are you talking about?" My response is overshadowed with unbelief.

"Well, Maxie called down here, crying. She's real upset."

"I haven't done anything to Maxine. I have no idea what you're talking about."

"Well she called down here, crying and saying that you won't talk to her. I don't know what you did, but I feel bad about how Maxie is being treated."

Whoa! They sure can play games. The usual sweep it under the rug as if nothing happened. This is sinister.

"Look, Mom. I'm not playing these games with you, Maxine, and the rest of the family. Dad molested Robbie, and you guys can play pretend all you want, I'm done."

She goes into pretense mode—tone deaf and all, which is the typical Coleman way. No accountability, and a confrontation didn't happen. "Well, I'm not on anyone's side," she whines. "I just want the two of you to get together and act like sisters. That's how we raised you."

Her plea grows more intense. "Don't you see what this is doing to the children? How are Robbie and his cousins going to grow up without each other? They need to be close. But they can't if y'all aren't getting along."

"Mom, I can't do anything about that, and you really need to stay out of—"

She loses her desperate tone, switches gears, then goes full throttle with a sharp command. "You need to stop! Y'all should act like sisters!"

My face grows warm.

No, she didn't.

Feeling irritated beyond belief, I know I have no option but to shut her down. "Mom, I'm done with the dysfunction!" I tap the off button.

They act like I'm a runaway slave. There's no making sense of the sickness.

This feels like a dark scheme. I'm sure the pile on isn't over, and I can predict what'll happen next—a call from the "big guns," also known as Gloria.

The announcer's voice booms on the shop-at-home channel, which is airing a segment featuring everything from cookware to gourmet appetizers. Picturesque shots spur me into thinking how things should be, and could be.

Thoughts of extended family and warm fellowship begin to creep into my consciousness. Thoughts of Robbie playing with his cousins at family barbecues and carefree visits in the summer.

It was all a facade.

But lately, everyone's been pretty scarce, other than the occasional call from Mom to see how I'm doing. The fiasco with Maxine at Cafe Noir feels like the shedding of a well-worn coat. The heaviness that was weighing me down has been replaced with an awakening of wearing only what's mine. I almost feel guilty for not missing her. Just for a brief moment. After all, she's my sister. I *should* miss her. The reality, however, is that I don't. And I refuse to feel guilty for no longer drinking poison. Funny how putting distance between me and my family has given me a new mindset. No Maxine. No Gloria. No drama. All's been quiet as a church mouse for the past few weeks.

I really should have done this years ago.

The predictable pattern is like an old stain—a stain so deep that the most vigorous attempt at bleaching doesn't even get it out. Then the dirty fabric gets swept under the rug. And nobody sees it. Only me.

The greenery which permeates into yellows and browns has prompted the shedding of hindrances for the newness of the future.

CHAPTER 9

As I cross the street into the entrance of the park, a fellow stroller and I exchange a cursory nod of acknowledgment. I make my way along the familiar path. On the trail, there are three women in the distance, heading in my direction. As the distance shortens, I recognize one of them while she strolls slightly ahead of the two older women. It's Tamika Simmons, another mom from Robbie's playgroup years ago. She seems as though she's self-absorbed in her power walk. We haven't seen each other in some time. Tamika and I had connected during the years that our children played together. In more recent years, our contact has fallen off for no reason other than life going in separate directions.

As the group comes within a few feet of me, I call her name, "Tamika?"

She glances up. "Darby? Oh my goodness. I haven't seen you in ages. How've you been?" The two other women pass us as Tamika and I linger to chat.

"What are your kids up to?" I ask. She mentions soccer and other activities that her kids are involved in. "How's that sweet Robbie?" Tamika asks.

A small inner voice tells me that I'm speaking to a safe soul. With caution I begin telling her how he's been struggling. The voice nudges me to proceed. "We found out that he was sexually abused."

"Oh-h-h," she groans sympathetically. "Was it by someone close to you?"

"Yes, my father."

Her reaction feels like time is suspended for several moments. Seconds after catching her breath, Tamika shares as well. "Before my father retired, he was a probation officer, so I became well aware of some of the behaviors of pedophiles."

"Yeah, it's usually not a stranger. Most times it's someone who the family knows and trusts. And it's someone who has access to the child. Never in a million years would I have imagined my father could do such a thing." Tamika nods, waiting for me to continue. "It explains the craziness that I grew up with. It explains the behavior of my two older sisters. I'm the youngest, and God only knows the miracle of how and why I was spared." Suddenly, I realize that I'm purging the events of the trauma I'm trying to escape.

"Darby, I feel just awful for Robbie. Is he in counseling?"

"Thanks, Tamika. Yeah, he is. He's making some progress."

"You know, Darby, you've caused me to remember something. I have a cousin who, years ago, said her father sexually abused her. He had already passed away when she revealed this, so her admission pretty much died as well. But I don't believe she made it up. I think you're extremely lucky that your father is still alive, even though he probably won't confess. They never do. That was one of the most frustrating things my father used to experience from working these kinds of cases—*rarely* do they confess. Even so, no other child has to be placed at risk by being around him."

"I couldn't agree with you more, Tamika. I really appreciate your input."

Her long arms reach out and squeeze me in a tight embrace. I'm feeling somewhat encouraged by this unexpected encounter with Tamika.

Everything's going to be all right.

"Give me a call, okay? Let's get together for lunch real soon." Tamika waves, then turns in the opposite direction as she picks up her stride to catch up with the other two women who are now small specks in the distance.

My own pace picks up while I reflect on the conversation with Tamika.

Ping.

Reaching into my pocket for my phone, I glance at the text from...Gloria? I haven't heard from her in ages.

Hi Darby. You were on my mind. Busy?

Before I can text back, my phone rings. I answer it.

"Hi, Gloria."

"Hey, Darby. Just thought I'd give you a call."

Oh here it is. That sweep-it-under-the-rug Coleman thing—as if nothing ever happened, no confrontation, and everybody's tone deaf.

I'm sure she's aware of the rumble that went on with me and Maxine. Now it's time for the pretense.

I proceed with caution, knowing that she's gotten wind of the drama that occurred at the rehab between me and my mom. Since I've backed away from Maxine, they only have one strategy left. So finally here it comes. I can imagine the three of them in a huddle plotting what to do next.

So, here comes their move, ready to be performed like a piece from a musical trio.

"Um ... ah ... whatcha been up to?" Her artificial sweetness rises with each word of pretentiousness.

Waiting it out, I feed Gloria nothing more than a cursory response. "Just the usual, Gloria. What's up with you?"

The blackout remains for several seconds before Gloria goes full in, like a wild attack dog. "I heard about the filth you accused Papa George of!" She comes in for the kill, as the reprimand increases. I envision spit flying in the midst of her rant. "He did no such thing to Robbie! You don't have any proof! And why would you want to lock another Black man up!"

She persists, each remark sounding more sinister than the last. "You're crazy!" Then she adds, "God's gonna strike you…!"

Shut her down.

I stab the red button on the phone. They've closed ranks, all right. Gloria's weirdness speaks for itself and piece by piece, it adds another layer to the ever evolving chaos. There's no making sense of the dysfunction—it's way too deep.

They've shown me that they could care less about Robbie—or me.

CHAPTER 10

"Mom! Mom! Look what I've got!" Robbie shouts as he dashes from the garage, and down the driveway to meet me. At his heels is his friend, Jeremy, who lives across the street.

"Oh wow, what's that you've got, son?" I ask, knowing that he sees through my mock curiosity. He looks up at me with his toothless grin.

Robbie cuddles the golden-brown puppy close to his chest. The puppy squirms and licks his neck, causing him to squeal. "Oh man, that tickles!" Robbie giggles uncontrollably. Jeremy shares his enthusiasm as he strokes the puppy's paws.

"Wow, Mom," he beams. "You and Dad said that you would think about it for my birthday. I couldn't believe it when Dad picked me up from school, and there he was, in a cage, on the back seat." He rubs his cheek against the puppy's fur. "Thanks, Mom," he says sweetly.

"Of course." I run my fingers along the puppy's back. "Well, does he have a name?"

"Yes. I named him Rocco."

"He's adorable, and he even looks like his name should be Rocco."

Shelly, an eight-year old from down the street, jumps off her bike, leaving skid marks on the driveway's pavement.

"Robbie! Did you get a puppy?" She joins Robbie and Jeremy, who are now huddled around Rocco on the garage floor. "Ooo-h, he's *sooo* cute! Can I please hold him?"

My heart is over-the-moon, watching Robbie with the fluffy bundle. I turn to go inside, leaving him and his friends playing with Rocco.

The fragrant aroma of herbs and garlic meets me when I open the door. Before heading to the kitchen, I drop my jacket and purse on the storage bench next to the back door. I'm caught off guard by an unfamiliar voice along with Quentin's.

Who's he talking to?

I approach the kitchen where Quentin stands at the sink, rinsing a colander full of pasta. On the stove is a pot bubbling with marinara sauce. And seated at the bar stool, several feet from the sink, is a stranger, who appears to be in his early 40s. He has closely cropped black hair, and smooth pecan-colored skin.

He and Quentin are immersed in the same dynamic energy, while bantering back and forth. I detect a hint of a southern dialect in the man's voice, as I listen closely to him and Quentin chopping it up.

"Hey Babe!" Quentin looks up as I walk over to the sink, then leans in for a kiss. "Let me introduce you to someone who you've only heard about," he smiles in the stranger's direction. "This is your cousin, Ethan."

Ethan smiles and extends his hand.

"Ethan," I say, as I pause to process the name. "I've heard about you. Let's see…you're my father's nephew, Aunt Camille's son."

"That's right. Your dad's sister is my mom, Camille, but everybody calls her Birdie."

"And let me see if I have this right. Aunt Birdie is the youngest of the bunch."

"Right again," Ethan laughs. "Well, there were ten of them, so it's hard to keep up."

"You're right about that," I chuckle. "And you live in Honolulu, right?"

"Yeah, I can tell that you're putting the pieces of the puzzle together." Ethan grins before adding, "I've been living in Honolulu for more than twenty years. Once I left Piperton, I never looked back." He glances over at Quentin, then takes a sip of the glass of water in front of him.

"Ethan had to come to California on business, so he promised his mother that he would look us up," Quentin explains while he takes the colander from the sink and sets it on the counter. "He called me a couple of weeks ago, and we thought we'd surprise you with his visit."

"That's right," Ethan chimes in. "It was pretty easy locating Quentin from his company's website. I reached out to him, knowing that I'd be passing through here soon on business. We've talked on the phone several times since then, and— well, this husband of yours is quite a guy." He nods towards Quentin. "He makes it pretty easy to let go of formal introductions. The next thing I know, he's invited me over for dinner."

The two laugh as if they're old acquaintances.

"Well I'm glad you're here. And yes, my Quentin is like that. He has a knack for bonding easily."

Quentin turns his attention to the marinara sauce on the stove—an attempt to conceal that he's blushing. He abruptly announces, "All right guys, dinner will be ready in about fifteen minutes."

"Okay, I'll let Robbie know."

The warmth in the room is met with a peaceful anticipation that I can't explain.

Rocco lays in his cage, off the dining room, playing with a chew toy. Every so often he tunes into our voices and starts whimpering. Robbie eats hurriedly and occasionally cranes his neck to get a glimpse of his new puppy down the hall.

"That's a cute puppy you've got there, Robbie," Ethan remarks while cutting his shrimp. "What breed is he?"

"He's a Golden Retriever. My dad got him for me this afternoon."

"Have you named him yet?"

"Yeah. His name is Rocco," Robbie says.

"I had a dog when I was growing up. His name was Brady." Our attention turns towards Ethan as he begins to share a part of his childhood. "My mom didn't want me to have a dog at the time—I was about your age. She was concerned that I was too young to take care of him. But her brother—who was also your grandfather's brother—convinced her that I was responsible enough. Uncle Clarence loved dogs and always had one type or another. One day, he brought one of his puppies over to me. And all the years I was growing up, Brady was right by my side."

"What kind of dog was Brady?"

"Brady was a mixed breed. I'm not sure exactly what he was, but he was a very special mutt," Ethan says fondly.

Rocco's whimpering gets louder. "Mom, I'm gonna go get him, okay?"

"Okay."

Robbie runs down the hall to get the puppy, while Ethan, Quentin and I settle in the living room. Robbie and Roscoe are the center of attention, as they play on the floor in the center of the room.

For some strange reason, the anticipation I'd sensed earlier, has been replaced by a solemn mood. I notice Quentin and Ethan exchange looks as if they have some sort of hidden telepathy going on. It's unnoticed by Robbie who is engrossed with Rocco.

Ethan picks back up. "Yeah, Brady, was given to me by Uncle Clarence. He helped me train Brady, and he also taught me how to ride a bike. I loved hanging out with Uncle Clarence."

Robbie's attention turns fully to Ethan, as he holds Rocco in his arms.

Ethan's mood shifts to sadness as he reminisces. "I had no reason not to trust him, he was my mother's brother—no reason at all." The cadence of his voice has slowed to nearly a stop.

Where's this going?

Without fully understanding what's going on, I interrupt Ethan and glance down at Robbie, who seems to be captivated by Ethan's story. I turn to Quentin, "Babe?"

"It's okay, Darb." Quentin calmly reassures. "Come here, son." He motions gently to Robbie.

Robbie scoops up Rocco and walks over to Quentin. He positions himself comfortably in his father's lap while Rocco squirms in his arms. He looks at Ethan inquisitively.

"Go ahead, Ethan," Quentin quietly affirms.

"Uh, um." He gathers his composure. "I loved spending time with Uncle Clarence. He used to make me laugh, and always had something interesting to show me. I trusted him, until…until the day he hurt me."

Everything in the room becomes still. Including Rocco.

"He molested me, Robbie," Ethan whispers candidly. "It was not because *I* did something wrong or that *I* was bad. He was the one who did this awful thing."

"Yeah, It…"It happened to me too," Robbie manages to say. His eyebrows convey deep thought, while we sit in the sensitivity of the moment.

"And I spent a long time being confused, Ethan adds. " He laid burdens on me that were never mine to carry. He never admitted it."

Robbie ponders for a moment, before asking, "What happened after that?"

"Well, there was a big uproar in the family with all the relatives chiming in. To make a long story short, they put a lot of pressure on my mother. It was all very, very sick—there's no other way to put it." Ethan's tone has now settled back to a relaxed place. "She and I moved a few miles away, over to the next county outside of Piperton. And in my senior year of high school, I got a scholarship to play football at the University of Hawaii. I moved there and I never looked back."

"Cool! You mean you played football? In Hawaii?"

Ethan grins at Robbie's enthusiasm.

"I sure did, Robbie."

Robbie jumps from Quentin's lap. "Ewe! Oh no! Rocco peed on me!"

⌣⟶

"Quentin, I need you to come lift Robbie." The evening has passed with Quentin and Ethan spinning vinyls in the living room.

Saxophone and acoustic guitar melodies play through the speakers on the console. The vibe has changed from the gloom of an hour ago. Quentin follows me back to Robbie's room.

"C'mon, big guy, you gotta get in bed." He lifts Robbie from the floor, startling Rocco, who has been sleeping beside him. I pull the covers over Robbie, who never opens an eye. The puppy stands and stretches his legs before shaking himself all over. Quentin puts him in his cage next to the bed, before we go back into the living room.

"Hey, you guys, thanks for having me. Dinner was great and it's been wonderful hanging out with you." Ethan says. "I better get back to the hotel." He stands and takes a few steps towards the front door. "The conference I'm attending starts early in the morning."

"Thank you for coming." Quentin extends his hand as he walks towards Ethan. "You have no idea how much this means." His voice breaks as the two embrace.

"It was no problem. No problem at all. When my mother told me what was going down with you all in California, it brought back so many memories. Apparently it was your mother, Darby, who called my mom, and told her that you said Uncle George molested Robbie. And she told me how you had pulled a gun on Uncle George," Ethan chuckles. "I'm sorry, I don't mean to laugh, but...I can't imagine that part."

"Well, yeah, I had a temporary lapse of sanity, but... wait a minute, you said that my mother told Aunt Birdie what happened?"

"That's right, why?"

"I'm sure my father mentioned it to my mother. And I have no doubt that my sisters are aware of everything , but I had no idea that our mothers confide in each other."

"Oh yeah. I'd often hear them on the phone when I was growing up. And now it seems that their bond had much to do with how Uncle Clarence and Uncle George were alike. As far as family dynamics go, remember I was raised in Piperton during part of my childhood, so believe me, I've seen a lot," Ethan nods with conviction.

"Thank you so much, Ethan." A knot has formed in my throat. "Thank you for coming and thank you for sharing."

"I was happy to. When Quentin asked me to tell my story to Robbie, I didn't hesitate to say yes. I've been through a lot of counseling. For a long time, I was confused and carried a lot of shame. I felt different from other kids, and thought that there was something wrong with *me*." Ethan sighs, "I came to realize one of the ways that evil works——through deflection. The shame was not my burden, It belonged to Uncle Clarence."

"Yes, I absolutely see that." I add.

"Even though it's painful, healing begins when the truth is exposed. I'm pulling for Robbie. Let's stay in touch."

"Yes, we will. We appreciate you." Quentin walks with him to the door.

I reflect on Ethan's visit later in the evening and add it to the other legendary stories of the Coleman family. As a child, I remember my father's mental turmoil when he got the news of his brother's death. He insisted on going alone to Piperton for the funeral, and he returned about a week later.

"So, after Ethan's revelation, and the family's commotion, do you know what became of your father's brother?" Quentin asks as if he's reading my mind.

"Yeah, I remember my father saying how much Uncle Clarence loved to fish, and that one day he was in a boating accident, and drowned in the Saluda River."

Ethan's story about his childhood causes me to reflect on my own.

CHAPTER 11

October 1979, Fort Costera, California...

L ike a blaring firehouse alarm, the bell sounds and signals the end of the school day. Classroom doors swing open, spilling children into corridors. The first week of October seems to churn slowly with the anticipation of Halloween. The scattering of kids every which way has quickly formed into several migrations. Those staying for after-school activities head in a different direction from those walking home through the neighborhood's army base housing—a community that feels secure knowing there's an armed guard posted at the entrance of its gates.

"Wait up, Darby! I'll walk with you, 'kay?"

"Sure, Cynthia."

Cynthia's reddish curls resemble the crimson leaves this time of year. I've never felt as though I'm on display with my friend. Being new at Fort Costera Elementary is difficult enough, as well as being the only Black student in a sea of white faces in second grade. Even so, I have a way of keeping quiet and hope not to be noticed.

Cynthia doesn't seem to be like some of the other girls in class, who have wanted to curiously feel my hair while wrinkling their noses and inquiring, "How'd you get your hair like thaa-aaat?"

But Cynthia on the other hand seems to take it all in stride. She had experienced living among a diverse group of kids while in Panama, where she'd attended school off base. Differences in hair texture and skin color were nothing new, so no big deal to her.

"When my Daddy was stationed in Panama, we got to go sailing, just about every day," she boasted. Like most kids of military families, there was much bragging about the places our father's tour of duty had taken us and the things we had experienced in those distant places.

Crowds of kids scurrying to bike racks and gathering into cliques is the norm. I was bewildered as to why Cynthia had sought me out to walk home with. Maybe it was because we were the two best readers in third grade. Or because we shared a love of walking among the crisp, dry leaves lining the sidewalk and hearing the crunch beneath our lace-up oxfords.

In the brisk air, jack-o'-lanterns line the doorsteps of the attached brick homes. Along the way, ghostly windsocks swing from the trees of neatly edged lawns.

The sound of a roaring motor and a familiar whistle always has a way of causing a kid's eyes to widen as if they've been put in a trance. Upon hearing the whistle, we glare at one another and our attention turns in the direction of the engine roaring from blocks away. The lips of my peers form words with no sound—the Jolly Roger. Like a flock of wild geese, the formation of cyclers reverse, skidding to the side of the street, where they wait for the truck to round the corner. The approaching vehicle has a mesmerizing effect, as if it were a Humvee rolling through a suburb. On top of the yet unseen white van, a pirate's flag blows in the breeze, causing a stir among the bicyclers in the front of the pack. The arrival of the sweet shop on wheels causes the local commune to come to a standstill. Calling it an ice cream truck won't do. Jolly Roger's specialty soft-serve confection is sold from his countertop window. The frozen treat is preferred to the local ice cream franchise located off base. He shows up only now and then, but when he does, one would swear that his appearance has the ability to hypnotize.

The migration of high schoolers who catch up with Cynthia and me are now among the pileup of elementary kids. In the frenzy and out of nowhere, Cynthia's older sister whirls between us, as she hands off a chocolate swirl in a cup.

"Here ya go, Sis. Gotta run."

"Thanks, Gail." Cynthia beams with delight.

"Do you have your key? I'm headed to pep squad practice. Start your homework, and I'll be home in about an hour, all right?"

Without looking up, Cynthia nods while spooning scoops of ice cream into her mouth.

"And make sure you lock the door behind you."

After issuing the gentle reminder, Gail dashes off to catch up with a group of older girls. I'm fascinated after witnessing this exchange between the two. I can clearly see why Cynthia admires and looks up to Gail.

Wow. She's nice—and not bossy.

Wow. My two big sisters never buy *me* Jolly Roger.

Cynthia and I giggle, until we make our way to the final stretch, where we part ways, going in separate directions.

My friend is gone. The turn onto the homestretch causes a gnaw in the lining of my stomach. Inevitable dimness creeps into my carefree mood.

Each step feels like lead in the bottom of my new saddle oxfords as I try to recapture my lighthearted mood from a few moments ago.

Home.

My dad's mantra is "What goes on in this house *stays* in our house."

I proceed up the walkway, my hearing growing keener with each step. I listen for cues that signal the mood inside. I turn the doorknob and prepare myself, as I tremble and hope. No matter what surfaces, there will be no further discussion of it outside our house. Inside of it either.

But all is well with the Colemans. Everything is perfectly fine.

CHAPTER 12

November 1979, Fort Costera, California

"Gather your things and rush home," Ms. Jacobson ordered the class, as apprehension fills her voice. Her news of an early dismissal has us overjoyed yet somewhat anxious. As a third grader, getting dismissed before the other grades let out is pretty exciting. Entering the third grade finally feels like being a big kid—no longer a little second grader.

Lining the walls, the stretch of classroom windows look out onto the playground. I crane my neck to see the brilliant blue sky quickly drifting away in the distance as gray coils of cloud surface along the horizon. Tetherballs that had earlier wrapped their ropes around poles now offer a dismal sway in the breeze. A forgotten jacket lays beneath a swing. An abandoned lunchbox awaits the coming of its owner. The fading sunshine of lunchtime has been replaced by the uncertainty being signaled along the horizon.

My classmates and I flock to the cloak room and grab our coats, like wild geese preparing to take flight. After sliding my feet into my yellow galoshes, I meticulously click the gold metal fasteners in place on my rain slicker. I pull the hood over my head and carefully tie the cords at the end, hoping that my hair doesn't get wet on the way home. Mom had pressed it a couple of days earlier, and I hated the thought of going through the whole ordeal again, sooner than necessary.

From the hallway, Cynthia's sister Gail peeks her head inside the classroom door. Her gaze darts around the room until it rests on her younger sibling, Cynthia, propped against the ledge, peering out the window. She and some other classmates stand against the ledge, fascinated by the whipping wind that causes playground debris to spin into whirls and glide away.

"Cynthia, C'mon! We need to get going!" Gail beckons to her.

I was sure my sister, Gloria, would not come for me, like Gail has for Cynthia.

"Can I walk with you guys?"

The dull gray sky has me somewhat spooked, and I certainly don't want to walk home alone. "Of course, Darby," Gail cheerfully responds.

Once again, I'm captivated by being in the company of these two, who were more like best buddies than sisters.

Cynthia and I waste no time in heading out the door with Gail, before we frantically convey a few goodbyes to the other students. Whipping our scarves around our necks, the three of us brace for the wind and ensuing rainstorm. The weather is a reminder that autumn is quickly fading and winter is approaching—ending the ease of idle walks and leaves crunching under our feet.

The usual animation of after-school activity among kids making their way home is nowhere in sight. No Jolly Roger ice cream truck ringing its bells, or kids bouncing balls along the way. The crowds have quickly dispersed in various directions.

The trees sway more forcefully now than they did moments earlier, when we were in the school's sheltered confines. Cynthia and I balance ourselves by locking arms, with Gail setting the brisk pace a few steps ahead. The motion of the wind quickens our steps and sends us barreling around the corner.

My dreaded moment is about to come. As we near the final crossroads, the two sisters bid me farewell, then head in the opposite direction. I think to myself how I'll have to go the next block alone.

"See ya' tomorrow, Darby."

"Bye, Cynthia." I remove my hand from my pocket and manage a somber wave.

Bursts of light interrupt the gloomy sky, which add to my feelings of isolation. I begin humming to myself while walking at a steady pace. My chapped lips have begun to feel sore from the rush of cold air on my face. I can't wait to get home.

The shifting in the atmosphere leaves me feeling unsettled, as the layers of clouds move in different directions. I brush the strangeness aside and find comfort in passing the familiar houses along the way. A bike leans against an empty flower bed. A skateboard has been left on a lawn.

Fortunately, I'm almost home, since I have to pee.

My pace quickens. I begin to feel a sense of relief, recognizing the chalk markings on the sidewalk. Only days before, I was carefree as I played hopscotch—the game serving as my companion. A welcoming bougainvillea bush sprawls against the front entrance of my house. As I rush up the walkway, familiar voices come from inside, pushing past my loneliness.

As I get closer to the door, I realize the voices are, in fact, shouts. For some strange reason, my dad is home early.

Neither of my parents notice when I open the door and step inside. No greeting. Not even a glad to see you.

I'm invisible.

Where's everybody else?

Standing in the front entrance, I become stiff as I watch the turbulent scene unfold in front of me. Dad and Mom are chest-deep in an argument. Their voices rise louder as one exchange is passed to the other, then reaches a pitch that seems to bounce off the ceiling. Each verbal blow grows angrier by the second.

What are they yelling about?

"You stupid bastard!"

He turns fiercely and yells at her to shut up as he raises one arm.

"Maxine does *not* need glasses," he barks. "Those people don't know what they're talking about!"

Why are they fighting over whether Maxine needs glasses or not? What's going on? And where is Maxine?

"George, you're an uncivilized fool!" Mom wails, then darts into the kitchen. She still hasn't noticed me standing in the entrance, on the other side of the kitchen.

The fact that she has called him uncivilized strikes me as odd. It seems extreme, since it's the exact opposite of all that they've worked so hard to achieve—the appearance that our family is indeed cultured and displays nothing but refinement. There is no sign of backwardness among *us*. Not the Colemans. George Coleman's family is as polished as Fort Costera is immaculate. Make no mistake about it—a white linen tablecloth graces our dinner table *every* day. And our yard is always beyond neatly manicured—well above the minimum required for base housing. Nothing but sophistication defines George Coleman's family.

"You'd better shut your mouth, Louvenia, I'm not going to warn you anymore!"

Mom is on the other side of the wall, still in the kitchen. The coffee percolator rests in its usual place on the kitchen counter. Its contents have long grown cold since the morning's brew.

Mom methodically lifts the lid from the percolator and removes the element which holds the old brewed coffee grounds. With only the element in hand, she walks back into the living room. With a single thrust, she flings the damp coffee grounds at Dad. Appearing to travel in slow motion across the room, the grounds travel through their midair flight and land with a splat on the wall behind the sofa.

My dad's mouth drops open as he watches the traveling coffee grounds. His astonishment escalates into rage. The physical fight is now on. He grabs her and shoves her onto the sofa.

Out of my peripheral vision Gloria comes into the room. But just as soon as she appears, she runs up the steps, wailing at what she's just witnessed.

Although I left the cold air outside, I'm now shaking like a leaf. I can't figure out what's going on. The heaviness in my feet and down my legs have me confused and frozen. As I shiver in the entrance, my stomach tightens into knots. The brawl goes on for what feels like hours across the living room. Is it ever going to end?

"You'd better watch it, Louvenia, before you end up blinding some of these kids!" My dad holds my mother from behind and at the same time has her arms strapped crosswise against her chest.

She scowls and screams at him, trying to free herself. At some point, I manage to take a step from beyond the entrance. I'm now in full view of both of them. The tussle, however, intensifies. They both land on the sofa.

Mom is on her back, looking up at my dad, who has both of his legs straddled across her. He's still restraining her by holding both of her arms against her chest. I still don't think that they're aware that I'm standing there, watching.

Still on her back, my mom fumes at my dad with indignation, before issuing what seems to be the ultimate comeuppance.

"You're ignorant and so are your people!" She smirks with all the disdain she can muster.

Your people? Does she mean the ones in Piperton that he looks down on? The ones he calls country bumpkins?

No. This has to be about something other than Maxine needing glasses.

I glance over to the huge dark spot left on the wall where the coffee grounds landed. The liquid from the moist residue flows down the wall in a slow, continuous stream.

Watching the dark stream, I shake my head. Instead it causes my own steady stream of urine to release, trickling down my legs and forming into a warm puddle on the floor.

CHAPTER 13

January, 1980, Ft. Costera, CA...

Even though I've made new friends right away, I still miss my old friends from Ft. Leonard, Washington. Cynthia has become one of my best friends at my new school.

There are some things that I'm not used to yet, like lining up after recess. At my old school the corridors were inside, right next to the classroom, so you never really noticed kids in other grades, because they were around the corner in another corridor. At Fort Costera Elementary, we line up outside on the blacktop, by grade. It isn't long until I start getting used to how things are done here.

My sister, Gloria, is in fourth grade—one grade ahead of me, even though she's two years older. When the bell rings, the playground monitor calls for each grade to go inside the building. Each class lines up according to height, with the shortest kid first in line. I've never seen so many kids at one time, as each class files into the building. Something feels weird.

In my class of third graders, I'm near the front of the line. One day, the playground monitor calls the higher grades to go inside first, ahead of the lower grades.

Gloria's class happens to be lined up next to my class. The bell rings. Kids dart every which way on the blacktop to their designated areas. One day Gloria's class passes my cluster of third graders as they file into the building. Some of them snicker and lick their tongues when they pass us. As usual, their line is formed by height, gradually peaking, with the tallest at the end of the line. That's when I notice something strange. Something I've never noticed before.

Standing at the very back of the line is Gloria—the tallest kid in her class! As I look around the blacktop, I'm surprised that she is the tallest fourth grader in the entire school! It's the craziest looking thing. There's Gloria bringing up the rear—her head held awkwardly down, like she's trying to lower her body and shrink, or something.

I feel unsettled by her clumsy stance. She looks as though she's uncomfortable that her height is so much taller than her classmates.

All I can do is wonder. How come she's so much bigger than everyone else her age?

Something doesn't feel right.

"Come here, Babycakes. Come dance with your Pa."

Dad lifts me up, and I place my feet on top of his sprawling ones. He often belts out songs without prior warning. That's my Dad, George Coleman. Sometimes when he's doing a household chore, he finds me watching him. He grins, then walks over to the CD player and puts on a song.

I clasp my palm inside his. He spins me around while we dance to an R&B tune. His favorite is, "Isn't She Lovely" by Stevie Wonder. A chuckle emerges from him while he spins me around.

I can pretty much predict what will come next. He begins to reminisce about when he first saw me, only moments after my birth.

"Yessiree, Babycakes. I remember when I first laid eyes on you while you were lying across your ma's chest. My unit had been out for a week on overnight field drills. You weren't supposed to arrive until the following week. They got word to me out in the field that your ma's time had come. My platoon sergeant came rumbling through the range in the jeep to rush me to the hospital. When I finally got there, they were wheeling Louvenia down the hall. You were already born, and when I first saw you, you were bundled up in your ma's arms."

He beams with a sentimental look in his eyes while he retells the story.

"I lifted the blanket on top of your head. Ooh-wee! I'd recognize that nose anywhere. A nose dead-on just like your good ole dad's. And I said, yessss, that's my baby girl, my Babycakes."

His stoic military stance dissolves as he muses over the story. His voice softens with momentary silence taking over. The breakout laughter about my nose is replaced by a delicate tone upon his proud pronouncement of "Babycakes." He's been calling me that pet name since the day of my birth. It's been one of many family tales, told time and time again. My name, Darby, came a few days later.

I don't like my nose, so I'm not especially fond of that part of the story. But I'm always drawn to the tenderness I hear in his tone when he tells it.

I wonder why neither he nor my mother share stories about the birth of my two sisters, Maxine and Gloria. There are no shared remembrances of the first sight of my sisters on the day of their arrival, or even as newborns.

Since I love hearing the nostalgia in his voice, I ask him to tell me more of his memories.

"Dad, what about when you first saw Maxine?" I inquire, anxious to hear another family saga.

The sound of the melody fills the room as he spins me with another whirl. I'm puzzled at first, wondering if he hears me. My body rotates in a spiral, and my view now faces the arched entryway of the living room.

Standing silently beneath the arch and against the side of the wall is Maxine, glaring at our every move. Her bottom lip quivers uncontrollably. How long has she been there, silently watching us, I wonder.

I look up at my dad and notice that he still seems to be in a faraway place. Meanwhile he hums the melody along with Stevie Wonder's harmonica. It doesn't seem as if he is aware that Maxine is standing at the fringes of the room.

Her icy gaze penetrates my skin, while her focus remains on the two of us. I feel timid and completely puzzled by her attitude. Her body is stiff as her fists open and close in tight balls. Her eyes narrow with intensity.

I decide to shift my inquiry from Maxine to Gloria, as we keep dancing.

"Tell me about when you first laid eyes on Gloria," I press my dad.

He doesn't answer. It's as though he doesn't hear me.

It's amazing how he reacts when he doesn't want to answer a question. I just can't figure it out. Sometimes he lifts his head real proud. Then, like he's got a bad taste in his mouth, he'll simply rise from his chair. He'll turn on his heels and leave the room, as if he's tone deaf—leaving me or anyone else, dumbfounded at being left in mid-sentence.

His nonchalant attitude, though, is a bit different from when I question my mom about something I'm not supposed to. At least she'll acknowledge that she hears my question. She'll respond with a soft-spoken retort in the form of her usual question, "Why do you want to know?"

As we dance, I realize that this is one of those times. He's not going to answer my questions. But why?

Don't ask. The message is clear.

So, I learned the lesson—don't ask questions. Forget about it. But sometimes I still remember. And I still wonder why.

CHAPTER 14

The sputtering sound of the green Toyota Corolla announces Maxine's arrival. Through the kitchen window, I watch as she maneuvers the car against the curb. She steps out, then removes her duffel bag from the trunk. With a toss of her long kinky strands, she struts up the walkway, wearing her favorite wool skirt and matching cardigan. And oh, those black, suede, knee-high boots. Wow.

She's a sophomore in college and lives in the dorms across town. She arrives home on most Friday evenings for the weekend, although the drive across town can't be more than twenty minutes.

"I'm ho-o-o-me." The front door slams as she issues her singsong greeting to no one in particular. She walks past the kitchen and heads down the hall without acknowledging me.

The next morning, the sound of clattering causes my eyelids to flutter. I raise my head while realizing that I have drool running along the side of my mouth to my cheek. While rubbing it with the back of my hand, I listen for what might be coming next. The floral scent of the sheets fill my nostrils as I pull the covers closer to my neck. I wait with anticipation to make sense of the business I hear coming from the kitchen. There are no voices. At least not yet.

Who's in there?

I listen intently, remembering that Maxine arrived home last night, just after dinner. I wonder if that's her in the kitchen. If it is, I'm sure I'll like what she's making. She's a good cook. Ever since she was a teenager, she'd sometimes make dinner. She'd try out new recipes that even tasted better than my mom's. Dad would always praise her about cooking and the stuff she did around the house. I guess that's why he likes for her to come home on the weekends.

Pretty soon I should be able to tell who's in there. If it's Maxine *and* Gloria, I'd better brace myself. Those two don't get along for more than five minutes, especially when Papa George is around. I'm sure it won't be long before something jumps off, depending on who is in *whose* space.

The voices are sure to grow louder. The volume and the tone will be my gauge. I'll be able to tell if it's safe to come out or whether I should stay in hiding.

So far it seems like the normal kitchen noise. The clattering sound of plates being taken from cabinets reaches my bedroom. It's followed by the clanging of silverware and the closing of drawers.

Yeah, I'll just play it safe here in bed for right now. I'm too tired to move, since I stayed up until early morning. My private read-a-thon had transported me to another place with the chilling mystery I'd checked out from the library. It kept me turning the pages well past 2:00 a.m. Gloria had fallen asleep nearly as soon as her head hit her pillow, so I didn't have to listen to her complain about turning off the light. I like having my own room ever since Maxine moved into the dorms. But on weekends when she comes home, I'm back bunking in with Gloria.

Uh-oh. I close my eyes as the sound of my dad's footsteps in the hall approaches—so distinct from anyone else's. I can tell by their heaviness and pace. I can even read his mood by the sound of his footsteps. If I hear pacing up and down the hall that signals for me to look out. That means he's on the warpath, with rant and raving sure to follow.

I quickly turn my back toward the door and pretend to be asleep before he opens it. He won't knock. Never has. Since I was little, I made it a habit to stand behind the door when I get dressed—just in case.

The door opens, and he whispers my name, "Darby?"

I lie still and pretend I'm asleep.

"Wake up, Babycakes," he says gently. "Maxine's making breakfast."

He's not as snarly when Maxine is home for the weekend.

I ignore him. I don't feel like being around the dining table with all the chitchat. It all seems so fake. Such a strange vibe.

I'd rather sleep and sneak into the kitchen when everybody's gone. Hopefully there'll be sausages and buttermilk biscuits left. Then I can slip back to my room, crawl into bed, and pick up my adventures through the pages of my book.

He closes the door after several seconds, hopefully convinced that I'm asleep and not interested in eating.

"Good breakfast, Maxine."

From the bedroom I hear his praise lavished upon Maxine. And to no one in particular—yet for everyone's benefit—he utters, "*She* cooks for her family."

Moments later I can no longer resist the aroma coming from the kitchen. I quickly slip into a sweatshirt and leggings and head down the hall.

Maxine is pulling a tray of buttermilk biscuits from the oven, as I enter the kitchen. She places the pan on the stove, then brushes melted butter over the tops of each biscuit. Everyone is seated in the dining room. I take a plate from the cabinet and sit in my usual seat.

Gloria side-eyes me, then directs her attention toward Papa George. "Diddy, Diddy, you know what?" she asks. Her giddiness is not lost on the fact that Papa George had complimented Maxine on the exquisite breakfast she's made.

Gloria's syrupy tone strikes me as phony. It's the one she uses when trying to one-up Maxine and get in Papa George's good graces. It's especially over the top when Maxine's around.

"Hmph," Papa George responds in his typical manner that shows he's listening, although he doesn't look up from his plate.

Gloria takes the cue as acknowledgment that he has heard her. She resumes her story with drama infused at key points.

He chomps away.

"My basketball team is in first place," she gleams. "We won the game last night. I scored twenty-two points."

Maxine enters the dining room and places the platter on the table. She doesn't look at or speak to anyone. It's as if she's in another world.

Miss Louvenia gazes in Maxine's direction as she returns to the kitchen. "Oh, that's so nice," she responds to Gloria's announcement while pouring coffee into Papa George's cup.

He closes his eyes while savoring every bite.

Yeah, it feels gloomy around here. I notice it starts around Friday evenings and goes throughout the weekend. On Saturday mornings—and especially on Sundays before church—everyone would acts especially nice around the table. I can't understand, but it feels so fake.

After breakfast I return to my room and bury myself in the world of Nancy Drew. I'm captivated by her newest adventure and the evidence she stumbles upon. As I turn the pages, I become further immersed in the cryptic case she's trying to solve. She's smart, independent, and shrewd as a bloodhound. What a gal!

My fascination with Nancy is interrupted by my mom singing from the laundry room. It's a familiar song that she sings every now and then. That old spiritual that she's sung for as long as I can remember. I lay the book down on my pillow and listen.

"Here bring your wounded hearts, here tell your anguish. Earth has no sorrow that heaven cannot heal."

She has an amazing way of intertwining the lyrics with her beautiful soprano pitch so that the two become inseparable. And those high notes. Whew.

There is so much intensity in her voice as one phrase blends into the other. She has sung that song for years. Mostly in the morning. She stands in the same place, against the kitchen sink, as she gazes out the window. Her voice rises higher and higher until it reaches a full on wail. That's when I know that she's lost in herself.

There have been times when I've walked in on her and realize that she's totally unaware that I'm standing there. It's as if the song is transporting her far away, while a pool of anguish seeps out of her. Over time I've come to realize that she's deeply bothered by something when she escapes to that unknown place. Totally unreachable.

"I'm out!" Maxine pronounces in a swift stride.

I gather that she's speaking to Mom as she passes through the kitchen. Mom's singing has abruptly ended.

Maxine doesn't say goodbye to me before heading back to campus. But that's typical. I try to catch her before she leaves. I leap from my bed and head down the hall to say goodbye.

Maxine's quick steps click against the tile at the entrance. The front door slams shut. Laser focused and moving fast, she heads toward her car, which is parked in front of the house.

My feet seem to have a mind of their own. I stop running after Maxine and watch her through the window of the front door.

Papa George is outside. He notices Maxine and looks up from trimming his roses. A stern look flashes across his face as he walks in Maxine's direction.

I glance toward the kitchen where my mom stands in a muted state, looking out the window. She's unaware that I'm standing there with a vantage point of her *and* the window of the front door.

The scene outside unfolds.

"Maxine!" Papa George calls out to her.

She ignores him and dashes down the walkway toward her car.

He catches up to her as she tries to open the car door.

He slams it shut.

What's going on?

I look over at Mom. She hasn't moved. She looks on, still standing against the sink, looking out the kitchen window, as if her feet are glued to the floor.

My head spins around with my attention back on the front yard and what's happening against the curb. Papa George's face is contorted. Maxine postures indignantly. He snatches her by the arm.

I'm lost.

She struggles, trying to free herself from his clutches. He's not having it. He pulls her. Maxine's blouse rips across her chest. My throat tightens. I turn around and run back into my room.

And the childhood memories keep rushing in like a tsunami.

How Maxine was able to hold up from it all, I'll never know.

CHAPTER 15

My consciousness is being flooded with childhood memories that won't stop. As I sit up in bed, the occurrences drift in and out like shadows to inform me.

There's a lingering feeling of oppression which seems to taunt me. Growing up, it was the normal mood in the household. This time I see myself as a dream chaser, determined to catch it. Shadows of incidents that are vividly playing around the time I was in high school.

The muffled voices grow angrier by the minute. I'm awakened by Mom and Dad's enraged voices, hurling hostilities at each other. As usual, it's my mother who carries the brunt of the aggression which, in turn, is directed toward my father. Their muted voices merge with the daybreak, injecting a quiet rage through the otherwise calm morning.

Not surprisingly, the two of them are pretty slick at keeping the issues behind their fight hidden. Their closed bedroom door is the barrier that helps keep the details concealed. But the intensity of their voices leaves clues. As far as I can tell, their fights are mainly verbal—and the tension is as thick as molasses on a winter day.

Why is it always in the morning? And what *exactly* is it all about?

Maybe if I tiptoe into the bathroom, I'll be able to gather some intel on what the turbulence in the morning is all about. Passing their bedroom door on the way will give me a better chance of making out what they're saying, and put some sense to this.

After several minutes of intense listening, I decide that it's too risky. I've seen it happen too many times. As predictable as a moth to a flame, their bedroom door is going to fly open. And sure enough, it'll be Mom raging down the hall, stopping for nothing and no one, indicating that she's had it. I sure don't want to be stuck in her path. Yeah, I'd better just stay in my room.

I wish I knew exactly what they're fighting about. For the most part they're hell-bent on appearances. They keep up a good front. The worst of their fights is in their bedroom and not in front of us. The tension usually builds when Papa George enters a room, especially if my mom is also in the same room. She may try to ease the heaviness by making a lighthearted comment and giggle in an attempt to undo what's been brewing. She's amazing at smoothing things over. When she does, it only lasts for a short period of time. Then, as predictable as the sunrise, the obscure fights start again in the morning. The arguments don't seem to get physical, but boy are they heated.

The bad blood between them has been baked into the walls of the house. It's penetrated so deeply that the walls must be burning internally from all the pressure.

Their bedroom door slams shut.

Oh good. Now I can get into the bathroom. I've got to go to school early for freshman choir practice. I cautiously open my door and peep through the crack.

Mom comes rushing down the hall, grumbling and shaking her clenched fists in the air. She's dressed for work, wearing her beige smock over her skirt and blouse. Her contorted eyebrows are full of disdain, even as her glazed eyes remain focused on the end of the hallway. I go unnoticed as she passes me, then turns and speeds through the kitchen. She slams the back door, which is followed by the sound of the garage door's springs as it lifts open.

Where's Gloria? She must still be in her room. She has a knack for lying low and surfacing only at the opportune time. And Maxine? Well, she's lucky that she's out of the line of fire too. She went off to college, but only across town. Even though she's less than ten miles from home, she decided to live in the dorms. Dad's always calling her on the phone, yelling at her to come home on the weekends.

I open my door, ready to duck down the hall. At the same time, my parents' bedroom door propels open and out comes my dad. He's dressed for work in his jeans and a plaid work shirt. I know better than to ask what all the commotion was about. I'd better not do anything other than pretend that I haven't heard anything. The military mantra of "carry-on" has always been in full effect in the Coleman household.

His commanding presence says it all. Don't ask me a thing. He mutters a stern greeting, followed by his orders.

"Morning, Darby. You and Gloria better not be late to school."

"Kay, Dad." I slide past him and into the bathroom.

With his long strides, he makes his way down the hall and out the back door.

As the minty toothpaste glides across my toothbrush, the walls seem to soften. The R&B sounds of Luther Vandross lighten the vibe after I turn on the radio that's sitting on the bathroom counter. The water flowing from the faucet lightens the mood as I sing in harmony along with the group. Rubbing Noxzema across my face, I'm pleased to see that the pimple on my chin has nearly dried up.

Just as the harmonies reach a crescendo, there's a heavy knock on the door. Without warning, the explosive thump is followed in succession by more rapid banging.

"Darby, come on outta there. You can't hog the bathroom. Other people have to get in, you know."

What the…?

It's Gloria. Like a snake, she seems to have slithered out of nowhere. And why is she always so mad?

I feel worn out, and the day has just started.

CHAPTER 16

May 2010, Los Vientos, California...

The vivid images of confronting Papa George are tormenting me. It's the singular thing I daydream about—coming face-to-face with him in a hostile standoff.

I'm ready.

I don't expect an admission of guilt. He's always blamed someone else for something large or small. Never him. No way.

In fact, I fully expect him to deny it. Drama and deceptive innocence may even kick in, as he pretends to be hurt that I have accused him of such a thing—molesting Robbie.

I can imagine his syrupy-fake response. "How could you say such a thing, Darby? I would *never* do anything to hurt Robbie!"

Ugh. How wicked. I want to throw up.

His pride and superior posture encapsulate him. I can only imagine his indignation at my accusation. Perhaps, the fury of his wrath will ignite. He'll expect that because of his rage, I'll become de-energized. He'll hope that I'll back down and the ugly accusation will fade away, like the smell of a cheap deodorant.

Swept under the rug. Buried. Kept secret.

No. Not this time. The sweep-it-under-the-rug thing is well established in dealing with Coleman family unpleasantries. The objective has always been to bury the hatchet and instead act with civility toward one another. "Y'all, stop that and act civilized!" Ms. Louvenia would pronounce while we were growing up.

The message was clear. Peace must be kept, and the Coleman's middle class image was to be upheld by any means necessary. This was the Coleman family mantra, which operated like a well-oiled machine. Never mind the circumstances surrounding a conflict. Individual feelings had to be sacrificed for the appearance of order and family civility. As a result, Maxine, Gloria, and I learned to be very proficient in our portrayal of family unity—all for the cause.

Ms. Louvenia was the designated peacekeeper. "Shh-Shh. *I said* that's enough" was her way of diffusing an impending disturbance. Her role was to shift into high gear, without command from Papa George, by pouring cold water on any situation that was about to erupt. Her further pronouncement of "Now hush!" was all that was needed for us to know that an issue was officially closed. She knew her role, and she performed it well. Any further discussion would be incapable of producing a desirable outcome.

Disputes among family members were something that were mostly left unresolved. The reality was that even through all the pretense and appearances, behind closed doors ours was anything but a peaceful family unit.

The most extreme noise level came from Papa George, who could be heard yelling about something or someone from any location throughout the house. An infraction could be as simple as a dirty dish left in the kitchen sink or as monumental as his dinner not being served on time. Make no mistake, at all times, he was the king of *his* castle, and expected his household to run properly, in military fashion. Of course, there would be no other way. He was Sergeant George Coleman.

Today, however, I envision driving the thirty-minute stretch along the interstate to my parents' home. Along the way, cars will drift freely to the side, allowing me to pass, as if I'm driving an emergency vehicle. The reality, however, is that I won't be pressed for time.

The steady pace will grow to a sluggish crawl. My empty stomach churns as I mentally prepare myself, walking up the familiar walkway lined by Papa George's hydrangeas. I can imagine the conflict that is about to ensue when I confront them together. Papa George and Ms. Louvenia. Shameless perpetrators—the cutthroat and his accomplice.

Yes, I can visualize it clearly. Exactly how it'll all play out. Words need not be spoken. They murdered my baby boy's spirit.

I brush past my mom when she opens the front door. Without acknowledging her, I move past her, dismissing her with a backward flip of my hand. Unfazed, I stride into my parents' home, steps clicking on the hardwood floor, as I proceed down the hallway leading into the den.

Papa George is laying on his back in his burgundy recliner. He's in the middle of his afternoon catnap, head propped toward the ceiling, mouth open. His dog, Trooper, dozes in his lap, while the continuous newsreel from the cable news channel penetrates the room.

As usual, Papa George's pride does not allow him to wear his hearing aids. The volume coming from the TV is raised to an enormous decibel level. The force of the sound waves move through the room, like bouncing rubber balls hitting playground asphalt.

I stand over him for several minutes, watching his chest move rhythmically up and down through relaxed breathing motions.

My face feels flushed.

Trooper peers up at me, studying the piercing expression on my face, then sheepishly scurries from Papa George's lap. Papa George rouses from his sleep, awakened by the sound of his own snoring. Startled, his bloodshot eyes open. He's astounded to see me glaring back at him. Seconds pass with each ticking of the clock above the mantle. His shoulders are relaxed and confident. The corners of his mouth turn upward upon realizing it's just me—his Babycakes—dropping by for a surprise afternoon visit. He smiles warmly, with his outstretched arms ready to embrace me.

No, not this time. This will not be swept under the rug.

I lean toward him with a deliberate move, hands firmly grasped around his neck. Calmly, I commence with a steady and forceful squeeze. He gasps and struggles for air. He kicks and swings his arms violently, trying to loosen my grip. He searches my eyes with bewilderment and fear. My heart pounds as my grip tightens firmly, both hands at his throat, imagining life gradually oozing from him.

"Darby. Darby! *Babe!*"

"Hu-Huh?"

"What were you thinking just now? Where *were* you?"

Looking at my hands, the reality of the here and now comes into being. Gooey dough covers my hands like a warm cocoon. The small balls have been flattened in the process of making home-made cinnamon rolls. With less intense motions, I knead the dough with the heels of my trembling hands. The racing of my heart slows to a steady thump. My thoughts drift into obscurity like vapor from a fog as reality emerges and comes into focus.

I take a deep breath. "Oh. Uh, nothing in particular."

"Babe, you okay?"

"Mm-hmm."

Quentin stares at me quizzically. As he moves closer to me, he affectionately touches my forehead with the back of his palm and whispers, "Babe, you're clammy. You are *not* okay."

I search Quentin's face and can only return his worried gaze.

CHAPTER 17

"Bishop Jefferson will see you in a few minutes. Please have a seat."

"Okay. Thanks, Charlene."

While waiting for the bishop, I think back on my conversation with Quentin and how he has begged me not to directly confront Papa George.

"Babe, I'll support you in whatever you decide to do, but I don't think you should confront him face-to-face. You know that he has always kept a gun in his house. The fact that he's a pedophile is an indication of his mental and emotional instability. Even though you're right in your position, you could end up being totally wrong in your response. It seems to me that everything hinges on how this is handled."

But waiting for things to be handled has ended. It seems that there will be no accountability for my father. The investigator on the case called yesterday to say that they did not have enough evidence to bring charges against Papa George. And Robbie's pediatrician did not find physical evidence of sexual abuse.

Weeks have passed, and as much as I try, I'm zombied out. I've again found solace in lying in the lounge chair on the deck, comforted by the sun, with each passing day. From dawn to dusk, a good day is measured by whether I manage to comb my hair and get dressed.

Quentin and I have been members of Grace Worship Center for a few years. Though we've never sought counseled one-on-one with Bishop Jefferson, I've always sensed that along with his wisdom, he would be easy to talk to, one on one. His demeanor is one of warmth and integrity, tempered with insight and understanding.

A judgmental stance is absent where he's concerned. He seems to operate from a place that people are just people. Whether they've made mistakes, like rippling drops or full-blown blunders, God loves us anyway—although there may be some consequences that ultimately flow from one's decisions and actions. The parishioners absolutely adore him. Yesterday I left a message with Charlene, his assistant, for a counseling appointment. She called me back this morning, saying that there had been a cancellation and a slot had opened up for ten o'clock.

As I wait for the bishop to come to the front office, I think about his magnetic sermon on Sunday. His message wove in the analogy of a card game and a metaphor about playing the hand we've been dealt in life. I think about his stance as he stood at the podium. His way of leaning into the lectern with the intensity building—a cue that you especially did not want to miss his next point.

"Life doesn't always happen for us. Sometimes it happens *to* us."

The pitch of his voice has a way of reaching a crescendo when he hits his stride.

"Each one of us struggles with difficulties in life. God knows the problems we are going to face, and He has the solutions to deal with them."

It's as though all the goodness that I've known my parents to be was just an act—a vicious betrayal meant to mask who they really are and with the goal of carrying out their barbaric scheme. Again, my thoughts turn to my suspicions that his deviant behavior is serial. This is too much. Way too much!

It's too, too big. I can't explain it in words, but I already sense layers upon layers of family secrets. Coded language, innuendos, and silent glances were often exchanged from one family member to another—their meanings kept secret and only known among them, especially at the breakfast table in the mornings.

"Darby, can I get you a cup of coffee or perhaps a bottle of water?" Charlene interrupts my thoughts.

"Thanks, Charlene. Water would be great."

"The bishop will be out shortly." Charlene hands me a bottle of water from the dorm-size refrigerator in the outer office.

Moments later, Bishop Jefferson's soothing voice fills the air as he steps from his office to the outer one. "Well hello, Darby. So good to see you. Come on back."

Following him to his office, I'm once again aware of the heaviness in my legs, which intensifies with my every effort to take a step. I thought I'd shaken this, but the burden has its hooks in me again, like an anchor determined to weigh me down and keep me at bay.

Bishop Jefferson's office is welcoming. The reddish-brown desk accentuates the warm tones throughout the office. The wall is lined with academic achievements, along with family pictures. A quilt hanging on the opposite wall is woven with Bible verses that refer to courage, faith, and love.

I take a seat at a small, round table across from his desk. He pulls up a chair and sits across from me.

"So good to see you, Darby. What can I help you with today?"

"Bishop, I'm not sure. I got a call a few weeks ago from Robbie's teacher. She asked me to meet her in the principal's office that afternoon, saying not to be alarmed, but there was something she had to discuss with me. When I got there, she was seated in the principal's office, along with Robbie and the principal. Robbie looked very distressed, and I could tell that something was very wrong. Well, Robbie stood up, and after much prompting, he finally said that my father … my father molested him."

Bishop Jefferson listens solemnly with his chin in the palm of his hand while I share with him the details of that bleak afternoon.

"I'm so, so, sorry, Darby."

"Bishop, I'm stunned. I'm horrified that my father would do such a thing. I know Robbie didn't make this up. It explains his behavior the past few months. He's been very withdrawn, and I've noticed that his appetite has changed. Drastically. He shows very little interest in the things that he used to be so excited about—Transformers, action figures, his friends … you name it, he no longer cares about any of it. He's so beat up, with a crushed spirit. We have him in therapy and see a little bit of improvement from time to time. My child is in a very dark place."

With that last sentence, a sense of powerlessness surfaces over me. My feeble attempt to compose myself is useless, as I relive the impact of my father's monstrous actions. Tears flow against the backdrop of convulsive sobs.

Bishop Jefferson ponders over my words. Pushing his chair from the table, he walks over to his desk and picks up a box of tissues. He places it in front of me in the midst of my spasms. After a while, I'm able to speak again. My weeping tapers off.

Reassembling himself back into his chair, he consoles me. "Oh, my daughter."

With a bold consciousness, I pronounce, "I don't like my father!"

The proclamation has ushered a fierce release from my body. As the tension escapes from my neck and shoulders, I sense equilibrium being restored to my entire being. Through my tears, I glance at the bishop.

His eyes are moist. Why does he look so hurt?

It hits me. There's no doubt that he's compassionate, but he may also be feeling deeply empathetic because he has a daughter about my age. A momentary hush overtakes the room.

Intentionally I dial back my emotions and attempt to convey what I believe my next steps will be.

"I need to confront him and let him know that I'm aware of what he did to Robbie. I need to hold him accountable."

"What do you expect will be accomplished by confronting him?"

Bishop Jefferson's question causes me to pause. "He can't get away with this, Bishop. I did tell my mom, though. She basically came unglued. So, I'm sure she replayed our conversation with my father."

"Have you ever thought that the fact that *he* knows that *you* know exposes him more deeply than you think? He *knew* it was wrong, yet he thought it was covered up. He can no longer bury it. It's as though you've snatched the covers off and held the issue up against the light. That accomplishes more than a confrontation would."

"I hadn't thought of it that way, Bishop."

My thoughts linger as I process this new perspective. "Uhm, as I said Robbie's in counseling, but I wonder if you could recommend a therapist for me. I know I'm stuck and feeling depressed most of the time." I become perplexed, noticing the corners of his mouth forming a slightly concealed grin.

"Didn't Quentin tell you?"

"Tell me what?"

"He came into my office after church on Sunday and shared with me what's been

going on with you guys. The more he talked, the angrier I could see him getting. He told me that you need some help and thought you could benefit from therapy. I referred him to a friend of mine, Dr. Floyd. He works with individuals and families who have experienced sexual abuse and emotional trauma.

"Didn't he give you the card I gave him?" Peering above his reading glasses, he looks at me pensively. He appears to be trying to hide a grin.

"Uh, no, he didn't."

That's weird. Why is he trying to conceal his grin?

Shifting his tone and choosing his words carefully, he delivers his next set of instructions with chilling, yet steady, caution.

"Darby, this has now been brought into the light. People have been killed over matters such as this."

I'm astonished.

That's the same thing Quentin was saying.

With soft persistence, he adds, "Darby, no matter what... don't get ahead of the Holy Spirit."

I nod and say, "Yes, I'm listening..."

CHAPTER 18

Stevie Wonder's voice fills me with pure bliss this afternoon. Singing while driving alone has always been one of my simple joys. It makes me so happy. He was one of my dad's favorite R&B singers. My dad would tell stories of how he would spin those vinyls over and over again on his stereo player. Later on, I learned the words to many of the same songs that he loved as well.

The light of the autumn afternoon beams through the sunroof as I careen along the highway. Bustling drivers and cars weaving are of no concern to me—so nice to drift and be carried with ease by Stevie. The lighthearted melody floats through the car and takes me back to a time that was innocent and uncomplicated.

Cars swish through the neighborhood faster than usual. The steady stream of vehicles turn the corner as if they are part of the same caravan. One occupant may be commuting from an office job. Another may be heading home from work as a blue collar worker. Either way, the lone person in each vehicle appears thrilled that it's the end of another work week.

I know my dad will be home soon. He's never late—4:30 on the dot. He might even be a few minutes early since it's Friday. And payday too? Yeah, he'll be early.

And just like that. The white station wagon pulls into the driveway. Dad beeps twice.

I jump from the front step where I've been waiting, just as he hollers through the window. "C'mon Babycakes, grab your sweater and let's get to the bank before it closes." I never consider why it's just the two of us—it just is. It's as simple as that.

We reach downtown Denton, with all the hustle and bustle of a typical Friday. The car slows down as we approach the bank. He looks along the line of parked cars against the curb.

"I bet there won't be any parking spaces."

"Yeah. You're probably right. We'll have to go into the parking garage."

He whistles as he takes my hand and we walk a few blocks toward the bank. Keeping up with his long strides is part of the ritual, as well as listening to the knowledge he imparts.

"Gotta save your money. Always put some away first." His dose of wisdom is administered as if he's talking to himself, yet I get the benefit of hearing. I listen along until we go inside the bank. I love the movement and activity. Most of all I love the echoes that bounce off the elevated ceiling.

We get to the counter where he hands the teller his paycheck and another slip of paper.

"Here you go, Mr. Coleman." The teller hands my dad back several bills that he puts inside his wallet.

"Here." That's the singular word he issues as he grins and hands me several dollars. There's no need for me to respond. With one hand, I stuff the bills in my pocket and take his arm with the other.

"Let's go on over to the chocolate shop." We head back in the direction of the parking garage, leaving the sounds of the bank behind. "Yeah, you better marry a man who's gonna be something in life—a hardworking man like your ole pa. But first, make sure you get your education." He squeezes my hand as we cross the street to the sweet shop.

As if by magic, Stevie has conjured memories of the days of my uncluttered youth. I smile as I remember the excitement of receiving the high-school graduation gift from Mom and Dad—a music player with headphones. I was overjoyed because I could go into my own private world while listening to Stevie Wonder and the likes of whomever I chose. No more interruptions of "Darby, turn that thing down!"

The euphoria of carefree driving and singing is pure rapture. Stevie continues as my accompaniment, and the tender symmetry triggers more memories of falling asleep with those headphones on. I would leave the headphones in my ears and can recall waking in the morning with them still in place.

Night after night, my bedroom door would creep open. I would lie in bed with my back to the door, headphones still on, and the music player under my pillow. I thought I might get in trouble for still being up, although I never did. From the time I was a young girl, my dad would shoo us off to bed and scream, "I'd better not hear any noise! I'd better be able to hear a rat pee on cotton!" I would shudder at the sound of his booming voice and scurry off to bed. I never got up during the night, not even to go to the bathroom. This was the conditioning from as far back as I could remember.

At this point in time, however, I was a teenager at home with Mom and Dad and my older sister, Gloria. Maxine was living across town on the campus of Elmhurst University. Her bedroom was no longer in use, so it had been handed over to Gloria. Stevie Wonder would continue the serenade through the headphones. I remember the door occasionally slowly opening, then closing. I simply pretended to be asleep. No one ever came in. Somehow I knew it was my dad. No words were ever spoken—just taking a few seconds to look in on me, and then he'd close the door. I never sat up in bed or even acknowledged his peering inside.

This was a normal routine—Dad checking on me, followed by the door softly closing as usual. Seconds later I would hear his steps outside my door, creeping slowly past my room on the vinyl hallway runner. The steps were light, not their normal cadence. Then I'd hear another door down the hallway creep open, then quietly close. There were no more footsteps to be heard in the calm stillness. I'd drift into undisturbed sleep, never giving it another thought.

Little did I know at the time, but now reflecting on all that was going on around me, perhaps this was one of many components of my saving grace—a key point in my own life—the fact that I figuratively was in another unsuspecting, faraway world.

To think that, even today, although I'm well into my thirties, I rarely get up at night to go to the bathroom. Even when I was pregnant with Robbie, I would wait until morning to go to the bathroom. It's amazing how I've connected this to the fear that was instilled in me from childhood. Once Papa George had commanded us to bed, it had better be quiet throughout the house. Quiet. "Like a rat peeing on cotton." I knew better than to get up—not even to investigate the strange footsteps I'd heard going past my room throughout the night. I wasn't about to risk facing his wrath.

Listening to the throwback song has caused me to reflect on a particular time in my life and place meaning as to what was going on. The reflection is one of many which is being retrieved from the storage of my mind. Things keep popping up and taking me back to what I used to think was insignificant.

It's astonishing how Stevie's lyrics have just guided me—how they've connected the dots that I was never able to do on my own.

The melody continues as I turn the corner and pull into the driveway.

Just an ordinary song. A song which has triggered a memory.

CHAPTER 19

After completing her reverse spinal twist, Paige shakes her newly cut asymmetrical bob into place and stands up. We both pick up our mats from the studio floor.

The throbbing in my temples the hour before our yoga session has now disappeared. Only days ago, waves of depression taunted my muscles with pangs of anguish, trying to pull me into an unknown abyss. Traces of tension have moved through my extremities and have now escaped. The welcoming beads of sweat trickle down my back, offering a cool release.

I'm getting stronger.

A few yogis migrate from the studio and into the outer gym, looking more peaceful than when they had arrived. I'm feeling the same way.

"Darby, I'm taking my parents' slot at the condo in a few weeks. Why don't you think about coming with me to Cape Larimar?" Paige interrupts my thoughts with her offer.

"Oh, Paige, that's so nice of you." As I roll up my mat, I can't help but feel grateful. I've been practicing living in the moment, even through the pain beneath the surface that I can't imagine will ever go away.

I'm intentional about looking for something each day to be grateful for. Right now, it's the feel-good sensation of stretched-out muscles and being in the moment with my dear friend.

Her appeal continues. "There's always so much to do on the resort. Bike rides around the cape, or you can just lie on the beach all day to your heart's content. I'll invite CJ and Camille. It'll be a girl's getaway."

We fall behind the others, who are already through the double doors and into the outer gym. The musky odor hangs in the air. Somehow it doesn't bother me today. The repetitive motion of feet pounding on treadmills joins with the rhythmic hum of its conveyor belt.

I ponder Paige's offer as we merge with the others who are already out the front door. *Will Robbie be okay without me for a week? And I need to book my next counseling session with Dr. Floyd.*

Paige pauses while fluffing her new do. "So will you think about it, Darby?"

"Oh, I sure will, Paige. That's so sweet of you. I'll give you a call in a couple of days. "OK, sweetie. Just know that I'm here for you."

We amble through the parking lot, sipping from our water bottles before hugging goodbye.

Driving home, I my thoughts drift to my first therapy session with Dr. Floyd and how pleasant it had been. So glad Bishop Jefferson referred me to his friend. I guess it's a good sign when you're disappointed that the session is over so soon. It feels longer than a few weeks ago that I first met with him. Not only is he a good listener, but I could sense the empathy of my inner turmoil on his face. I hadn't considered my feelings about my family's dynamics before now. I'd simply accepted them as they were. I hadn't identified the layers of dysfunction—my feelings of being shaped in a family with a sexually abusive father. I'm floored that this was my environment. I'm even more floored that I was not sexually abused. For some reason, evil skipped over me. I can't figure out why I was spared. But now it feels as though it's bigger than that. I don't have the words yet, but it's bigger than my revelation about what Papa George really is.

Exhale.

My blinker clinks as I turn into the subdivision. A runner in her early twenties trots across the street that's bordering the park. As her pace picks up, her brown ponytail swings back and forth while her golden retriever runs alongside her. The neighborhood's burgeoning energy is clearly awakening, as it approaches another midmorning Saturday.

Pulling into my driveway, I'm appreciative of the air flowing through my lungs. The patterned brickwork leading to the front entrance meets with the textures of the potted succulents lining the walkway. Like the green-and-purple cabbages leading to the archway, the different shapes emerge, expanding from one plant to the other.

I'm grateful.

Before I insert my key in the lock, the sound of Robbie's laughter makes its way through the door, leaving me hopeful for the return of his former self. I can see his grin before it appears on the other side of the door, feel his gangling arms stretching tightly around me, see his sweet face.

As I walk from the entrance into the kitchen, Quentin turns and smiles in my direction, stirring a pot simmering on the stove. Robbie jumps from the stool against the kitchen island, rushing toward me. My vision has become reality.

Inhale. Today's a good day. Exhale.

I'm grateful.

CHAPTER 20

"**Y**es, Robbie seems to be a quiet child. But that's okay. He gets along well with his classmates. He seems to be doing okay," his teacher informs me. "And I can see that he loves geography. Occasionally he'll isolate himself, but when I notice this, I'll draw him out. He loves to help. I make sure to ask him to do me a favor by cleaning the chalkboard or some other task. "Thanks, Mrs. O'Neill. I appreciate it." Twirling my hair around my finger, I'm a bit relieved that he's adjusting to fourth grade.

"My pleasure, Mrs. Shields. Please call me anytime."

Just for today. One day at a time.

Looking out the kitchen window, onto the raised deck, I see that the empty lounge chair and its lush cushions, waiting to provide comfort in the afternoon sun. Traces of the previous gloomy days threaten me from beyond the patio.

No. Not today. I'll keep things moving, thanks.

I hang up the phone, thinking that at this point in time, this is the best I can hope for—hoping that I'll continue to see improvement with minimal setback. Continue the counseling and and keep praying.

I'm so glad to have a moment to myself. I should get dinner ready. It's already four o'clock, and Quentin and Robbie will be home soon. I'm glad Quentin called earlier to say he'd pick up Robbie from school. No doubt they've stopped off somewhere, probably eating something that they shouldn't be eating, right about now.

I better do some laundry first. I walk into Robbie's room, pull the hamper from his closet and start sorting his clothes. As usual, the stack of dark clothes is larger than the whites.

I find more white polo shirts from the bottom of the hamper and spray the collar with pre-wash. I think I'll do the whites first.

One after the other, I go through the shirts, making sure not to miss any stains before they go into the wash. Then it occurs to me. None of the collars are chewed on! That's what I used to find! And I couldn't figure it out. His psychologist said recently that was probably how he had dealt with the stress and anxiety of all that he was silently going through.

As I pick up the pile I feel grateful. It's a step in the right direction. I head towards the laundry room while the sound of knocks come from the front door. Why are they knocking? Those two and their silly jokes.

Heading to the entrance, I decide to throw them a curveball by going into my three little pigs' voice.

"Knock, knock. Who is it? You probably have the wrong how-ouse."

Hee. Hee.

I feel a little foolish to be staring back at the mailman when I open the door.

"Hi there. Certified mail. Just sign right here." He suddenly hands me a green postcard to sign, while pointing to the signature line.

"Oh. Okay."

I close the door, and turn the envelope right side up. It's addressed to Mr. & Mrs. Quentin Shields. Handwriting looks familiar.

It's my mom's. Certified mail? What's going on?

Trying to contain my nerves, I hastily open the envelope, making every effort not to tear the letter inside. Unfolding the letter, I see that the words are typewritten. That's weird.

> *Dear Darby and Quentin,*
>
> *We are deeply shocked and hurt by your accusation of sexual assault against Robbie. You know that your mother is very sick, and I'm not well either. We all need to get together to talk about your charge. We can't believe that Robbie would say such a thing. He knows I would never do anything to harm him.*
>
> *How could you accuse your mother of luring him to our house?*
>
> *I'm alarmed that you are vilifying my name. I've worked hard in the military and the community for our family's reputation. For you to drag the Coleman name through the mud is beyond belief.*
>
> *We need to settle this. Perhaps it would be best if we get assistance from a neutral party. Someone of your choosing who you respect, maybe your pastor.*
>
> *Please let us hear from you immediately. This is weighing heavily on us all.*
>
> *Dad*

The weight of stress churns through my gut as I sit at the kitchen table. I reflect back to my visit with my mother in the rehab facility several weeks ago. As she lay in bed, her performance about my accusation had been so telling. Although I believed she was an accomplice, I never accused *her* of anything. How telling that this letter mentions Robbie being *lured* to their home. Yep, that's exactly how my mother aided in the assault.

This is beyond pathetic. Neither of my parents uses a computer, so Maxine would have had to factor into the equation. Why has Maxine inserted herself where she doesn't belong? I didn't address her. This is an obvious attempt to cover for Papa George, just as I had anticipated. I had suspected a cover-up, but Maxine's assistance is telling as well.

Taking the indirect route of telling Mom has forced Papa George to make a move. He's taken the bait, and everyone else has lined up and closed ranks.

Who knows what other secrets there are? What other grandchild may have been sexually assaulted by him? Both Maxine and Gloria have had their kids around him—and often.

I can't help but notice his hurtful tone. And sure enough, appearances mean everything. *I've worked hard in the military and the community for our family's reputation.*

Oh, I want to throw up!

His pitiful plea of innocence is disgusting. "I would never do anything to harm Robbie."

Oh, blah, blah, blah.

Tossing the letter across the counter, I take a deep sigh and turn my attention back to making dinner.

And calculate my next move.

I admire my delicious looking creation bubbling in the casserole dish. Robbie plops down at the table next to Quentin, butters his dinner roll, and eagerly takes a bite. He looks up, noticing that I'm still tossing the spinach salad, then sheepishly lays the roll on his plate.

Quentin blesses the food.

"Looks good, Mom. I'm so-o-o hungry."

"I'm glad. You guys took longer than usual getting home. I was beginning to think you had stopped off for a snack."

Remaining silent, the two exchange glances, communicating only with their eyes.

"So how was your day?"

"Pretty good. We finally wrapped up the commercial project that'd been taking so long. I expect that things will be slowing down for a while, going into the fall."

Robbie rises from the table, carrying his plate to the sink, just as the doorbell rings.

His eyes follow Quentin, who has risen from the table to answer the door.

"Mom, I'm done with my homework. I left it on my bed for you to check. Can I play video games for a while?"

"Okay, just for thirty minutes."

Quentin returns to the kitchen with Robbie's friend. The two boys immediately head to the den.

The buzz from my phone grabs my attention. Picking it up from the kitchen counter, I glance at the text from Shannon, Dr. Floyd's receptionist.

Hi, Darby. Got your message earlier. We've had a cancellation, and it looks like we can fit you in at 5:30 on Thursday. Please let me know if that works.

Oh that's great. I really had hoped to get an earlier appointment to see Dr. Floyd, especially in light of this latest fiasco with my family.

I text back *Y* for yes.

Reaching over to Quentin's plate, I help myself to a heaping forkful of the cheesy macaroni as I contemplate Paige's offer of two days ago. My fingers wrap around one of my kinky coils before twirling the end around my index finger.

"Babe, the other day, Paige mentioned that she's going to Cape Larimar in a few weeks. She vacations there every year at this time and stays at her family's condo. She invited me to come along with her. It'll probably end up being a girl's trip, along with CJ and Camille. I don't know if I should go, though."

Quentin swallows the last of his water, gazing intently at me.

"Darby, I think it'll be good for you to get away. You should consider going. Robbie and I will be fine. And it just so happens that I won't be traveling for the next few months."

From the den, repetitive jingles blast from Robbie's video game console. Every so often, the beeps and buzzes completely fade, only to be heard by the excited shrill of his and Jeremy's "Oh no!"

As my fork reaches toward Quentin's plate, within an inch of its target, it abruptly clashes with his fork in a mock duel.

"Thanks, sweetie. I'll give Paige a call tomorrow."

With a grin, he proclaims, "That's *my* macaroni."

CHAPTER 21

Days later I sit on the edge of my bed, taking inventory of my beachwear. I'm excited about the girls' trip to Cape Larimar. The summer whites in the back of my closet beckon, as though they're anxiously waiting to leap out. Placing my beige espadrilles into the suitcase along with several shorts and tank tops, I ponder Papa George's letter.

Certified letter. Humph.

His attempt to intimidate me causes my face to grow warm. What does he expect me to do? Shrink? His cowardly response is typical of the bully who flees when he's confronted. It's obvious that the truth I've unleashed has set off a Coleman firestorm. Yet it feels as if there's so much more. What else are they covering up? They've closed ranks, and they've all piled on. There's more to this story. Their weird behaviors say so.

I've been feeling so much better lately. I'm thankful those dreary days are for the most gone. Each day brings new hope.

I need a little break from packing. I head downstairs into the kitchen to survey the contents of the refrigerator. Chilled mocha frappuccino looks good. Roasted almonds in the pantry. Twisting the top off the bottle, I take a long sip of the cold, chocolatey brew.

Along with packing, I contemplate the household things that need to be done before I take off for vacation. My mind lingers over Papa George's letter. Picking up my phone from the kitchen counter, I decide to use the direct approach. I tap the contact button for Mom and Dad's landline. The phone rings several times before my mom's cheery voice answers.

"Hello?"

"Hi, Mom. How are you?"

Pause.

"Oh. Hi, Darby. I'm … I'm good."

Her stumbling cues me that my call may be confusing. She's probably wondering, "Didn't you get the message that King George has summoned you?"

"Can I please speak to Dad?" I ask, hoping she picks up on my polite insistence.

"Yes. Sure."

Pause.

"Hello?" The raw force of Papa George's voice moves through the phone with its usual strength.

"Hello, Dad. Just wanted to let you know that I got your letter. You'll hear from me by mail very soon," I say with the frosty formality of an unspoken "Don't call me, I'll call you" phrase.

"Well, don't let it be too long," he responds, as the intensity rises in his voice.

I don't let him go any further.

Click.

Of course. Just like your letter said—it's weighing heavily on you.

Instead of heading back upstairs to finish packing, I take a detour into the den.

Adjusting myself at the desk, I open my laptop and type a response to Papa George's letter.

Dear Dad,

This is to follow up on our conversation today. I appreciate your input that we need to move this along soon. I believe that you are sincere in wanting to address the accusation of sexual violence against Robbie.

I accept your offer to meet at a place of my choice. Quentin and I are open to meeting with you—along with my therapist.

Prior to our group meeting, he has suggested that it may be helpful if you and Mom were to meet alone with him, or even you, solely, with him.

His name is Dr. William Floyd. Please give him a call to set an appointment. After your initial session, he advises that the four of us get together to meet with him. Please do not bring along other family members. Thanks in advance for respecting these boundaries.

I too, am committed to alleviating any further destruction.

Sincerely,

~Darby

Seconds later, the paper slides from my printer and onto my desk. After retrieving the page, I grab my flip-flops and head down the hallway to the garage, en route to the post office—with the task of sending my letter the same way it came.

Certified.

Yeah, I'll meet with you, Papa George. No problem.

CHAPTER 22

Lifting the last piece of luggage from the curb, the Uber driver slams the trunk as we pile into the car. From the airport's curbside, he pulls away while the police officer motions the fleet of cabs and other vehicles into the congested traffic. I'm thrilled with anticipation of the next four days together with my best friends.

"This humidity is raging!" CJ gathers the hair at the nape of her neck and twists it into a messy bun. "I'm glad I decided to get my hair braided. The last thing I want on my mind is to worry about sweating out a perm."

Camille gulps her water from the nearly empty bottle she's been carrying. "So what's going to be first on the agenda? I'm looking forward to a beachside massage."

"And yoga on the beach at sunrise. I'm already smiling at the vision."

"I see the yoga, but not the sunrise." Paige's response leaves us roaring.

Swaying palm trees line the expressway, as the car careens on the fifteen-mile stretch headed to Paige's parents' condo. Charming cottages and tiny bungalows line the beachfront of Cape Larimar, spanning for miles along the coast. The well-traveled arteries from the interstate flow like veins from a heart, leading to an abundance of lush golf courses.

Cape Larimar—the golfer's paradise.

The Cape, sometimes referred to simply as Larimar, has beaches along the towns of Clifton, Oakville, and Piperton. The Cape's recorded history dates back to the early 1800s, when its first settlers migrated from the border towns. Beginning in the mid 1900s, large corporations bought the land, moved the settlers out, and developed massive resorts. Swarms of tourists flock to Cape Larimar during spring break and through peak season—just past Labor Day.

Paige's parents bought their vacation condo two generations ago, when property values were seemingly affordable. Along with a conclave of other Black families, the Bryants settled on the northern end of The Cape and have vacationed here for the past several decades. Finally, the car turns off the interstate and onto a more secluded road. Condos stretch along the tree-lined roads and through the hills of the resort. Off the beaten path, we journey another mile before arriving at the Lighthouse Resort. Carefree bicyclers travel along the narrow paths of the resort with their bike baskets full of beach gear or a picnic lunch.

We travel up the steep hill, and finally pull up to the Bryants' stucco condo, tucked behind a grove of massive oak trees. Below, the glistening waters of the ocean has us captivated.

The car grows silent.

Oh well, our first morning at Cape Larimar has passed, and I didn't make it to yoga at sunrise. I didn't feel like rising that early anyway.

Frisbees sail through the air as swarms of eager children clamor to retrieve the disk and send it gliding to bunches of bustling kids along the shore.

Along the ridges, billowy foxtail grass gently sways toward the ocean, enraptured by the midmorning breeze. The warm sand prickles my toes and shifts under the pressure of each step as I take in the savory air.

Paige guides the way, followed by CJ, then me, and Camille bringing up the rear. Wearing earplugs, Camille hums softly as the four of us trail through the sand dunes, on the planks of the tiny strip of boardwalk leading to the beach.

Despite our later than planned start, the four of us head toward the water's edge, in search of the perfect spot, not to be bothered by the surrounding activity on the beach.

"How about right here, you guys?" Paige turns around, facing the three of us, as sweat trickles from her brow and collects on her nose.

"Looks fine to me," CJ answers before we drop our tote bags, beach towels, umbrella, and folding chairs.

Camille removes one earplug from her ear, then looks around, wondering, "Are we gonna park here?"

"Girl, where've you been?" Paige answers as we bust into stitches and plop down into the chairs. While we laugh the morning away, the waves wash along the shore and into the lull of the day.

***

"C'mon!"

As I look up from my book, CJ and Camille rise from their recliners beneath the umbrellas and race, all the while giggling as they make their way toward the ocean. They leap into the incoming waves, later motioning for me to join them. With the gentle movement of the water, the two glide among the rippling waters.

As the afternoon lingers on, I'm content to lay here, sipping my wine spritzer and reading my book. From the other side of the umbrella, the intermittent sound of Paige's snoring escapes from beneath the brim of her straw fedora hat while she slumbers with one arm dangling over the side of the recliner.

Glancing down the beach, past the vast dunes and into the distance, a strange sense washes over me. In the distance a cheerless displaced part of the beach lies, just an empty and barren piece of land on the water's edge. The faraway part of the shore sits isolated, with remnants of several old, weathered fences tossed among its dunes. I can't help sensing that there's something vaguely familiar stretching from that part of the shore. It's as if it breathes a quiet confidence, despite its lonesome state.

Somehow it feels like I've been here before. How weird.

Paige turns over from her back and onto her side as she opens her eyes and yawns. "Oh wow," she mumbles. In a single motion, she wipes the moist corner of her mouth, toward her cheek, laughs, then sluggishly sits up in her recliner.

"Yeah, girl. You must have really needed that nap." I chuckle.

"So where are the other two? Are you guys up for trying that new all-you-can-eat seafood buffet we passed on the way in?"

"Probably later. It doesn't look like CJ and Camille are ready to remove their fins and head to shore," I add, taking a sip of my wine spritzer.

Looking out into the ocean, Paige nods. "Oh yes. It's not easy coming in, once you're relaxing out there, letting those waves take you away. You can easily forget every care you might have had while you're lying in those floaties. That's why I love it here.

Ever since I was a child, being on The Cape has always had a way of helping me put things into perspective."

"Mm-hmm." I ponder my previous thoughts while I take in Paige's comments and the perfect silence. "You know what? I had the strangest feeling earlier. As I looked down the beach, in a brief flash, I imagined blurred glimpses of people moving along the beach. I envisioned only Black people on the beach, lounging and swimming as usual. But it was so strange. There *were* varying shades of blackness, none of them white or of a different race. And it was as if the scene I was envisioning happened in the past. The styles of bathing suits, beach chairs—everything was of another point in time. It felt like I'd been here before—like déjà vu."

"Well, that may not have been your imagination," Paige announces matter-of-factly. She nods in the direction of the barren shore. "That used to be the part of the beach for Blacks. During segregation, it was fenced off from this part of the beach, which was once a 'Whites Only' beach. After integration, they closed the 'Blacks Only' beach. Then people started to dump trash there. Later, they cleaned it up, and after that, there became only one beach—Cape Larimar beach. The old part's been secluded for decades."

"What's beyond the secluded beach?"

"About fifty miles north of the secluded beach is the town of Piperton."

"Piperton? That … that's the town where…Papa George is from!" A stream of air rises unexpectedly in my chest and releases with a rush. "I *must* have been on that beach before! When I was a little girl, probably four or five, we made a road trip several hundred miles to Piperton to visit my dad's home. At the time, we lived at Fort Costera, and this was the *only* time Papa George took us to visit his childhood home. He called Piperton 'The Country'. I met my Grandmother Coleman on that visit. Growing up, Papa George made it clear that Piperton was a good place to be *from*."

"Wow, Darby, this is amazing." Paige leans in attentively with her mouth gaping open.

"I have a vague memory—and it's cloudy—of holding my mom's hand as she took me to a porta-potty on a beach, with a long line of Black women stretched outside the potty. That must have been during that *same* visit to Piperton, my dad's home. We must have driven the fifty miles from his home in The Country, then down this way to the 'Blacks Only' beach at Cape Larimar."

"All I can say is, wow." Paige's response carries with it her own state of nostalgia. "I have so many fond memories of Cape Larimar as a child," she reminisces. "I remember wading in the foamy waters when they washed in. I distinctly remember holding up the bottoms of my Bermuda shorts, because I never wanted to go further into the water and have them get wet. I'd hold them up only as far as where the water touched my knees. I also remember my father surprising me from behind and swooping me up. Then he'd carry me on his shoulders for a long walk further down the beach. There's a picture in one of the Bryant family photo albums of me on his shoulders as he walked down the shore."

Listening to Paige recount this part of her childhood leaves me wondering.

Did my father ever carry me? The soreness in my heart signals that I never really knew him. I only thought I did. Staring at the horizon leaves me with a peculiar feeling that there's much more to be uncovered beyond the anguish of the past several months. The hush-hush tones from my childhood leave my spirit unsettled, as they search for hidden meaning.

The wound that's lodged within the depths of my soul is being challenged. Every tear I shed is enticed by the waves, longing to be swept into the sea of forgetfulness and further into an endless mass.

CHAPTER 23

The hum of the vibrating phone jolts me from my sleep, then abruptly stops before I can answer it. I open my eyes, find my bearings, then I realize where I am.

All's quiet as a graveyard.

Through the blinds, a dim ray of light peeks into the bedroom. The room is decorated in a beach motif with seashell-patterned comforters sprawled across each of the twin beds. In the corner of the room, several anchor-shaped throw pillows are tossed about on a blue chaise lounge. Realizing that it's not quite daybreak, I crawl out of bed and reach for my phone, which is lying on the dresser. With CJ as my roommate, I'm relieved that she's deeply dozing, undisturbed by my phone.

I glance at the screen. *That was Jackson. Dang. It's only 7:30.*

I love to tease him by calling him my favorite cousin. He's actually the *only* Coleman cousin that I've gotten to know, other than my recent meeting with Ethan. Still my favorite. Even though I'd never met his father, I still visualize Papa George's faraway gleam as he shared pleasant memories of him and Jackson's father growing up.

Jackson and I got to know each other as adults, after he reached out to me nearly fifteen years ago. Since then, we've visited each other across the country–me on the west coast, him in the south–

and have become good friends. He shared stories of being raised mostly in Europe and moving between different military bases until coming back to the US as a teen. I can only imagine that he caught hell as a world-traveled Black teenage boy settling in the rural south.

Now it's as though we've grown up together and have never missed a beat. CJ shifts in her sleep again, in the midst of my thoughts about familial ties and how fondly Papa George would share boyhood stories of Jackson's father, whose nickname was Buddy. The more I heard the stories, the more fascinated I became in wondering about the other Colemans. Papa George didn't mention much about the rest of his family. Just a few short clips here and there. Growing into adulthood, I longed to get to know these obscure people.

"I always knew that my little brother, Buddy, was going to get from 'round Piperton and make something of himself," Papa George would reminisce proudly because Buddy had followed in his very footsteps.

Funny how even then, I picked up that Piperton was referred to as "round there" and not viewed in a positive light.

CJ stirs in her sleep, jolting my thoughts once again. Not wanting to disturb her, I tiptoe out of the bedroom and down the hallway of the condo. After a few quiet steps, I tap the phone and dial Jackson's number.

"Hey, early bird, it's Darby," I whisper.

"Hi, cousin. So I take it, you all are enjoying yourselves on The Cape? How's everything going?"

"Wonderful. It's not hard to fall in love with Cape Larimar."

"Yes, indeed. It *is* something special. Sorry that I called you so early. So, you remember when we talked a few weeks ago, I said

I'd come pick you up and we'd hang out. I'm going to be about twenty miles south of the Cape a little later. How about I swing by and take you over to Piperton for a visit?"

"You've got to be kidding! I'd love to. I haven't been there in over thirty years, since I was a little girl. And I barely remember that visit at all. I didn't realize until yesterday that Piperton is just a stone's throw from Cape Larimar."

"Oh, Darby, you're so funny. I can really tell you're enamored with this region, West Coast girl." His teasing between chuckles reminds me of the stories Papa George had shared about Jackson's father, Buddy, and his lighthearted nature. Jackson must have inherited that trait.

"I'll pick you up in a couple of hours, and we'll head over to The Country."

"Okay, great. I can't wait! See you soon." As I hang up, the thought occurs to me. The Country? I thought it was only Papa George that called Piperton The Country.

The landscape gradually shifts as Jackson and I leave The Cape, heading toward Piperton. The vitality of the seashore shifts to the weariness of the rustic countryside, while the humidity and hazy winds drift across my skin. On the hour-long drive, we pass the time by singing melodies of neo-soul and R&B classics with Alicia Keys and Sade as our lead vocalists. The satellite radio station is on a roll as we laugh and sing our hearts out. The musical sing-along culminates with "Reasons" by Earth, Wind & Fire.

Jackson shares that generations ago, this same interstate proudly displayed a different scene—one where big rigs swerved along the highway with loads of timber, the booming commerce in the region decades ago. The once-thriving economy of the area is long gone, leaving Piperton with a bleakness, where only a scattering of small military bases exist in neighboring communities. The Saluda River, which runs alongside Piperton, seems to be the only constant in a landscape that has continually declined throughout the years.

Pulling off the interstate and onto a narrow back road, I take in the landscape with livestock grazing along the fenced-in pastures of family farms. The putrid smell fills my nostrils, leaving me holding my breath and panting for fresh air. Trailers and small shacks fill other open spaces along the farmlands.

Street signs are nonexistent along the road. No landmarks to leave an impression. It pretty much all looks the same—thick woods lining both sides of another narrow, secluded road. At some point, it becomes clear to me that Jackson is familiar with driving this neck of the woods. His sense of familiarity may have to do with being born on one of the neighboring military bases.

As if reading my mind, Jackson says, "After we left the base in Aviano, Italy, Dad decided he wanted the family to be closer to his relatives. So that's when we moved back to the States. Even though I was almost out of high school, I adjusted to being back in the South. I would occasionally drive out to The Country to visit and that's when I got to know all of our Coleman cousins and other relatives."

The car gradually slows down, then turns off the asphalt and onto a gravel road, deeper behind a thicket of young trees. Finally, the car stops on a dusty lot, several yards from the steps of a humble dwelling—the house that Papa George grew up in.

I can't believe I'm really here.

The atmosphere is overwhelming in an odd sort of way.

I'm spellbound.

Sparse patches of grass and crooked front steps seem to knowingly welcome the two of us as long-lost kinfolk. I'm captivated by the sense of it all. I've only heard my dad speak of this fabled place in somber tones. My eyes immediately gaze forward, toward the mysterious bungalow. I'm torn between both a sense of welcoming, yet unfamiliar distance. It seems as if the Coleman family stories once told in quiet whispers now seep through the porch's crevices, begging to disclose more than the tales told during my childhood—and yearning to come to life.

"We're here." Jackson turns off the ignition as he smiles and studies my expression.

A few seconds pass while I look out the window, taking it all in. The humble Coleman homestead—Papa George's boyhood home. I'm in awe of being in Piperton. The place known as The Country, the place that Papa George would solemnly mention from time to time.

A tin roof sits on top of the tiny shotgun house; its dull green color has long lost its luster. White trim borders the two front windows. On one end of the porch, two cushioned chairs sit on either side of a small accent table. At the other end of the porch, a wooden bench swing gently sways in the breeze. Its chain links hang from the ceiling, creaking as if they are wind chimes. A few well-worn cushions lie across the swing, as if it's someone's regular place for afternoon napping. I've already sensed that time in The Country tends to move at a snail's pace.

On one side of the house, the remnants of a cornfield stand. And beyond the field, a singular dirt path leads deep into the woods. The mention of a juke joint in the woods crosses my mind.

I envision the gathering of relatives conversing throughout the years on this very porch, along with mason jars of sweet tea—or maybe moonshine. I can almost hear the laughter as the stories and tall tales are being spun like whirlpools.

"Chewing the fat," was how Papa George described the banter and socializing that routinely occurred on most afternoons. Bragging rights went to the person who could get the others to believe the lies he'd concocted.

Although weathered and in much need of repair, it looks like the old place has stood the test of time—generations of long ago.

Oh, if this porch could talk.

Papa George had proudly shared stories that at age twelve, he had helped build this family home. He talked about how he and his siblings would sit on the stoop on hot summer nights and watch fireflies flicker in the darkness, while beetles and crickets chirped in the night air.

As I take in the surroundings, Jackson makes his way to the house. A huge oak tree sits in the barren yard, where fresh tire tracks make known the comings and goings of other visitors.

A well-worn screen door has been left slightly open. From inside the house, the sound of a TV blares through the door, past the porch, and mixes with the country airiness.

The buzzing of insects and bristling of leaves seem to signal to anyone inside the house that I'm an outsider. I'm suddenly conscious of the sound of my car door closing, which seems like an intrusion in the mysterious surroundings.

Jackson struts up the boarded steps before tapping the decaying wood frame around the screen door. No one responds.

After a few moments, he hollers through the front room, "Hey, Gator, you in there?"

Finally, footsteps can be heard approaching the front door. The lean silhouette of a brown-skinned man appears behind the screen. He yawns as he unlatches the screen door and pushes it open. He rubs his eyes with his fists, then sweeps his hands through his hair, front to back, before tossing on his baseball cap. Stepping onto the porch, he offers Jackson an energetic hug. Jackson returns the hearty embrace, and after several seconds the two loosen their grip while exchanging fond expressions.

"Hey, Jackson! It's good to see you, man."

This is Cousin Gator. There's got to be a story behind his name.

Stepping onto the porch, Gator appears to be in his mid-forties. Naturally distressed jeans hang slightly from his waist. His belt is pulled comfortably in what appears to be its last notch. As I study his features, I can't help but notice his nose—yes, that Coleman nose. The unmistakable Coleman feature that Papa George loved to tease me about when I was growing up.

These genes are downright amazing.

As I take it all in—by what I hope is an unassuming stance—the two make their way down the steps toward me. Jackson leads the way, with Gator following closely at his heels.

Jackson nods in my direction. "Hey, Gator, I brought somebody with me. You know who this is?"

Moving next to Jackson, Gator glances at me, then back at Jackson. His puzzled expression and subtle side-eye, signals suspicion of the stranger who Jackson has shown up with.

"Nahh. I can't say I recognize her."

The reluctance in his voice implies that I'm an outsider who will need to be vouched for. From what I've observed of the relationship between the two, I should be good to go, once Jackson makes the introductions.

"Man, that's our cousin, Darby. Uncle George's daughter!" Jackson is obviously beside himself at unveiling this previously unknown fact to Gator.

A broad smile quickly stretches across Gator's face. The restraint he showed moments ago immediately dissolves into acceptance.

"Shonuff?" Gator asks.

Whew, I've made the cut.

"Girl, I haven't seen you since you were a lil ole thang, when Uncle George and Aunt Louvenia brought you 'round here years ago. Y'all were on your way to Fort Costera," he adds.

Before realizing it, I'm engulfed in a bear hug. I hope my laughter doesn't sound uneasy.

Gator goes on with his story, "Your Daddy never came 'round here too much after he joined the army. But when he was on leave one time, he came through here lookin sharper than a daggum razor, yes he did! He had on that dress army uniform. I musta been about five."

A look of admiration wells in Gator's eyes.

"Well, my Dad has talked about Piperton so much when I was growing up. It's been such a mystical place to me that I'm having a hard time believing that I'm really here. It's weird that this place is unfamiliar, yet seems familiar to me at the same time."

"Yea. He brought you and your sisters down here. You were just knee-high to a duck. He bends and gestures with his hand, which stops at the height of his lower leg.

Trying not to appear overly reserved, I pointedly inquire about what's been burning in my mind. "So, um, how did you get the name, Gator?"

Jackson and Gator howl in unison. I can sense that the answer is one that has rolled off Gator's tongue on several occasions. He grins and slowly proceeds.

"I used to love to fish at the river when I was a kid. I'd stay at the river for hours and hours, all day long. I loved fishin' so much that I'd lose track of time," he shares wistfully. "Come close to dark, Mama would send someone out lookin for me. After awhile she'd tell me that alligators were in the water and that one was gonna get me. Them uncles of ours were worse and told me that them gators would bite my legs off."

Jackson chuckles.

Gator continues, "That did it. That scared me so bad that I quit goin' off fishin' by myself. I can't remember who first started it, maybe one of our uncles, but everybody started teasin me and callin me Gator. So I didn't fish too much after that—at least not by myself. After that I took up playin' basketball, but the nickname stuck. They been callin' me Gator since I was 'bout eight or nine. My real name though is Willie Earl. Or William. That's what the teachers called me at school."

I knew there was a story behind the nickname. I file it in my mind, along with the other stories about Piperton and the Coleman clan.

With a faraway look, Gator finishes his story, "Yeah, there're a lot of tales you get told when you grow up in Piperton. A lot of the ones that have been passed down are hogwash, though. But you only realize that once you're grown."

The pensive look gathers on Gator's brow, then travels to his eyes, blending into a look of nostalgia.

He catches himself. "C'mon, I'll take you 'round to the family plot."

Gator places his arm around my shoulder and guides me along the patches of grass, gravel, and dust. Instinctively, I place my arm around his waist as we walk several yards toward the empty pasture next to the house. Just beyond the family burial ground, a tired country church sits. The rustic white is part of the charm—steeple included. Without peering inside its windows, I know that it is a one-room structure, and that surely my father once worshiped here.

The aura of the surroundings seems to speak to me. Whispers and hushed tones.

Across the road from the church, a vacant firehouse stands. One side of the dilapidated building reveals specks of peeled whitewash, partially hidden by overgrown brush. The lush ivy seems to thrive in the moist air and conceals much of the structure. A decrepit flagpole still stands at the end of the cracked driveway, although absent of Old Glory. It's hard to imagine that the rundown building once housed a fire engine and served this sleepy Black community.

Gator notices my attention has diverted to the old building.

"Yeah, that's the old firehouse. It's been closed for nearly twenty years. Back in the day, the Ku Klux Klan would go over there and sit inside on many a Sunday morning. They'd do all their hecklin' and keep up a commotion to disturb the churchgoers until the service let out. Those rabble-rousers kept it going over there—drankin', harassin' and havin' themselves a good ole time," he says.

I shudder, thinking of the dangers, both told and untold.

Our pace lessens when Gator stops in front of a graveyard marker. Bending down he pulls up weeds and vines, which have overtaken a simple marker embedded in the ground. After he removes much of the growth, the marker displays the name of our grandmother, Coralene Coleman.

"There's Big Mama." He points to the marker. "She been gone

a long time. I was mostly raised by her, right in this here house." His head motions to the simple dwelling behind us.

"Yeah, my dad told me that I met her once, although I was too young to remember."

Moving from one Coleman memorial to another, the familiar names mesh with the lore that has gone before them. Connected to those tales is Papa George. And me.

In the distance stands a wreath whose flowers have long wilted, though not quite finished drying. A more recent Coleman passing, apparently laid to rest in the familial setting.

The heat beating down on my head is becoming a bit much.

"I'm gonna head back to the front of the house," I say.

"Yeah, I'm right behind you. I bet Jackson is lyin' up on that porch swing takin' a nap," Gator teases.

As we leave the cemetery and approach the side of the narrow, old house, the sound of the TV once again drifts from its windows and into the meadow. Jackson is sitting on the front steps, engrossed in his phone.

"You guys stand right there so I can get a picture of the two of you," Jackson says. He motions for Gator and me to stand underneath the old oak tree and face the house.

"Ready? Smile!" Jackson looks intently at the screen, then taps the button.

The stately branches of the tree stretch upward and spread outward—a vivid contrast to the younger ones below. I finally feel attached to a family beyond my immediate one.

I'm intrigued by it all.

CHAPTER 24

Rushing from work and into the busy traffic has me feeling like an acrobat trying to escape the circus.

Five thirty was the only opening Dr. Floyd had when I got the text that there'd been a cancellation. Quentin is picking up Robbie, so that makes it a lot easier. With several miles to go before my exit, the expressway traffic bottlenecks with no movement in sight. My frustration begins to mount along with the gridlock.

This is just great.

Pulling off the expressway at the next exit, I reroute through the bustling city streets. At each traffic light, I'm more aware of the moisture collecting in my armpits.

Finally, the pace begins to pick up and the traffic moves at a steady flow.

As luck would have it, I screech into the parking lot of Parkview Landing's commercial complex with three minutes to spare. Small and midsize companies surround the main entrance, competing for the easiest access and best view of the nearby canyon. Occupants of the building begin to pour out, eager to experience the few hours of light left in the day.

I proceed several steps off the beaten path through a side entrance. Nestled in the sprawling complex, Dr. Floyd's office sits beyond an airy atrium on the first floor. My shoulders automatically relax as I open the door and step inside Bethesda Counseling Services. Since it looks like the receptionist has left for the day, I press the button on the wall that will let him know that I've arrived in the outer office. Relieved that I've made it on time, I exhale and take a seat in the waiting area. The waterfall mounted on the wall works like a sedative, as it sends streams trickling down to a pool of water nestled with scattered rocks.

My childhood indoctrination has tried to haunt me and filter my rational thoughts. Irrational chants have tried to seep through, mixing in with the rational. At this point, I need help sorting through the overwhelming pain, and anger. I feel so torn and broken in so many places.

When I was growing up, Papa George had our household indoctrinated and under siege with his bold chant, "What goes on in this house stays in this house!"

It made no sense, but I never gave it another thought. What could be so bad in the household that he would put so much emphasis on containing it? Now I understand why. The abuse of Robbie has unleashed sheer rage in me and an unbridled license to commit what Papa George would consider the gravest of all sins—"Don't ever put your business in the streets." And especially don't let white people know what's going on in your family. The anguish that is trying to overtake me is not too concerned with cultural differences at this point.

In the weeks since Bishop Jefferson referred me, I've realized that people and families have many of the same dynamics regardless of their race. I've concluded that families consist of some of the same personalities, some functioning in families much like the one that partly shaped me.

My first meeting with Dr. Floyd had been remarkable. Appearing to be in his late '60s, he sports salt-and-pepper colored hair, which complements his gray beard. His gentle eyes convey warmth and wisdom, making him easy to confide in. The gurgling of the water fountain ushers me deeper into thoughts of that initial session.

Dr. Floyd had said very little during that visit, and I immediately felt at ease by his approach.

"This is just about me getting to know you, Darby. There aren't going to be any intense questions. What makes you happy?" he had asked.

Really? He sounds like Mr. Rogers talking to a captivated audience of children, during circle time. How strange.

"Let's see. Singing by myself in the car. The sound of raindrops against the window."

It felt as if he were guiding me, to God only knows where. The more I talked that day, the better I felt. I had shared that what had me feeling over the edge was finding out Robbie had been molested by my father. I'd gone on to share about the letter that my father had sent with its threatening tone and his denial.

He seemed genuinely sympathetic. For the most part he only listened, and provided little feedback or commentary. He suggested that I ask my parents to meet alone with him, followed by a visit with me, Quentin, and my parents.

Before I knew it, he was saying in that comforting voice of his, "Well, I think that ends our time for today."

Heck, I wanted to sit there and empty my guts some more. I had no idea how redirecting all those emotions would leave me feeling both energized and empowered. That hour went really fast. There's nothing like a good purge.

Judging from how I felt after my first session, the time I'm investing will be well worth it. Feeling more self-aware in an unusual sort of way, I'm sensing that I'll resume regular sessions with him for the next few months.

Noticing the water cooler in the corner, I reach into my tote bag for my vinyl bottle and fill it to the brim. Dr. Floyd enters the reception area with his previous patient. After the two say their goodbyes, he turns to me in the same welcoming manner I'd experienced during my first visit.

"Hello. Come on back," he says.

I notice the smile lines in the outer corners of his eyes that seem to appear quite naturally. His navy sweater vest and heather-gray pants add to his peaceful demeanor.

We walk the stretch of the hall to his office. Now that I'm inside, the empowerment that filled me in that first session energizes me again. I can move through whatever obstacle comes my way. My silhouette moves along the wall in harmony with the soft lighting. Tucked into the corner is an unassuming desk, next to an array of floating bookshelves. The atmosphere is enhanced by a shaded window that sits behind the sofa and adds to the simplicity. Instinctively, I kick off my pumps, sink into the couch, and lay my arm against the well-cushioned armrest. Dr. Floyd takes a seat in his chair directly across from me.

"So how have you been since our visit a couple of weeks ago?" he asks.

"Much better, thanks. I'm beginning to feel like the heaviness that was weighing me down is getting lighter."

"Good. And what are your best hopes for our talk today?"

"Well, for me to keep feeling better and to be able to get by. I'm no longer lying in the lounge chair on my deck, crying all day.

I feel like I'm coping a bit better. I've returned to work, and I'm able to at least function."

He nods his head with reassurance. "It sounds as though you're going in the direction you've set for yourself."

"Yeah, I think so."

The easy silence floods the room for several seconds.

Dr. Floyd's voice interrupts the quiet with a tone that shifts to a delicate warning. "I got a call from your father, since you and I had discussed that I should meet with him and your mother. They came in to see me a few weeks ago—along with your sister, Maxine."

Oh wow. I can't believe they were moved by my reply to Papa George's letter, saying that I wanted them to meet with my therapist. I'm surprised they followed up. I wait for Dr. Floyd to continue.

"Your father can't understand why you've made the accusation that he sexually violated Robbie. He says this is a very heavy load that you've placed on him and the rest of your family." He pauses, before concluding, "Your father says he's very concerned about your mental state."

"Oh, cry me a river. I could have handed you a script for how this was going to go."

I can see my mom—frail, yet sweet looking, probably dabbing her eyes with tissues during the entire visit with Dr. Floyd. Oh, what a performance that must have been.

"Well, that's no surprise either. Now *he* turns the tables and plays the victim, as if *he's* the one that's been violated." The thought causes a tinge of heat to rush across my face. It moves downward through the back of my neck and finally rests upon my shoulders.

Pause.

"You know," he adds persuasively, "Your mother is also a victim in this."

"Yeah, I thought about that. She's an accomplice *and* a victim."

"Your sister wanted to come into the session. I asked her to wait in the reception area while I counseled with your parent."

An unexpected chuckle escapes from me. "No surprise there either," I say. "As usual, there's Maxine inserting herself where she doesn't belong." My shoulders stiffen at the thought of the three of them colluding.

She's such a control freak.

The room is still as I take in the subdued glow of the table lamp and the shadow it casts upon the wall.

"You know? I've been thinking that this is much bigger than Robbie. I've been thinking of my nieces and nephews and how they also were put at risk by being around my father. The fact that my sisters allowed this—after what he did to them—is sick."

"Yes, that's true. Your nieces and nephews were also placed at risk if your father had access to them. No one knows why they pick a particular child, but they're always looking around for a victim."

His statement makes me shudder, as I think about my father's mannerisms. How he'd approach a room that other people might be in. How he'd cautiously look around the room as if he were casing it before entering. After he had entered, he seemed to warm up.

"He molested Robbie, and I believe my two sisters. What do you make of that?"

"It's about power, Darby," he gently concludes.

Dr. Floyd lifts his hands from his lap. In a solemn way, he begins rotating them in a circular motion. "Incest breeds, Darby."

My fingers glide down one of my locs, then makes its way to the end, where I twirl it around my index finger and contemplate his words. In those few seconds, I study his circular motions, which seem like the motion of an infection spreading around. And his words seem strange. As though they're something I need to process later. I can't seem to get a grasp on this strange vibe.

"I had a cousin reach out to me—actually he reached out to Quentin. He's my father's nephew. Anyway, he came over when he got to town, and spent some time with us. He had heard through the family grapevine about what we've been going through. And— long story, short, he said that my father's brother molested him as a child in Piperton.

Dr. Floyd sits nodding, as he solemnly comment, "Hopefully this news will help Robbie."

I reach for my water bottle on the table next to me. The effect of the cold liquid settles me adding hope that Ethan's story will be helpful to Robbie. The quiet lingers. Its pause is fueled by seconds upon seconds.

The lull shifts me into the realization that I haven't told him about the trip I'd taken since our last session. It was more than I imagined it would be. I am *so* over talking about my parents and Maxine's antics.

I begin sharing with Dr. Floyd one of the highlights of my trip.

"Oh, I just came back from Cape Larimar. I took a trip with some friends before I returned to work. I took my friend Paige up on her offer to stay at her parents' condo. We had a blast, relaxing on the beach and just hanging out."

He leans forward, intently focused on hearing about my trip. "Good for you. It's important to know what you need for your well-being," he says.

"I got a chance to visit the house in Piperton where my father lived most of his life. It's just a couple of hours from Cape Larimar. I'd never been there or met my dad's side of the family.

"Oh, nice," Dr Floyd responds.

"Yeah, when my dad went into the army, they moved around a lot. So I never got the chance to meet his family." I go on to share about how Jackson picked me up, and we made the drive to Piperton, an hour away. The excitement of having gone to this mythical place has my words spilling on top of each other. At that moment I realize how chatty I'm being.

"Mmm." Dr. Floyd nods

"So then, I met another Coleman relative. His nickname is Gator. He lives in my grandparents' old house. He showed me around the farm that my father had described when I was growing up. I'd been there once before, but I was little and I can't really remember the visit."

"I see," he quietly says.

"Piperton and my father's home has been like a piece of folklore that has come to life." I pause to catch my breath, in hopes that I'm conveying what a big deal this trip was for me. "Oh, and I walked with Gator through the family cemetery, right there by the house. Many of the relatives are buried there. It was pretty fascinating."

I'm trying to get a read on Dr. Floyd's expression but there isn't one. Only a poker face. With his hands folded in his lap, he leans slightly forward, which I take to mean that he's captured it all. After a lengthy pause, he begins speaking, though his tone seems to carry a specific purpose. With a self-assured posture, he softly declares, "Yeah. *A lotta secrets* in that graveyard," he utters emphatically.

The inflection in his pitch feels as though he's making a distinct point. And it's causing me to think of secrets as being the same as lies. What was it my father used to always say? "If you tell one lie, you have to tell another one to cover it up."

I take a long swig of water and ponder what he's saying. I can't process it all—at least not right now.

After an uncomfortable silence, the only sound is the chime of the clock, which changes the mood, bringing it back from the obscure moment that has faded as quickly as it came.

His genuine smile returns. The creases emerge at the outer corners of his eyes. He reverts back to his usual warm tone. "Well. This ends our time for today."

CHAPTER 25

The certainty of each new day forces me to adjust to this new unfathomable reality. My world has been crushed to its core, yet somehow, I manage to take it day by day and keep things moving.

Some days feel like an evil beast continues to lurk under the waters with the mission of swallowing me whole.

As I head down the stairs to make breakfast, I think about watching Robbie yesterday afternoon when I arrived to pick him up from after-school care. I stood watching him in the field next to the playground where he played with two other boys. They were laughing and pretending to chase leprechauns into gopher holes. The glimpse of him playing at that moment gave me so much hope that somehow he's going to be okay, even though he's been affected forever by the violence he's suffered.

The gut-wrenching deception by a family who I thought loved me is unbelievable. Who are these people? Mom. Maxine. Gloria. Their collective pretense has added fuel to my father's actions.

My mind is racing. Each day I manage to pull myself through, with the anticipation of a welcome respite when I lay my head down at night. Sometimes I get relief; other nights I don't. I've been up for an hour, yet I feel so groggy. I laid there, listening to Quentin's restful slumber and wishing I could do the same. I'm groggy and my mind is on overload. Thank God it's Saturday.

I thought that a family should protect its youngest and weakest members.

I can almost hear the sinister laughs of my sisters, while they must have thought, "How could she be so dumb? How could she not know?"

Oh, God, help me. I don't want to get stuck today. I need to keep moving forward. I need to talk to Aunt MayBelle. Talking to someone who knows and loves my parents may give me another perspective. I can't imagine what she'll have to say.

Refined and compassionate, Aunt MayBelle is the epitome of southern charm. Sassy, yet sweet, she makes sure folks don't call her Mabel.

"May. Bell. Accent on the May," she loves to assert.

She and Mom had been close growing up. When each married and moved from Pikesville, they made it a point to keep in touch with weekly phone calls. I could pretty much predict the timing of Aunt MayBelle's calls. As a child, I would usually be the one to answer the house phone. Catching up on the latest news happening in Pikesville was their usual ritual.

My mom would take the call, then huddle up in her bedroom on Sunday evenings with the door closed. Sometimes it was partially open, with just enough space for me to peek through the crack. Propped up pillows and her chenille bedspread were her backdrop as she settled in for the next hour. From the other side of the door, my ears were glued to her end of the conversation.

"Ohhh, MayBelle, I didn't *know that*. Didn't nobody tell me."

Yakety-yak.

Younger than my mom by twenty months, Aunt MayBelle loves to be precise about the length between their ages. And she loves to tell stories about them growing up in Pikesville, near S'vannah, where she now lives. That would be Savannah, Georgia.

I love to hear the way she enunciates every word, with each syllable sounding more sugary than the last. She begins many of her captivating stories with "Oh, I must tell you 'bout the time when Louvenia and I…" Her nostalgic tales usually leave the listener fixated on her syrupy spiel, along with the actual details. Without a doubt, anyone listening hangs on to her every word.

Now in her late sixties, she still carries herself with the ease of a gazelle. Her smooth, caramel skin creases in a way that is amicable to her nature—unless something ruffles her. She considers leaving the house without makeup to be a serious lapse in judgment. "At least wear a little lipstick" is her firm belief.

Yes, a nice heart-to-heart with Aunt MayBelle is always comforting.

After what seems like longer than a few seconds, she finally picks up the phone.

"Well hello, Aunt MayBelle. It's Darby."

"Hey, Bay-bee!"

I love the way I can picture her smile when she hears my voice.

"And how are you doing?"

"Oh, pretty good for an old gal, Sugah."

She makes *me* smile too.

After she catches me up on the latest, the conversation takes a natural turn. "What's new with you, honey?"

"I don't have good news, Aunt MayBelle," I proceed cautiously.

"What is it Bay-bee?" Her voice grows more concerned.

"Aunt MayBelle, it's Papa George. I found out that he's a pedophile."

The sound of her deep inhalation is followed by no sound at all. I wait for what I hope are enough seconds for her to gather herself, before I continue.

"He molested Robbie."

"Lawd, Lawd. Oh Jay-Sus!"

"Yeah, it's been a few months since we found out. I've been trying to put myself back together, piece by piece. It's not easy, but somehow despite my world falling over the edge, I'm trying to hang on."

"Oh, Bay-bee. How dreadful!"

"Robbie's in counseling and seems to be adjusting from the trauma. But my poor, poor baby, there's no undoing what's been done to him."

"Oh Bay-bee, this is terrible! I never would have imagined George would… but you never know. I remember my grandma used to say, 'Don't turn your back on a man or a billy goat.'"

"Yeah, I'm still having trouble believing that this is my world— family secrets and lies. I've started therapy too. I can't sleep at night, thinking about this evil thing."

"My goodness." She hesitates. "And that…" She pauses. "That … that means Louvenia must have known. I mean how could she not have known, as close as she is to your lil Robbie."

"Oh yeah, she did, Aunt MayBelle. They all did. They won't admit it. But since I've exposed the truth, their strange behaviors confirm it. It's pretty sickening. They've closed ranks. You know how it goes. Now I'm tagged as crazy. But that's okay. It explains all the puzzling things that used to go on when I was a child."

"Bay-Bee, I am so sorry for your Robbie," she offers.

"And of course when I asked questions about bizarre incidents, I was chewed out. So after a while, I learned to not question my parents about things I thought were strange. Papa George made sure we didn't ask questions, and we sure knew better than to tell anyone about family business. It was such a scapegoat atmosphere. And of course I was the scapegoat."

"Those strange occurrences in the household became the normal way of living," Aunt MayBelle completes my thoughts."

"You're right, Aunt MayBelle. I have a hard time believing that a grandfather molests his grandchild out of the clear blue—unless he's been successful with the previous generation. That means my sisters were victims also. It finally all makes sense. Lights turned on in the middle of the night. Footsteps down the hall. I could go on and on."

Her voice grows quieter. "Honey, in a lot of those small towns like where yo' Daddy's from, they believed in family members sleeping together. That's what they did. They believed it made their family unit strong. But no matter what he believes, how he could do this to a child is beyond treacherous. Lawd, Louvenia never let on to me about George's ways."

"Wha-what?"

Chile, I had no idea," she says. The pace of our conversation has slowed and is no longer weighed down. "Yo' Daddy was always *something* else."

It's as though she now has a license to speak freely and can throw caution to the wind. Something tells me to listen as I try to collect myself. I'm dumbfounded at what she's revealing.

She continues purging, "When he came round here, he was always acting high and mighty like he was better than everybody else." Her voice rises with indignation. "Honey, he sure 'nuff was highfalutin. He had made a career in the service, and did well, so he had his nose stuck up high in the air. Everybody pretends to like him—outta respect for Venia, but folks can't stand yo' Daddy," she reveals.

"Whoa," I manage to respond.

"George and Louvenia have done well, and that's good, but so have others. Plenty of folks 'round here have lovely homes and have raised educated children just like y'all. No reason for George to be all up on his high horse. It doesn't call for all that. *Now* look at how he really is. Lawd, have mercy."

I had no idea Aunt MayBelle didn't like Dad. It never crossed my mind that Mom's relatives thought badly about him. Whew!

"Aunt MayBelle, I needed to talk to you. I'm so… I'm so done with family secrets."

"I don't blame you, Bay-Bee," she consoles.

"The more I share this awful news, it's like a heaviness gets lifted and I start climbing out of a dark hole. Even though this happened to Robbie, at the same time it's trying to bury *me* too." From nowhere, my sobs erupt. "Aunt MayBelle, this … this whole thing is trying to take me out."

"You keep on, honey. Keep on going to counseling and taking care of Robbie and Quentin. Keep on doing just like you're doing."

Between sniffles, I manage, "OK. Thanks. I love you, Aunt MayBelle."

"I love you, too, Bay-bee. Now you be encouraged," she says.

As my thumb moves to tap the off button, I hear Aunt MayBelle mumble to herself. "Oh, my Lawd. That man needs to be whipped like a government mule."

CHAPTER 26

I place the picture of me and Cousin Gator on my dresser, beneath the glass along with my favorites. Every so often I look at it in awe, where it lies alongside the pictures of me, Quentin, and Robbie. My thoughts trace the events surrounding the day I met him when I was on the trip with Paige and the girls at Cape Larimar.

Throughout the spring and summer, I had fought deep waves of depression as the reality of family secrets and lies became embedded into my reality. And then there are days I feel like a recovering addict having a relapse. Quentin's suggestion that the trip would do me a world of good was spot-on. Thank God my days have become brighter, like I'm coming out of a fog, yet drawn to a mass that's taking me to an unknown place.

Jackson taking me to Piperton was the highlight of my trip. The two-hour trek to Papa George's hometown still seems surreal as I stand in front of the dresser, contemplating the events of that humid day. It seemed like the ticking of time had stood still in the little country town. It turned out to be just the way that Papa George had always described it.

Jackson introducing me to Gator helped me feel connected to the Coleman side of the family. The three of us had stood in front of our grandparents' house, talking and laughing throughout the afternoon. The same house where Gator was raised and has lived since their deaths.

Over and over I searched my childhood memories as I listened to the family stories. Something seemed vaguely familiar. Like a fine mist, the recollection of chickens roaming the dusty yard clouded my mind. I was told that I'd been there before as a small child, but I only have a faint remembrance. And then there was the cloudy memory of shadowy figures on the beach at The Cape. All of it is like venturing into an unknown, yet strangely familiar, past.

I pace the room, walking several feet away, but once again I'm drawn back to the dresser. My gaze is fixated on the photo of me and Gator standing beneath the old oak tree in the front yard of the humble dwelling. Today something feels off, but I can't put my finger on it.

Gator has much more than a striking resemblance to my dad. Of course there is the distinct ebony shade, which is common to most of the Colemans. The facial lines from both sides of his nose to the sides of his mouth have the same depth as my father's.

I remember watching him as he led the way to the family cemetery in the back of the house that day. He walked with the same long stride as Papa George in his younger years. It reminded me of my walks with him when I was a young girl and the game we played where I tried to match his pace.

Wow. This lineage is amazing.

Papa George rarely displays a toothy, let alone broad, expression of joy. His signature smile is usually a solemn one. Even the happiest of occasions elicit only Papa George's signature half grin. I'm so unsettled every time I stare at the photo lying on the dresser. Gator's image in the picture seems to gaze back at me with a disturbing expression.

Perhaps it's the fact that he was wearing a baseball cap that day, same as my dad's, that makes the likeness even stronger. The gray hairs shadow Gator's beard just as they do my dad's. And to think... this is my dad's nephew? I feel eerie as I survey the similarities.

As I stare at the picture and muse about the visit to Piperton, a flashback of my last session with Dr. Floyd comes to mind. In that session, I shared about the Coleman family burial plot that Gator had shown me.

"A lotta secrets in that graveyard," had been Dr. Floyd's bewildering declaration.

I had gone on about how excited I was to visit my father's childhood home—a place that existed mostly in my imagination.

Now as I take in the picture, a vision of Dr. Floyd's circular hand motions loom in front of me, bringing to mind his passing remark, "Incest breeds."

Those words conjure up notions of a virus that can't be contained. One that spreads, and goes around and around. No one knows who'll be the next one to catch it.

Could my cousin really be....my brother? No-o-o!

My face begins to feel flushed, as a burning sensation travels to the top of my head. Placing my palms to my cheeks, I stand in front of the dresser—my mind racing and the two words echoing as if they're in a chamber. *Incest breeds.*

I contemplate the haunting possibility, yet I'm afraid of speaking the unspeakable. The thought lingers, as if it's daring me to speak the unspeakable.

"Gator is my brother," I whisper alone in my empty bedroom.

I can't believe I've said those words. It starts to seep in, traveling further from my imagination and into my reality. The possibility stirs and spins deeply inside me.

Pacing the floor in front of the dresser, my lips continue to murmur, "My cousin is my brother."

Finally, speaking to no one but myself, the disturbing conviction rises from my gut and is released like the unexpected burst of a balloon. "That boy is my brother!"

My phone buzzes on my bed, shocking me out of a near-like trance.

It's Paige!

"What's going on, girl?"

She barely finishes greeting me before I blurt out, "Paige! Oh my God, I think my cousin, Gator, is also my b-brother."

"Huh?"

"Yeah, I know it sounds crazy, but I just have this awful feeling. I can't explain it."

"You mean? You mean you think … you think your father is also his father? This is..."

Her stammers are interrupted by dead air which seems to thrust me further into the possibility. The silence gathers her up as well.

"Darby! My God, this is *unreal*!" Paige continues. "I mean, do you really think so? All I can say is, wow. How in the world can you... what are you going to do?"

The hush fades as we sit in the darkness of my suspicion.

CHAPTER 27

Their bleak figures move through the darkness as they watch my every move. Their gray silhouettes seem to function as a unit and show no distinction between each other. He takes command and leans in toward me. He thrusts his protruding neck in my direction, coming within inches of me. His breath emits a pale vapor into the air, as the warm mist spews droplets against my face. The deep intensity in his voice takes hold, along with his authority, leaving me petrified.

"Someone has to break the curse that has plagued your family," he explains. "It has gone on for more generations than you'll ever know. You must shine the light on everything that will be revealed to you." The other shadowy figures gather around him as reinforcement. He continues, "There will be much that you will uncover. It's up to you. This is *your* mission, Darby." Astonishingly his tone changes to a whisper before he murmurs. "You, Darby, are the one that must break the generational curse. This is *your* assignment."

"Wh-what?" I can't breathe. *They're after me. Leave me alone.* "No-o-o-o!!" What? Who? Whose voice is that? "No! No! Go away!" Is that me? Telling me? I need to get away. I have to go. My words. Mmph! They're stuck in my throat! *"Leave me alone!"*

"Babe? Darby!" The calm voice is familiar, which immediately frees me from the stalker's pursuit. Soothingly, Quentin rubs my back, then wraps his arms around me. I'm relieved that I'm now in the safety of a cocoon.

The pool of moisture in the well beneath my eyes summons me to move away from the darkness that has tried to engulf me. Instinctively, I position my arm across my chest. I'm stunned by the pools of sweat that are drenching my gown. It clings to me like a sheet of sticky plastic wrap.

Gradually the murky gloom is left behind, and I emerge into the reality of this moment. The familiar, reassuring silhouettes of my bedroom are in the dimness around me.

Still the same. *They* seemed real. *It* seemed so real. With his steady arms around me, Quentin continues, "You okay?"

"I feel like I'm in a haze—like some deep thing is trying to take shape and come into its own existence, pulling at me."

"You're dealing with a lot. Everything's going to be okay."

As the beating of my heart steadies its pace, its tempo becomes a calming melody. Quentin's embrace lulls me cautiously back to sleep.

"Hey, Mom. Whatcha doing?" Robbie stands next to me, scrunching his nose as he looks at the computer screen.

Clicking on pictures of babies and their outfits online has had my attention for the past hour. "These little girls' dresses are so cute. I'm shopping for some outfits for CJ's baby shower. "You know, the baby will be here next month."

"Yeah, all that girl stuff. They look funny, Mom."

I reach over and kiss his head. He grins.

"If you say so, baby boy."

"Can I go outside and play ball with Jeremy?"

"Mm-hm, for a little while."

With that sweet giggle of his, he heads out of the study and down the hall. Seconds later, the sound of a ball thumps on the pavement before swishing through the hoop. The sound of their playful rivalry drifts from the driveway and through the office window.

A banner ad appears at the top of the computer screen.

TRIAL OFFER FOR A LIMITED TIME. Research your family history.

These ruffled onesies are too cute. I ignore the ad and focus my attention again on which outfit I'll get CJ's baby.

Into the shopping cart they go. I type in my credit card number and complete the transaction.

Done. The gift will arrive in time for the baby shower. The banner ad scrolls again, catching my attention.

TRIAL OFFER—14 Days

New! Military Records. Research your family history.

Hmm. Military records. Wonder if Papa George has any records in this database?

I open a trial account and begin searching and surfing for family birth records, starting with my own. I input the various filters into the fields, beginning with my name, year of birth, and parents' names. The program processes for seconds before the record selection appears.

There it is. There's my birth certificate. I don't know what I expected, but I guess I just wanted to test the site's accuracy.

It pretty much has the same information as the hard copy I've had nearly forever, with all the vital information. The time of birth and the doctor's signature are missing. Everything else is the same—even US Army Hospital at Fort May, Tennessee.

Papa George's legendary story comes to mind of how he felt when he first laid eyes on me.

Curiously, I continue playing with the software, inputting the names and other known vital information of relatives. One after the other, a birth certificate is produced by the operating system. *This is fascinating.*

Then it dawns on me. I don't think I've ever seen Maxine's or Gloria's birth certificates.

Moving my finger across the keyboard, I type in Maxine Coleman, along with her birthdate. Before pressing the search button, I input Ft. Chandler, NC, in the city and state field and wait for the vital information load.

And wait.

It's taking forever to load and retrieve the record. And then it stops rotating.

NO RESULTS FOUND.

That's weird. I know I got her birthdate right. And her place of birth too. I try the same thing with Gloria. Inputting the same fields with her vital information. I think about the stories of Gloria being born in the town of Benton, just across the Saluda River from Piperton. This is pretty easy. Typing in "Benton" is exactly what I'll do.

The data loads. But seconds later.

NO RESULTS FOUND.

I don't know what to think. Why is *my* birth certificate in the database but not Maxine's or Gloria's? This is so strange.

I continue to input friends and other relatives based on their birthplace and date. Each individual's birth record appears after a few seconds. The hours pass until I remember what first started this exercise in the first place.

Oh yeah, the newly added military records.

The flashing letters at the top of the screen: "MILITARY RECORDS" pulls me into its allure.

I'm magnetized by this new category of military documents. Typing in the various fields in hopes of finding a military record of Papa George feels like going on an expedition. I have no idea what I'm searching for—just knowing that I should find something. Like all things associated with the military, it seems so official. I've never seen any of his documents and this will be amazing to... A few clicks and...click.

What's this?

Quentin pauses in the doorway of the study with streams of sweat dripping down his face. "You've got a very troubled look on your face," he whispers.

"Ah yeah. I'm tired. I've been at this for hours."

Click.

"I've had enough of this," I say while rubbing my eyes.

I shut down the computer.

As I sit in my home office, I spend most of the morning scouring the internet on how to go about doing a paternity test. The nagging thoughts continue, despite how much I try to talk myself out of them.

I want to know the truth.

I steady my nerves while I go to the company website I've become familiar with. I'd researched several, but for some reason this one stood out to me as the first one to call. Their website shows accreditation seals from several national laboratories.

Yeah, here it is. I'm going to go with it.

I pick up the phone to call AccuDNA. I dial the 800 number listed on the site. After listening to the menu of prompts, I tap number eight to speak to an agent.

"Thank you for calling AccuDNA. This is Kelly. How can I help you?"

"Hello. I need a paternity test. For me and another individual to see if we share the same father. The thing is … um … I know I won't be able to get a sample from the father … I mean … um … the one I believe is the father of both of us."

Pause.

Without interruption, I continue, "So I'm wondering how to go about this, knowing that our father will not participate by agreeing to give a sample." Now that I've thrown caution to the wind and decided to go down this path, I'm feeling more nervous than I thought I'd be. I must sound like I'm babbling. "Does that make sense?"

"Yes, that makes perfect sense." Kelly's cheerful Midwest accent comes through as she begins to explain the process. "Actually, we don't need the individual who you believe to be the father. What we'll do is send a kit to you and a kit to the other individual. Inside the kits will be everything you need along with instructions on how to collect and return the samples. Each of the kits will be numerically coded so that we'll be able to match the samples. Once we have both samples, it'll only take about a day to get the results. And after the test results are ready and the final payment is received, we will email you the results."

I'm amazed.

"That's it?"

"That's it. Would you like to place a deposit today and give me the names of the two individuals? Then we can get both kits sent right on out."

"Um. Uh. Well, I need to talk to the other person to see if he'll agree to do it. I mean … I mean it's going to be hard for me to tell him. You see um … he's my cousin, and I think he's really…" *I can't believe my voice is fading.* "I think he's really my brother."

Kelly chimes in without missing a beat. "Oh, I'm not here to judge, ma'am. It's all pretty scientific to me; that's all."

"Thank you. I'll talk to him first, then get back to you, Kelly. Thanks so much."

As I tap the phone off, I sit in the silence and ponder how in the world I'm going to convince Gator to take a DNA test.

CHAPTER 28

"I'll be right back with two glasses of water," the server says as she hands Paige and me the menus before dashing off. Our Saturday morning yoga session has been followed up by breakfast at Larry's Diner, which is beginning to fill up with some of the other regulars. My eyes scan up and down the menu, feeling unsure if I want my usual veggie skillet with hash browns.

If my suspicions are right, then Robbie has been a pawn in a web of deception and cover-up that may span generations. The full extent I will never truly know. The knots in my stomach tighten the more I think about it.

"I'm feeling so stretched out," Paige says. "I can't wait until James gets back. He usually doesn't have to travel so long, but this time was an exception."

We continue chitchatting while looking over the menu.

My hand rubs across my forehead as my fingers press down in circular motions. The tensions I was relieved of moments ago during yoga have now come back to harass me. Trying to gather the courage to pose my suspicion to Gator has me unnerved. How will I open him up to this ugly possibility? Like all of the relatives in Piperton, he thinks so highly of Papa George. And who does Gator believe his father is, anyway?

Paige looks down at her buzzing phone. "Oh, it's James. I'll be back in a minute." She rushes toward the entrance, with the phone to her ear, while the other hand covers the other ear.

Just thinking about the wicked charade makes me want to throw up. The vile notion of a family that inbreeds conjures up images of corn pipes, moonshine, and wayward people.

Whoa. I guess this means that I come from a line of Black hillbillies. I never even considered that there *was* such a thing.

Paige comes back to the table and settles into her seat, just as the waitress approaches. "Here you guys go." The server places a glass of water in front of each of us and takes our order.

"I'll have French toast," Paige says while handing the menu to the server. "And a mimosa."

"And the veggie skillet for me. Um … no. Actually, I'll have the spinach omelet with wheat toast. And yeah, a mimosa for me too."

"Great. Your orders will be right up," she says before spinning off once again.

My world has been opened up for sure. Somewhere there are Colemans who could never have imagined that the secret they thought was buried is about to be resurrected by scientific evidence. Surely the elders of the Coleman clan who still live in Piperton know this gruesome secret. Yet I'm not expecting some sort of explanation from anyone.

Dr. Floyd's words infuse my thoughts, along with the circular motion of his hands. "Incest breeds." Heck, that sounds like a virus that spins around, and who knows who'll catch it. And if Gator is my brother, that's proof that the virus traveled.

It explains why Papa George used words such as "backwards" and "ignorant" to describe the small country town and his clan. "My people" is how he referred to them. Could this really be? Was incest a regular family way of life which was accepted? If I'm lucky, I'll be able to get proof.

"Here you go. Spinach omelet for you and French toast for you." The waitress places the plates in front of us. "Can I bring you anything else?"

"No, I think we're good," Paige answers..

Maybe I'll never know, but like a ghostly figure resurrected from the past, the possibility haunts me, nevertheless. And now it's staring at me front and center—the prospect knocking at my door. Is this really part of my world? Really?

How in the world will I persuade Gator to take a DNA test? I cut into the omelet, moving the cheese around the plate, next to the toast.

"How's the omelet?" Paige interrupts my thoughts.

"Huh?" Along with the clang of dishes around the room, her question causes me to drift from my mind's fog, bringing me back to the present.

"Girl, where were you?" She looks up at me wide-eyed and expectantly as she pauses from chewing her French toast.

"I was thinking about Gator and wondering if he'll agree to take a DNA test," I answer.

"I have no idea what he'll say, but I've got to ask him." I lay my fork down. "I have to follow this trail and see where it leads. It's nagging away at me, and I know it won't let up until I know the truth."

"Darby, somehow I feel as though you're receiving divine guidance." Paige stops nibbling her bacon as she conveys her point.

Her intense gaze brings back the memory of the conversation I had with Bishop Jefferson. It's like he had a premonition that this whole thing is much bigger than Robbie. I was too distressed that day in his office to really have a sense of what he'd said.

"The main thing I remember about meeting with Bishop Jefferson was his counsel: 'Don't get ahead of the Holy Spirit'." I separate the spinach from the eggs on my plate.

"I did some research on incestuous beliefs," Paige says. "It was only if the girl became pregnant that it was frowned upon. In that case the family would send her away to a faraway relative, because of the belief that the family would be looked upon with shame."

I'm no longer hungry. "Yeah, it's possible that my father was the one who was sent away. But instead of going to live with relatives … oh my God!"

"What?" Paige asks with astonishment. "He was drafted by 'his Uncle Sam! That's what he was fond of saying!" I pick up the tulip-shaped glass and take a gulp. "He joined the army! I think it's likely that this was the chain of events. And I need Gator's DNA to see if my theory has any truth to it!"

I feel as though I've talked myself into a revelation.

"Darby, I just hope you're prepared for the backlash that's sure to come if the DNA results point to your suspicions."

Paige's sobering thoughts had already crossed my mind. "Yeah, I know. I've gotten past the point of wanting to kill Papa George." I place my forehead into the tips of my fingers, pressing gently. "I'm grateful that counseling has helped and that I'm no longer in that space. The truth, Paige, is that I'm afraid my rage is buried somewhere I can't tap into—if that makes sense."

"It does, Darby," Paige affirms.

"The difference now, though, is that I'm determined to chase down the truth. And fling it right at him and the entire family." Paige stares into the distance before sinking against the cushioned back of the booth.

"What I can't understand, though, is my two sisters. They've allowed Papa George access to their children, fully knowing that he's a pedophile.

Our server stops at the edge of our booth while balancing a stack of plates on her left arm. "Can I get you guys a refill on your mimosas?"

"Thanks. I think we're good," Paige responds.

Still balancing the plates, the server reaches into her apron pocket and places the check on the table. She proceeds down the aisle as more diners gather in the entrance.

"This is a lot, Darby. It's absolutely unbelievable." Paige exhales.

The energy at Larry's Diner noticeably shifts as the early morning breakfast set winds down.

My face grows warm as I declare, "I'm determined to chase down the truth. Somehow, I'm going to convince Gator to take a DNA test, if it's the last thing I ever do."

Quentin pulls a bottle of water from the refrigerator, kisses me between swigs and hurries out the door with Robbie. Glancing at the clock on the oven, I take note of the time and think about what Gator might be doing at the moment—the difference being three hours ahead in Piperton, 10:30 a.m.

I find his name in my contacts and press the button. The tone rings steadily. I think it's about to go to voicemail. I'll just ask him to call me, nothing more than—

"Hey, Cousin. How you doin', Darby?"

I can almost see the smile on his face. His genuine and cheerful demeanor. He strikes me as the kind of person who doesn't allow much to bother him. A roll-with-the-punches kind of guy.

"Gator! I was about to leave you a message. I'm glad you picked up."

"Yeah, I heard my phone ringin'. I had left it inside. I was just out back pickin' some collards for dinner. So I ran in to answer it. You're up and about early. Isn't it only about 7:30 there in California?"

"That's right. And the thought of fresh greens for dinner sounds right up my alley. If I had the patience or the know-how to grow my own, I sure would."

The bond causes us both to giggle and puts me more at ease.

"Well they ain't too hard to grow. You gotta know what you're doin','though, when they start gettin' a bit thick. Thinnin' them out is the trick—that's the secret to growin' good greens so that they'll stay tender and don't get tough."

"Yeah. Yeah. I think I've heard my dad say something like that."

The unexpected connection puts me further at ease. Suddenly the memory of picking greens alongside Papa George in his garden invades my head.

He chuckles at the mention of Papa George.

"Darby? You still there?"

"Um … um … yeah, I'm here."

Gator's cackle tells me what I had already suspected. I've struck on something for which he has a high regard—his Uncle George.

"How *is* Uncle George?" He seizes upon the opportunity to inquire about my dad, who existed mostly as a mythical figure to him. "Tell him I'm gonna get out there to California soon. Imma be the one who actually comes to see him."

"Ah. Um. He's well." *If he only knew the details.* That we've been estranged for several months.

"Uncle George. He came 'round here a couple times when I was a little boy," Gator continues in a wistful tone. "I musta been seven or eight. I think he stopped in on his way from somewhere overseas. Folks 'round here were sure proud of him. He must have been in his late twenties." The admiration in Gator's voice thickens. "I remember Mama tellin' me that this was the uncle I'd heard so much about. The one who had left Piperton and done well for himself. So I was glad to finally meet him. Everybody looked up to him, even though he hadn't been 'round here in a long time."

"Yeah, I missed getting to know my Coleman cousins." I find my tone, mimicking his—the longing for something that was so unfamiliar. "I only met Jackson a few years ago, when he reached out to me. Since then we've caught up on our childhood—him growing up in Italy, and me at Fort Costera. It's like we haven't missed a beat. I'm glad I got to go to Piperton when I was at Cape Larimar last month. Jackson bringing me there was one of the highlights of my trip. And I'm glad I got to meet you."

"Make sho' you don't make it your last visit, now. You ain't a stranger no more."

"I won't. This may sound strange, but it seems as if I got to know my dad better, just because I visited Piperton."

"No. It don't sound strange one bit. It sounds like you under-stand him better by seeing where he came from."

Gator is so easy to talk to. But I can't. I can't rattle him with my suspicions. The bond we're starting to form would vanish. I know it.

"Gator, when's your birthday?"

"It's June 15th"

"And the year?" *I hope he doesn't feel like I'm interrogating him.*

"1965. Why do you ask?"

"Oh, just curious.

Pause.

Before pondering much more, I throw caution to the wind and press forward.

"I wonder if you would help me out with something. I'm tracing our family's lineage. I've done some research where our family's origin may be traced to the particular region we came from in Africa, and in some cases research may be able to determine the tribe."

The silence allows me to press on. "So, I was wondering if you would participate by agreeing to submit your DNA. It's really simple. All you'll have to do is swab your cheek with a Q-tip. You'll get a kit in the mail with the instructions and where to send in your sample." There. I got it all out.

"Sho, girl. You know I'll help you," he says without hesitation. My heart feels like it's about to leap through my chest. Trying to sound like it's no big deal, I continue with the spiel on how easy this will be.

"Thanks, Gator. I'll give the DNA company a call and give them your address. You'll get the kit in the mail in a couple of days."

"No problem."

Our conversation ends with the usual pleasantries.

Feeling dazed and convicted, I slide into a seat at the kitchen table and weigh the enormity of what I've just done.

CHAPTER 29

R obbie runs down the hall with a chant. "Mom, we're out of milk."

"Okay," I answer as I add ketchup to the shopping cart before typing milk into the search field at the top of the grocery site.

Lowfat. *Click.* It drops into the shopping cart.

I point the cursor to a newsfeed and scan the national news. As I scroll down, ads display alongside the articles.

What's this ad?

Free seven-day trial? Really? Hmm. Now that I think about it, I looked at the genealogy site a few days ago. I've always wanted to search my lineage, given that I know so little about my grandparents, and practically nothing else beyond that. On Papa George's side, it's a good thing I got to know Jackson. Other than that, I've only heard the mentioning of a few names.

The information on my mom's side is only slightly better.

I click on the ad for the free seven-day trial and put a reminder in my phone so that I'll remember to turn it off before it charges my card.

Click. Click.

Oh, this is so cool.

Scanning down the different types and categories of records to the side, my eyes pause at the category BIRTH RECORDS. I click on it and review the boxes that request bits of information.

Hmm. I suppose it's going to retrieve the record when I input the parameters. Let's see. BIRTH NAME: Darby Coleman. I place the cursor on various boxes and type in the relevant information and wait while the system loads the information to retrieve my birth certificate.

Several seconds pass before the electronic document appears. It's an abstract with all of the correct information taken from my birth certificate.

Let's see. I'll try my dad's. I've never seen his birth certificate, so this should be interesting. After loading his birthdate, place of birth, and other information, the display reads: NO RECORD FOUND. No surprise there. He was born in my grandparents' house.

I go through the same exercise for my mom, typing in her birth name, Louvenia Jackson and all the other necessary information.

NO RECORD FOUND. Okay. Okay. Let's keep things moving.

I think I'll try Maxine's information. NO RECORD FOUND.

Gloria's information. NO RECORD FOUND. Huh?

I don't get it. Why isn't there a birth certificate for either one of them? Maxine and Gloria were both born in hospitals.

Or were they?

I go back to the homepage. Glancing to the side where the categories of records are shown is a flashing category: MILITARY RECORDS ADDED.

Well, this is cool. Papa George was in the army, so I wonder if any of his records are in this database. I click on the category and input the required information.

The record pops up. At the top it says, DRAFT RECORD. Name, Date of Birth.

Nothing. How come? What's going on?

I don't understand. This information isn't correct. It's far from accurate. The indignation stirs inside of me. How dare this company put out false information. Papa George didn't enlist in the army. I search the site looking for the contact button so that I can let this company know that I don't appreciate their misrepresentation of a document that I know is not accurate. How bogus this is!

I grew up with Papa George's laughter about how his uncle came to get him. He'd laugh and belt out his thunderous roar when I'd innocently ask why this uncle wanted to take him from his home. I only remember the story told in clips, not in long-version form. He'd be so overblown in laughter, I figured he couldn't get through it all. The stories always ended the same—with him leaving the room after telling us a piece here and a piece there. That was his art of storytelling—never the long version and never in one sitting. I was usually enraptured when he was in the mood to share, knowing surely that I was going to be entertained.

Papa George was drafted. It took me much of my childhood to realize that his uncle was Uncle Sam. By the time I figured it out, I must have been a preteen.

His way of opening up was simply to say that he was drafted and didn't realize the world of opportunity that would open up to him—first of all by leaving Piperton where there was none. He was able to get his GED in the army and received training as a medic.

I'm wondering if there is any such thing as a draft record. I click on MILITARY RECORDS again. I hadn't noticed before, but a subcategory is listed beneath it—Draft Records.

I click on it and input "Joe Johnson" and the year 1960. That's such a broad name and likely should be enough that a record may pop up.

The loading icon spins for several seconds. A record appears. It shows someone by the name of Joe Johnson, his city, and the date he was drafted.

This is crazy.

I go through a series of mock exercises a few more times, for the heck of it. Does this site have records of drafts *and* enlistments? After making up a few more random names, I find the records of individuals who have draft cards.

This is too much.

After nearly an hour, I leave my desk and go into the kitchen for a break.

In a few minutes, I pick up where I left off, clicking on ENLISTMENT RECORDS. My fingers move across the keyboard, while the jitters in my stomach grow louder.

Is there another part to Papa George's story that he covered up? Am I entering wrong information into the search fields? Will I find another pack of outright lies?

As I input new data into the search fields, the rumbling in my stomach speaks of premonition. I'm going to find something new. Something untold.

Click. Enter. The colored wheel spins. The data loads. Several names appear.

Oh wow. I found him. I click on the link—George Coleman—then drill into the record. It lists his date of birth, March 8, 1945. I scan the document until my eyes rest on 'ENLISTMENT DATE: March 15, 1965.'

What the...?

So my dad enlisted. He was *not* drafted. The place of enlistment is noted as Pine Bluff, Arkansas.

I'm overwhelmed with the lies. Another piece of my foundation has crumbled. How well I know this story. There's nothing left to my imagination. I can no longer question the legitimacy of the information.

If the digital document could speak, it would say, "Surprise. I thought you'd never find me. It's been a blast stringing you along for thirty-five years."

I'm paralyzed as I stare at the black-and-white type that no amount of lying can attempt to undo. The secrets. The lies. The whispers.

The laughter.

The wheels of my mind keep turning. And turning. And my eyes keep going back to the year that my dad enlisted—1965—the same year that Gator told me he was born. Wait. Gator told me that his birthday is June 15th. So there's only one conclusion for me to draw. Papa George got the heck out of dodge three months before Gator was born.

Oh hell!

"My uncle Sam came and got me," he'd proclaim. "Even though I ended up going to Nam, nearly getting my ass shot off, the army has sho nuff been gooood to me." This was the family legend that we were raised on.

The emphasis was always on the word "good." It would be dragged out and enunciated. And the implication was that we were not to forget the life we could have ended up with in Piperton, had it not been for his vision in seeking a better life through the army.

Oh, blah, blah, blah. I'm stunned, yet I want to throw up. Another lie which has been part of my foundation.

It's unbelievable that now the issue has resurfaced decades later. Oh my God!

All of his jokes and snickering about shotgun weddings—it was as if *he, himself,* had dodged a bullet. He literally would double over in laughter when he broached the subject that was so peculiar to me. He'd start with talking about the way things were "down home." As usual the wistfulness of what he'd left behind was infused into the story.

The revelation in front of me is nothing short of sinister.

CHAPTER 30

The morning's conference call winds down, just as I look up and notice Gavin Cohen standing in the doorway of my office.

Leaning against the doorframe, Gavin is dressed as usual in a stylish continental suit by his favorite designer —a nice complement to his olive complexion and lanky frame. He winks at me and listens attentively to the voices coming through the speaker phone.

As the VP of digital content for our publisher, Vanguard Media Group, Gavin is working closely with each of the magazine's executive editors. He's got a lot of influence throughout the print media industry. So he's leading the charge for the entire media group to grow their digital publication. With Gavin's help, I've established *Dynamic Parent* magazine's online strategy.

Today's call has me jazzed that our online traffic is growing at a steady pace. I'm betting that it won't be long before subscriptions pass our print publication.

"That wraps it up, folks." Vanguard's President, Phil Eisenberg, adjourns the call. "Thanks, Phil. I look forward to presenting Dynamic's continued growth strategy on next month's call." The line beeps repeatedly after each executive editor makes their closing remarks and then hangs up.

After the repeated beeps, Gavin leisurely takes his cue and steps inside my office.

Tapping the speaker button, the line disconnects and I turn my attention to Gavin. With a smirk on his face, he positions himself by plopping down in the cushioned chair in front of my desk.

"Well, look what the wind blew in. What brings you into town?

"I'm just making my quarterly rounds to each of the affiliate magazines. And you know that *Dynamic Parent* magazine is my favorite—hands down." He lifts his mug, takes a sip, and continues in his self-satisfied mood.

No matter what frame of mind I may be in and no matter his heckling, Gavin's presence always puts me in a lively mood.

"Well, aren't you quite comfy. What's got you looking so smug? I swear you look like the cat that just ate the canary." My light-hearted agitation sets the conversation in motion.

He shifts fully into gear, ready for a few minutes of back-and-forth banter. Knowing that it aggravates me, he taps his fingernails, accordion style, one after the other along the glass top of the desk.

"Mm-hmm. I've got every reason to be a little cocky. Oh, if you only knew." Leaning back, he clasps his hands behind his head.

"If I only knew what?" I ask, giggling and trying not to appear curious about his delight surrounding his mystery. I look back at the computer monitor, hoping to send the message that I'm absorbed with what's on the screen.

Yeah, this'll work.

"You're gonna be giddy, once you get the news, " he continues. He peers over the top of his mug and takes a slow sip of his coffee—a deliberate effort to heighten the drama.

"So, how are things going with developing new content for Vanguard?" I persist in staying the course—my strategy in not letting him bait me.

"Things are moving along well these days. No complaints here. But I've got to run now." He makes the abrupt announcement as he peeps over the top of his hipster eyeglasses. "I've got to review some proposed articles coming down the pipe from one of the other magazines, *and* if there are no fires to put out, I plan on starting my weekend early."

He's not going to get the best of me. No way.

Fully intent on maintaining my strategy, I unenthusiastically reply, "Ummm, okay, have a nice weekend."

With that, he shifts his body weight from one side to the other. He can no longer contain himself and starts to dish.

"I knew you had it in you, Darbs," he teases. Now in his full-blown giddiness, the crinkles across his nose appear. "And when Phil lets you know, just remember, you didn't hear it from me." With this disclosure, he goes into full-blown chatter mode, declaring, "Yep, there are advantages to being the publisher's nephew." Still punchy, he abruptly rises from his chair

"Ohh-kay. I appreciate your vote of confidence but, hear what? What are you talking about?" I want to give him breathing space, so I wait for him to continue dishing.

He bolts for the door. I try to get his attention before he rushes from my office. He's too quick and is practically sprinting down the hall.

"Gavin!" Left standing in my doorway, I whisper down the corridor, hoping to stop him in his tracks.

Halfway down the hall, he turns, blows me a kiss, and exits to the left.

He got me. And he's loving that he's left me hanging.

Pure Gavin.

Monday morning's scan of emails reveals no fires to put out. The message count is below one hundred, which means I can relax and chill for a bit in the constant ebb and flow. I've learned that sustaining this corporate environment is all about knowing how to pace yourself.

Browsing the sender and subject line, I ponder which messages will get my immediate attention. A new message from Phil's assistant grabs my attention.

Click.

Drilling into it, I'm relieved to find that the memo is brief.

Please mark your calendar for a Town Hall meeting this Friday at 11:30 (EST). Vanguard's President, Phil Eisenberg, will be making an exciting announcement live from New York. The broadcast will be simulcast live in each publication's main conference room. Everyone at each location is encouraged to attend. You won't want to miss Phil's captivating message!

What's this about? I can't remember the last time Phil scheduled a live broadcast with all the publications.

My curiosity is interrupted by the grumble in my stomach. I yield to its cue and decide to step away from the grind of the office. Grabbing my jacket, I head for Sacha's Bistro, half a block down Second Avenue.

The usual sounds of company banter spin through the atmosphere as I step into the elevator. Colleagues make smalltalk about projects and upcoming deadlines. One busy bee steps in, another steps off. At last, the elevator reaches the first floor, I step off with all the others, heading in various directions.

"How ya doing, Darby?" The lobby's security guard looks up from his post and signals a forewarning. "Better bundle up. The wind is kicking out there."

"Thanks, Kayani."

The continuous hum echoes throughout the foyer

For some strange reason, I'm sensing that the buzz is higher than usual for a typical Monday afternoon.

The wind whips my face as the breeze rushes through my nostrils. I can't help but feel grateful. Let's see, three things. I go through my mental gratitude exercise. Grateful for the ability to breathe, grateful for Quentin and Robbie, grateful that Robbie has a good therapist. Grateful that I feel like I'm adjusting. The hole in my soul is being mended. I'm starting to make sense of some things. The abuse has shattered my world, but with my suspicion about Gator, it's starting to feel like it's bigger than Robbie.

A swift gust brushes my cheeks as I round the corner to the bistro. As I tighten the cashmere scarf around my neck, I reminisce about the last conversation I had with Gator. He had assured me that he would take the DNA test to help me trace our family's lineage. I sure don't want to keep bugging him, but he should have received his DNA kit by now. Wonder if I should call him again?

Along with the wind, a whisper of conviction moves across my nose, turning to an icy chill. My readiness at persuading Gator to participate in the DNA test doesn't sit well with me. The certainty of what I've done travels and settles into my throat. With no hint of reluctance on his part, only a genuine need to be of help, I'm feeling guilty about not revealing my *real* agenda—suspecting he's my brother. My neck begins to itch with the burning conviction of having manipulated him. I just—no I *need* his DNA sample. Badly. The need is insatiable, and the intensity is growing as I search for meaning beyond what's happened to Robbie.

Maybe that's why the universe has stalled on presenting the evidence that I feel in my gut. Gator has had plenty of time to send in his DNA sample. Why has this stalled?

The guilt continues to rise within me, mixed with the anxiety of such a vile secret—Papa George fathering a child with his sister? I simply cannot wrap my mind around it and am haunted by the prospect. I've got to know. Why didn't I just come out and tell Gator my suspicions?

The double doors of Sacha's Bistro slide open. In what looks like the awakening from a weekend slumber, most of the lunch bunch wades through the doors and back to the slew of office buildings scattered nearby.

The hostess looks up from her stand as I move inside the entrance. "How many, please?"

"Oh, only me. I'll just grab a seat at the bar." I motion in the opposite direction of the dining room, and head into the bar where customers are sparsely seated at bistro tables. The gray carpeted floor is highlighted in shades of gold and muted blues. The sub-dued lighting mixes with the natural lighting from the floor-length windows, casting a swanky aura over the atmosphere.

I revel in the melody of a jazz saxophonist piped throughout the room. I slide into a cushioned stool against the oak bar, then hang my purse on the hook beneath the carved edge of its mantle.

The bartender examines and wipes a glass while watching the programming on the TV overhead. Several customers scroll through their phones with a half-eaten meal lying in front of them.

After a moment, a cheerful waiter greets me from behind the bar. "Have you looked over the lunch menu? The avocado toast is Monday's special. It's delish! I'll be right back and take your order."

"That's okay, I'm ready. I'm gonna take you up on that avocado toast, with a side of coleslaw."

"You got it," he says before dashing off.

My phone buzzes. I lift the purse from the hook. Phil Eisenberg's name illuminates the display on the phone.

"Hi, Phil. How are you? *I wonder what he wants.*

The natural buoyancy of his voice meshes with its command.

"Darby, I'm well, thanks. I'm beyond elated about the wonderful news I received late Friday afternoon." His tone is regulated yet enthusiastic. "I got a call from the president of the Amy Awards. It seems Vanguard Media is in the running for this year's Publication of the Year award."

"That's wonderful, Phil! All of Vanguard's magazines are incredible. I'm glad that *Dynamic Parent* contributes to our young family demographic."

"Oh, *Dynamic Parent* more than contributes, Darby." The conviction in Phil's voice is unlike any tone I've ever heard from him before. "The President of the Amy Awards said that the major factor in their decision was the significant impact that *Dynamic Parent* has made on its readers."

I can hardly believe my ears. Racing thoughts travel through my mind, then settle at the memory of the long hours I've put in. The late nights. The pressure to meet deadlines. The stress. The weight of it all.

And now this. When I think about the load I've carried all of those days, weeks, and months, moisture collects in the corner of my eyes, then releases freely into a steady stream as it flows to my chin.

"Um, ahem." Clearing the knot from my throat, I manage to respond, "Thank you so much, Phil. I appreciate that."

"Well, you and your team have surely earned it, Darby. And there's one other thing. I want you to come to New York next month—to the Amy Awards gala, represent Vanguard, and accept the award on behalf of Vanguard Media and our entire portfolio. That is, of course, if we're announced as the finalist. My assistant will call you later with all the details."

"Certainly. I'd be honored, Phil," I manage to whisper between sniffs.

"Oh, one other thing I think you'd like to know." He pauses. The emphasis in his voice takes full effect. The Amy Awards President said he wanted us to know that one of the key factors that the committee wanted to acknowledge was the series of articles that *Dynamic Parent* did on stranger danger. What parents need to look out for—the whole thing. Absolutely outstanding. That's what really put Vanguard over the top. Good job, Darby!"

I can only murmur, "Thank you."

"OK, Darby. You have a good Thanksgiving holiday and keep up the good work."

"Thanks." My heart sinks at the irony of it all.

Stranger danger. No. No-o-o. The perpetrator is someone who is close to the child. Someone who has access. He's not a stranger. He's someone the child trusts.

The tears flow freely as I fumble for a tissue at the bottom of my purse.

"Ma'am. Ma'am?" The cheerful waiter side-eyes me. " Here's your avocado toast."

"May I have the envelope please!" The announcer's voice is full of drama as he readies the audience for the Publication of Year award. "And the award goes to *Dynamic Parent* magazine, a Vanguard Media publication! Accepting the award is Dynamic Parent's Editor-in-Chief, Darby Shields."

I feel overwhelmed from the thunderous applause as I rise from my seat.

Don't trip going up the stairs.

The announcer turns awaits me as I make my way to the stage. He greets me and hands me the shiny award which is a bronze replica of a magazine.

I step towards the podium and adjust the mic. "I'm honored to accept this award on behalf of *Dynamic Parent* and Vanguard Media." I continue with the usual acknowledgments and mention Phil Eisenberg and the mission of all of the collective publications of Vanguard Media.

"*Dynamic Parent* strives to be a trusted resource that empowers parents on everyday issues that moms and dads face in caring for their families. The response to our issue on stranger danger exceeded our expectations and our reader's feedback indicates that it was because of the real examples we provided of kids being victimized on the internet."

A knot in begins to form in my throat.

"We want to continue bringing stories that arm parents with valuable information. We'll be extending the topic of stranger danger, because, unfortunately, children are often in the gravest danger by being in the midst of an unsuspecting family member— a trusted person who is no stranger, yet who happens to be a predator. Unfortunately, it's a situation that's all too common, yet not commonly talked about. And…and, unfortunately, that's

why he—or she continues to victimize children within the family."
My voice is shaky as I end the sentence.

The room grows silent.

"We look forward to…surpassing our reader's expectations.
Thank you."

I feel as though a weight has literally lifted from my shoulders
as I exit the stage.

CHAPTER 31

Their muffled excitement travels through the house followed by the sound of Quentin's and Robbie's footsteps scurrying out the door. They had planned their mission last night after dinner, determined to snag some Black Friday specials on video games.

Turning on my side, toward my nightstand, I glance at the red display on the clock—6:00 a.m. I'm going to enjoy having the house to myself for most of the day. I'm looking forward to being a slug and binge-watching movies.

Pushing back the covers, I start to crawl out of bed, but the stark chill sends a shock up my leg, causing me to rethink my movement. Rocco's footsteps click on the floor signaling that he's headed this way. He pushes the door open with his nose and plops down on the floor beside me. I snuggle back under the comforter, close my eyes, and drift back to sleep.

After what seems like a few hours, I open my eyes and prepare to settle into the post-Thanksgiving lull. The stillness causes me to think about yesterday.

Paige, her husband, and their two boys celebrated the holiday with us. I catch myself smiling. The warmth spreads over me as I reflect on the mood and the previous day's events. At one point I had looked around the room, taking it all in, feeling grateful that everything in my environment appeared normal, just as it should. I couldn't have asked for a better day than yesterday. Robbie and the boys had a blast playing together.

I'm able to embed the day's image into my mind. Embracing each instant has been a big help along with keeping a gratitude journal.

Leaning against the kitchen counter, my fingers glide along my chenille robe while I watch the small circular bubbles bounce against the glass of the electric carafe. I survey and ponder the stash of teas in the cabinet. Earl Grey, Peppermint, Lemon Ginger.

The undisturbed quiet has my thoughts, once again, filtering to Gator and our conversation about taking a DNA test. The thoughts, however, bring me anything but peace. I'm embarrassed, even though no one knows but me.

The last slice of Paige's special homemade pecan pie sits on the counter. Normally I'd be thrilled that I spied it before Quentin or Robbie. Somehow I can't get excited about it.

Grabbing my mug, I head to the family room. The atmosphere in the house feels weighty as I click the remote in anticipation of the weekend Christmas movie marathon.

I feel anxious. I need to know. Soon.

I scroll through the screen's TV guide. The Christmas movies have suddenly lost their appeal. I put down the remote, pick up my phone, and dial the DNA company's number. Navigating through the automated call system is beginning to grate my nerves.

"AccuDNA." The cheerful greeting catches me with a mouthful of tea.

"Mmm. Hello," I manage after gulping down the tea. "I'm calling to check the status of DNA samples that were sent in."

We sift back and forth, going over the preliminary questions to confirm identity. "I'll need to put you on hold, ma'am. What's your name again?"

"Darby Shields."

"And when did you send it in?

"About ten days ago. I should have the results by email by now, right?"

"One moment please. The click of the agent's button prompts an annoying hold music. Minutes pass. And pass. Gator should have sent in his DNA sample by now. Why haven't I received the results yet?

I head into the kitchen, switch the carafe on again, and wait for the water to boil. Why do I feel like there are more dark secrets—more deceptions, and cover-ups?

I glance at the pie on the counter. What's taking so long?

Removing the phone from my ear, I check the time before unwrapping the plastic that covers the pie dish. It feels like I'm in an endless cycle of nowhere in the three minutes that have passed.

My cares ease for just a moment as I bite into the pie, savoring the rich sweetness along with the crunchy pecans. I contemplate the outcome of what's in motion.

The music halts.

"Ma'am? Hello? Hello?"

"Um-hmm?"

"May I please have your passcode?"

"06223."

Seconds pass.

"Yes, we have your sample, Ms. Shields." My heart flutters. "It's been here for a few days. But we don't have the other party's to match it to. This was a test to determine shared paternity, correct?"

"Yes."

"Hold on. I'll check again."

Shared paternity. The two words travel through me like the sting of an infected wound.

So Gator hasn't taken the DNA test, after all. My face grows warm at the thought of what I've done.

Oh, why did I have to lie to Gator?

I wonder if my gut is gnawing at me because of the possibility of my cousin being my brother? Or is my stomach gnawing for not being completely open with Gator?

Probably both.

Did my father *really* impregnate his sister?

Regardless of the calamity the situation will bring if it's true, I can't rest until I know.

"Ma'am? Hello?"

"Oh! Yes, I'm still here," I answer.

"No, we don't have the other party's sample. Maybe he overlooked it in the mail. "Uh..." I'm dumbfounded.

"It's just a pale blue envelope that the test comes in," she continues. "There's no logo or return address on it. Would you like us to send it out again?" she asks.

"Yes, if you would, please."

After confirming Gator's birth name and address, I hang up and contemplate what to do next.

The afternoon has blurred into watching one hokey Christmas movie after another. The plots all feel the same. Hours have passed since my conversation with the DNA company.

I pick up the phone lying next to me on the sofa, and tap on Gator's number.

"Hello?"

"Hey, Gator. This is Darby."

"Hey, gurl. It's good to hear your voice. How you doin?"

The genuine sweetness of Gator's voice comes through, as usual. Everything is going to be okay. The self-talk soothes my nerves. *Don't overthink it.*

"I'm doing well, Gator. How was your Thanksgiving?"

"Real good. I made a fried turkey. 'Sho was good. I know folks probably smelt it up the road." He chuckles.

"Sounds wonderful." I envision the thickets and underbrush alongside the rickety backwoods road of our grandmother's house—the place where so many of our relatives hadn't traveled beyond the confines of Piperton. I imagine Gator frying a turkey on this back porch with his scraggly dog, Jeff, nearby. The aroma in the country air…

"I'm surprised you're not out shopping with the rest of the mall rats," he interrupts my thoughts.

"No. Not today," I respond. "I'm not about to get caught out there in that madness."

Recognizing that this is the moment, I shift the conversation. "Hey Gator, did you ever take the DNA test that we talked about?"

"Yeah, I *think* I did."

You think you did? What's up with that?

"Oh. 'Cause the company hasn't received your sample. Maybe it got lost. Another one is on the way to you, though. You should have it in just a few days. Can you please do me a favor?"

"Sure."

"Will you call me once you get it in the mail?"

"Yeah. That's no problem. I'll be sure to call you." His response carries a degree of inquisitiveness, unlike when he first agreed to participate.

"Gator?" The tremble in my voice unsteadies me. My tone lingers.He picks up on my uneasiness.

"Yeah, what is it?"

Cautiously, I press through. "I don't know how to say this, but I think you're my broth...brother."

"What?" The intake of breath is so pronounced that it sounds like a convulsion. "You mean? You mean Uncle George?"

"Yeah. I think my father is also *your* father."

"Nah, nah."

"I know it's hard to believe, but..but...I hate to tell you this, Gator."

"Wha... what?"

"My dad molested my son, Robbie. I'm pretty sure he molested my sisters too." I let the momentary pause give Gator time to reflect. "I couldn't help but notice how much you resemble my father, it's downright amazing. And so now that I know about this other side of my father, I don't think it's a stretch to consider that he molested your mom."

"Oh-o-o. I'm so sorry bout yo son. This here is a lot you're droppin on me." He pauses for several seconds. "Yeah, gurl," he picks up. "If you want me to, I'll take that test, just so it'll rest yo' mind. I hate to think my mama suffered from something like this, so it would rest my mine too. I'll call you when it comes in the mail."

"Thanks, Gator. Have a good weekend and will you please call me when it comes in the mail?"

"I 'sho will.

CHAPTER 32

"Shelly, the manicurist at my favorite salon places my left hand under the UV light, then lifts my right arm toward her. She begins with a hand massage, starting from my palm, then moving upward. Her fingertips press into my skin in a kneading motion. Some of the tension begins to release. I hadn't realized how wound up I've been.

She turns in the direction of the door, as a woman dressed in brown sweats selects a bottle of nail color that's lined up on the shelves against the wall. "I'll be right with you," Shelly acknowledges, before turning her attention back to me.

"I can tell the mood of my regulars. It seems like something's a little off with you. It must be about family, or money, or both." She giggles.

She places my right hand under the UV light, then steps away to assist the woman still standing at the entrance.

I hope Gator hasn't chickened out. It's been almost a week and he should have called me by now.

After a few minutes, Shelly's back to tend to me. "Toes for you today?"

"Not today. I've got to run." I rise from my seat and reach for the wad of cash tucked in the outside slot of my purse.

"Be careful. You don't want to smudge. I'll see you next time."

Stepping outside the nail salon, the dreary clouds mix with the evening's dusk. Together they cast an imposing sense of dominance into the atmosphere.

On the drive home, I muse about the DNA test's outcome—if Gator decided to follow through.

The smoky smell meets me as I enter the house. Quentin and Robbie haven't noticed that I'm home. The kitchen window is cracked open, which explains the smell of smoke. They are seated across from the fire pit. A package of graham crackers and some partially eaten chocolate bars are lying on the table between them.

Robbie holds his skewer up to Quentin to examine. "I think this one is toasty enough, Dad."

"Hi, guys!" I shout through the window.

"Hi, Mom."

"Hey, babe."

Being in no mood to roast marshmallows or eat s'mores, I remove the few dishes from the sink and load them into the dishwasher. Another package of graham crackers sit on the counter, but this one has been left open. I remove one from the package and nibble on it. The crunch factor has an appeal that's oddly reassuring. After the last dish is loaded into the dishwasher, I head upstairs to the solitude of my bedroom. The muffled conversation of my two guys on the patio drifts upward and through the window.

In the dark room, the glow from the fire pit travels above, casting its shadow onto the walls of the room. Their activity outside has created a serene ambiance that has ushered me into an inner peace.

I'm relieved that I fessed up to Gator about my suspicions and needing his DNA.

With a clear conscience, I dial his number.

"Hello?" He picks up after only the second ring.

"Hey, Gator, It's Darby. I thought I'd give you a call to see if that DNA kit has shown up in your mail."

"Yo' ears must have been burnin." He laughs. "I went out to the roadside a couple hours ago to bring in my mail. I'm so bad about checking it regularly. So now I have a stack on the counter. Let me look and see.

"OK, thanks."

The sound of papers being shuffled and moved about drifts through the speaker of his phone. The commotion continues for several seconds.

"What'd you say it looks like?"

"Um… a plain blue envelope, probably a little thicker than normal."

More rustling and shifting about.

"Let's see… I think I got it!"

I'm amazed at his excitement, as if he's won the lottery.

Now that this moment is here, I'm not quite sure what to say next. But for some reason, I feel prompted to make an appeal.

"Gator, would you mind if we do this over the phone? I'll talk you through it."

"Ah… um… yeah. Sure."

The sound of paper tearing is reassuring.

"Inside the envelope are four Q-tips wrapped inside plastic. You'll need to be careful that you handle them with the stick, and not let your fingers touch the cotton portion."

"Okay, I got one."

"So, take that Q-tip and swab the inside of your mouth, against your cheek. I'm going to count to twenty while you do that."

After several minutes, he's completed the entire process with the swabs.

"Now"—the sound of a tap on what I imagine is the counter signals that the job has been completed—"I've just sealed the envelope and I'ma mail it back first thing in the morning," he assures me. "I promise."

"I really appreciate you for doing this, Gator. It's something I just *have* to know."

"Since you want me to do this, that's why I'm doing it." His solemn voice fades with each word. "It don't mean nothin."

The control I thought I'd had in my voice begins to weaken. "Gator, we're going to get through this." My throat tightens as I push through the next few words. "Everything's going to be all right. I'll call you in a few days," I manage.

His voice diminishes to just above a whisper. "That'll be just fine."

CHAPTER 33

Quentin must have gone on his run, I realize when I fling my arm across the pillow next to me. I begin to mentally fill in events for the day ahead while lying in the stillness. Instinctively, I reach for the phone on the nightstand and scroll to the weather app. Mostly cloudy, with a slight chance of rain. My fingers tap on the email app. I scroll past random messages until my eyes become fixated on the subject line of one.

AccuDNA

That's right! It's been seven days. Gator sent it in! The realization causes me to sit upright in bed.

I manage to steady my fingers when I tap on the email.

> *Darby Shields,*
>
> *Thank you for choosing **AccuDNA** for your paternity testing needs. We are pleased to inform you that all samples have arrived at our laboratory and testing is complete.*

My stomach tightens. My face grows warm, yet feels in conflict with its accumulating moisture. Pants of air in my chest battle for control.

Breathe.

I've waited so long for this moment. Now that it's here, I'm wondering if I've done the right thing. I hadn't anticipated the sheer panic that I'm now feeling.

After several deep breaths, I click on the link and watch as a pdf file opens with the results of the report. A boldfaced heading is at the top of the page: **DNA TEST REPORT**

Data which indicates the different types of tests run is shown in the left column, along with their results. The numbers and percentages are all meaningless data to me.

Dang. Do they think a scientist is interpreting this data.

My eyes frantically scan the message for information that I can interpret, before landing on two columns: **DNA Sample #1. DNA Sample #2.**

And finally, the paragraph at the bottom of the page:

Interpretation:

DNA testing was done to determine siblingship of the alleged siblings. Based on testing, the probability of half siblingship is 98%. The likelihood that they share a common biological parent is 49 to 1.

The reality registers in my head, but is felt in my heart, whose beats compete with my deliberate deep breaths. The percentage stares at me—98%.

The phone drops and nestles between the covers. I need to just stand in place for a few moments and take it all in. This is too much.

After several minutes, I hear the sound of Quentin's footsteps coming down the hall. He's singing as if he's in a world far away. His silhouette enters my mind much sooner than he actually does. The steps become closer as he approaches our bedroom.

Headphones. Sweaty face. Uninterrupted.

His lightheartedness is interrupted by a look of fearful concern as our gazes lock.

"What's wrong?" The despair on his face must be the mirror image of the distress on mine. He removes one of his earplugs, as if he's preparing for the worst.

"I want to show you something." I toss back the comforter and pick up the phone. With a tap, the screen illuminates as I hand it to him. "Tell me what this says."

Like a fixture, he directs his attention to reading the email. His natural frown lines have become more pronounced. His eyes tighten, as if squinting will change the data that is illuminated in the palm of his hand.

Part of me wants him to interpret it differently—that I've misread the data, interpreted the report wrong. That my gut feeling for all these months has had no meaning. That it was all part of my vivid imagination, with no credence with which to base it on.

"Gator's your brother. That's... that's what...it says. The odds are 49 to 1." Each word is enunciated with the agony of truth. He tosses the phone back onto the bed. It lands with a soft thump.

The newly released declaration hangs in the air.

"Gator's my brother," I mumble.

The drive home from work has me stuck in traffic longer than usual. The gridlock worsens near the exit to Coventry Mall, as shoppers clamor for the last of the pre-Christmas sales. The stiffness in my body has only begun to lessen since Saturday's revelation. Letting the truth settle into my soul for the past few days has allowed me to gather my strength and gear up.

My heart aches for Gator. I can't imagine that he'll take this too well. It's taken me a day to digest the reality of the DNA report and also to prepare for telling Gator—even though I'm not sure I really am.

At the same time, I'm fully armed and ready to confront my father. I've got more than I could ever have imagined. He won't get a chance to give some devious response when I slap a DNA report in front of him. The report is all I need to show that he molested my child *and* that he's covered up a sinister past for my entire life—that he fathered a child with his sister. My head is still reeling at the truth of it all.

My thoughts jump to Ethan and his story of being molested by Uncle Clarence. Was this a typical way of life in Piperton? And just *who* is my father anyway? He's sure not the father I thought I knew; that's for darn sure.

He was the father who I loved to take drives with through the hillsides of Denton. I couldn't wait to turn sixteen because he had promised to teach me to drive a stick shift. After our drives, we'd head to the ice cream store. He'd often joke, "When you look for a husband, look for a hard-working guy like your old pa." Then he'd add, "But make sure you get your education first." He emphasized having integrity along with compassion, and was fond of saying, "Don't lie, because if you tell a lie, you'll have to tell another one to cover up the first one, and then more lies to keep covering up."

And he was the dad who loved to call me Babycakes.

How ironic. He's George Coleman, the bully. I'm ready to take down the bully.

Pulling into the driveway, I'm buoyed by the small window of time I have to myself. Quentin and Robbie are probably deciding what takeout they'll stop at on the way home.

I think I'll give myself a facial and soak in a bubble bath.

I flip the door latch, my phone buzzes in my purse.

"Hey, girl, are you on your way home?" Paige's enthusiasm brings a smile to my face.

"Your timing is scary. How'd you know I just pulled into my driveway?"

"Oh, you know, I've just got that extra sense." She giggles. Her bubbly nature and humor soothe a bit of the tension in my neck. Instinctively, I close the car door and settle in for a catch-up conversation in the driveway. This couldn't be a better time to fill Paige in on Saturday's hoopla.

"What's been going on with you? We keep missing each other, and you haven't shown up for yoga."

"Yeah, I've been preoccupied. Pretty much a zombie. I'm just now getting my bearings and starting to regroup." The silence sits before I continue. "I got the DNA results on Saturday."

Paige cautiously responds, "Uh oh. I'm holding my breath, and I'm not kidding anymore."

"My hunch was right. I wish it wasn't, but Gator's my brother."

The lull in our conversation has heightened. It's as if the wind has forever known of the Coleman family secrets, whispered throughout the generations.

"Darby, I don't know what to say. This is mind-boggling." "

"My head is dizzy from putting the pieces together. These generational secrets have everything to do with the present and are affecting me and my family today. Growing up, I'd hear footsteps walking down the hall late at night when I'd gone to bed. My father would shoo us off to bed. Much later, during the night, I would see the light from the hallway shining beneath my door. After a while, the light would go off. I never knew that there was a hidden meaning to it, and I just put it all out of my mind."

Paige's compassion naturally encourages me to persevere with the childhood clues that are being pieced together. Knowing that she's listening intently, I begin to purge more of the mysterious memories from my childhood.

"All I can think about is how my father kept us away from Piperton. He used to tell us what an awful place it was and that he didn't want us exposed to the Jim Crow South. I believed him. I had no reason not to."

My voice feels dull, and weakens before trailing off. Somehow I manage to recapture my thoughts. "All the secrets. All the lies. Now it makes sense. My life has been one big lie."

One purge connects with another and another—feeling like the onset of a cleansing process. "I can't describe the feeling." I'm puzzled at the effort it took just to say those words. Like an ambushed soldier, I'm caught off guard by the lump in my throat. My stomach stirs with agitation, now that I recognize the secrets and lies that I was raised on. Like a reckoning, I'm aware that a sinister energy has emerged because of what I've just uncovered.

"Oh, Darby, I feel so bad for you." The concern in Paige's voice tapers to a whisper. "Are... are you going to be okay?"

"I don't know. I really don't know. Quentin and Robbie will be pulling into the driveway pretty soon. I'd better go inside and get myself together. We're headed to our timeshare at Mount Charcot in a few days for Christmas. Somehow I've got to release this load before then. It's too heavy a weight to carry."

"Release this load? It sounds like you're thinking of confronting your father." Paige's concern is apparent because of the subdued tone in her voice.

"I've got to let my father know that his jig is up! The pretense and charade he's played for my entire life is over. He fathered a child with his sister, so he's *always* been a pervert. I wonder if my mother knew that when she married him."

The atmosphere somehow becomes infused with a sense of order.

"But first I've got to tell Gator. And I need to go see Bishop Jefferson before we leave for vacation."

"Darby, this is incredible. What you've uncovered is unreal." Paige's response is mixed with hesitation and unbelief. "It's like you're in a story, walking through the forest, picking up bread-crumbs as clues. And the breadcrumbs are leading you to the truth."

"Yeah, it feels surreal. Too bad this is no fairytale."

As I pause in the front entryway, I decide to get it over with and send Gator a text.

Can you please call me when you have a chance. I take a deep breath and push send. Flexing my neck and shoulders, I head upstairs to change into athletic wear and put on a yoga recording. My phone vibrates just as I take my T-shirt off. Gator's image illu-minates across the display—the one photo I have of him, cropped from the photo of the two of us standing under the old oak tree in Grandma's dusty yard.

I exhale. The memory of that day...when it felt as if the porch was whispering vague memories in my direction.

"Hey, Gator. How's it going?"

"Doin' good. Sho doin' good. Ain't got no cause to complain. How 'bout you?" His predictive response merges with his spirited tone, and conveys that he doesn't have a care in the world.

"Thanks, Gator. I'm good. I just got home from work, and I was about to get a workout in."

With a chuckle he adds, "I can tell that's your normal thing."

"Yeah, I try." The pause resumes, but not for long before I pivot to the disturbing truth. "I got the DNA results back. I'll forward a copy to you."

Our conversation hits a natural lull. I move forward with caution.

"Gator, my father is also your father," I whisper. My words hang in the air suspended for what feels like an indefinite amount of time. "You…you're my brother," I say as delicately as I can.

The jovial tone in Gator's voice is diminished and replaced with uncertainty between the cracks. "Really?" The fracture moves like the severing of a fault line below the surface of the earth.

"It's true. You're my cousin *and* my brother." A mild whimper drifts through the line, followed by erupting sobs growing progressively louder. "Gator, I'm so sorry to lay all this on you."

Unsure of what else to say, I remain silent, which seems like the right response. After a while, Gator manages to speak.

"Yo daddy thinks he's better than everybody else," he manages between sobs. I sense that more unleashing is coming, in both words and emotions. "The last time yo daddy was down here, you know what he told my mom?"

With nothing to say, I manage a solemn "no."

"This is what he told her, 'Jerlinda, I was thinking of taking you back to California with me for a visit, but I changed my mind, since you don't talk so good.'"

"Oh-o-o, I'm sorry." I try as best I can to console him. My father's arrogance flashes into my mind. The country boy who escaped, yet who scorned the relatives who didn't.

The sobs elevate, with the pain and resentment mounting. "That's what he told my mama. Uncle George—*yo* daddy—always was one to thumb his nose and look down on some folks. That's what he told my mama—to her face!" The dam has fully broken, and the unrestrained sobs gush out.

"Gator, I'm sorry. I just had a feeling that there was more to my father's story. I've been chasing the truth down, not really knowing what I was after. Just a feeling that there were secrets and lies that needed to be uncovered."

"Can I ask you...well, who do you believe your father is?"

The mood shifts again before Gator gives a pensive explanation. The loud sobs have diminished into a whimper.

"Never met him," he solemnly declares. "Mama loved this man to *death*. Name's Ben Jenkins. I didn't ask much about him; I knew that was her business, and I knew my place as her child. She knew him from high school. And he left her at the altar," he explains wistfully.

I say nothing.

"Broke Mama's heart, yes, it did." The uncomfortable silence persists, before he picks back up to end the story. "I was born three months later. After that, she moved to Arkansas for many years. Worked as a domestic. Came back to Piperton and lived the rest of her life here in Grandma and Grandpa's house."

"Oh," is all I can manage.

Gator's purging goes on. "I always heard the stories round here from our aunts and uncles. How yo daddy left Piperton and went into the army." He pauses to catch his breath. "They used to say how highfalutin he got to be. Had his nose stuck in the air cause he had done well and was livin' high on the hog."

Gator's breathing deepens, followed by an intense blowing sound. I imagine him with a wad of tissues in his hand, trying to compose himself after the sudden left hook that I've thrown.

"Gator, I'm sorry about all of this. The silence and the sobs have invited a comfortable space. "Like I told you, the suspicions about my father's past came when I found out that he molested my son. This whole thing is beyond shocking."

Between sniffles, Gator responds, "Yeah. With all this about Uncle George, it looks like another side to him is showing up." After a brief silence, Gator's seething starts again. "Folks down here look up to yo dad. When I was a little boy, he'd come through Piperton every once in a while, on his way from overseas. He always had that dress uniform on—stepped real high in it. You could tell he was *real* proud." He sniffles. "I'm sorry, this is all so…" He stops to blow his nose again.

I feel torn about releasing the truth, and bringing Gator so much pain. His fury picks up, drawing momentum from his anger.

"And folks was real proud of him too. That he had made something of himself and didn't stay 'round here drinking moonshine and wasting his life away, like a lot of them done."

His weeping is now muted."I looked up to Uncle George. I wanted to be like him, since that's all I heard about 'round here. But with what you're telling me now? I don't care if I ever see his uppity self again."

"I understand," I manage to respond, knowing that it's a scant offering for the agony my father has caused.

"This is real hurtful, Darby." The tone of his voice catches me off guard. His voice is more composed and measured when he repeats himself. "Real hurtful."

My instincts tell me to let him get as much of the pain out, before responding.

"Gator, I'm so sorry for the lies and the secrets, and for the pain this has caused."

"I gotta go."

Abruptly, the connection ends, squelching me into its hollow space.

Much of the uncertainty that had been lodged in my heart unveils itself, then travels through my body as the tears surrender to the dull ache.

⸻

"Good morning. Grace Worship Center. This is Charlene," the cheerful voice greets me after the third ring.

"Morning, Charlene. This is Darby Shields.

"Hi, Darby," Charlene responds with her usual charm. "How can I help you?"

"I wonder if Bishop Jefferson has a few minutes open on his calendar later this afternoon? I'd like to drop by to discuss an urgent matter with him. We're leaving on Friday for Christmas vacation and won't be back for over a week. If there's any slot at all, I'd really appreciate it."

Charlene responds with hopeful assurance. "OK, hold on a minute, and I'll take a look."

The clicking sound of keyboard strokes fills the lull for a few seconds before hold music pipes in the voice of Yolanda Adams. She lulls me along with her melodious tone. For a few seconds, I journey with her, gravitating to a moment of peace. I'm enraptured as, effortlessly, she persuades me that everything's going to be all right. I had spoked with Bishop some time ago about my suspicions that Gator was my brother and the DNA test I was hoping he'd take.

"Hello, Darby?" The startling interruption brings me back to the task at hand.

"Yes?"

"Bishop has an opening at three thirty this afternoon. Will that work for you?"

"That's great! I'll see him then. Thanks so much, Charlene."

A gush of relief washes over me as I hang up and turn my attention to the proposals for next quarter's issues. Immersed in the spreadsheet looming in front of me, I review the budget for each of the plans.

Gavin sticks his head through my cracked door. "Hey, Darby. Congratulations on the Amy Award and also on that passionate speech you gave. I heard there wasn't a dry eye in the house. I knew you had it in you."

"Well, thanks. When did you breeze into town?"

"I'm just here for a hot minute for a couple of meetings. But don't change the subject. I've seen how you've turned this magazine around. You have put *Dynamic Parent* magazine head and shoulders above all the rest."

"Thanks, Gavin. Stop now. You're making me blush."

"Want to head out to lunch?"

"I can't. I'm going to leave early, so I need to finish up this budget report."

"Okay, I'll take a rain check for the next time I zoom in." He spins on his heels and begins heading down the hall, before rethinking his move. "And you need to stop working so hard," he finishes before dashing off.

The need to tie up loose ends before Christmas vacation has created an urge to share what the data has revealed, but I haven't fully digested it.

The reality of what I'm about to divulge brings to mind my conversation with the bishop, when I informed him that my father had molested Robbie.

Bishop had suggested that I consider what I may or may not gain by confronting my father. I was stunned that he would ask me to consider whether there would be any other option. He had counseled me that my father's realization that I knew was likely doing more to punish him than my wrath could. The idea being that my father knew was like pulling the covers off him.

Whew. If he'd only known.

I couldn't wrap my mind around the guidance he had given. But now that I am armed with the unimaginable—the uncovering of what the DNA has revealed—it's nothing short of supernatural. This is so much bigger than Robbie. None of this would have been brought to light if I had not felt this unexplainable sensation of being pulled like a magnet in Gator's direction. This whole ordeal seems like a spiritual awakening. I can't even explain it to myself. And I'm tired of even trying. Strangely, the magnetic pull is beginning to feel comfortable like an unspoken voice that is guiding me.

Even though it's been a few days since learning about my father's secret past of impregnating his sister, it's still shocking. The person I've known my whole life is really a stranger living a double life.

What if my father had snapped and pulled his gun on us? Would I be alive to get the DNA and the truth about his secret past? The what ifs are flooding my mind, with no way of escape.

I stand at the door of the delivery entrance and wait to be buzzed in. Unlike a typical Sunday, the church's parking lot is empty except for a handful of cars. The late afternoon sun shines against the glass door. I press my cold hands against it, anticipating the soothing warmth transferring from the glass and into my palms. My anxiety begins to release as I press the button and wait for a response.

Seconds later, the loud click signals that the door has been unlocked and I can enter.

The phrase "quiet as a church mouse" applies to this setting, as I round the hall to the inner office where I know Charlene will be waiting.

She sits at her desk, eyeing the security monitors mounted on the wall across from her. Her shoulder-length braids are elegantly wrapped high atop her head. The aromatic diffuser located on the shelf above her desk has the office seeped in the scent of eucalyptus. Seems so fitting, with Christmas only a few days away. She turns towards me, smiles, and resumes her typing while nodding toward Bishop Jefferson's door down the hallway.

"He's expecting you. You can go back."

I count the familiar steps in my mind while walking down the stretch of hallway. Tapping on the partially open door, Bishop immediately responds, "Come in."

Bishop quickly pulls his chair back from the desk with a look of concern. He stands and studies my expression. "Can I get you a bottle of water?"

I nod, collapsing into the leather chair in front of his desk.

He moves swiftly across the room, then grabs two bottled waters from the small refrigerator. His bewildered expression clues me in that he's braced himself for whatever news I have to tell him. Seems that he's taking his cue from my demeanor.

He takes his seat behind his desk, faces me, and recomposes himself.

He leans forward. "Did you get your cousin to take a DNA test?"

"Um…hm."

Unable to respond, I meet his gaze. The silence in the room communicates the answer. Finally, he seems to gather his courage to ask me. "It's positive?"

"Um...hm." I nod.

With a loud sigh, he falls back into his chair, lifts the water bottle, and takes a long gulp.

"Darby, have you thought about how you want to handle this information?"

"I've already told my cousin that he's my brother. That *my* father is his father *and* his Uncle George. I was so shaken that I also had Quentin look over the results to make sure that we were both reading the same thing."

"I see."

He allows his chair to swivel back and forth. It seems that the spinning is giving him some level of comfort from the disturbing news that I've unveiled. I wonder if he's ever guided anyone through such a cesspool of iniquity as the one in front of him.

"And what about your other siblings? Do they have any idea?"

"I highly doubt it. I wonder if my mother even knows."

"Now that I have what I never knew I was looking for, I'll confront my father about molesting Robbie. The DNA about my brother Gator is like a divine bonus that's landed in my lap. I guess it shows that since this was never contained solely to Robbie, it was meant for me to expose the bigger story."

Bishop sits mutely without any response.

"We're leaving in three days for Mount Charcot. I need to get this out of the way before then. You'll remember that he sent me an overnight letter last year, to meet with whomever of my choosing—to iron out why I had accused him of molesting Robbie. I sent him an overnight letter, in return, saying that I wanted to meet with Dr. Floyd. The stipulation was that he and my mother would meet with Dr. Floyd first, then we'd have a follow-up meeting with Dr. Floyd, my parents, and Quentin and myself. He backed out of that second meeting."

"So what do you want to do?"

"I want to call another meeting. This time with you, my parents, Quentin, and myself.

Bishop Jefferson lowers gaze while contemplating my proposal. "So you're saying the sooner the better."

"Yes. We need to get this over with and get everything out in the open, preferably before the end of the week."

Bishop pauses, releases a sigh, then reaches for his water bottle.

"OK. Leave your parents' number with Charlene. I'll have her give them a call. Hopefully, we can all meet before the end of the week."

CHAPTER 34

The parking lot at the social security office is nearly empty as I pull up and gauge how long my wait might be by the number of parked cars. I'm feeling pretty pleased that I've arrived ahead of the crowd. The last place I want to be is stuck in a never-ending line at a government agency. I can't understand why they're slow as heck. But I'm glad I decided to run this errand before going to work.

Sifting through my briefcase, I find the envelope at the bottom where I'd placed my original social security card. Last night I made sure to look for it in our personal documents so that I wouldn't have to hustle this morning to find it.

"Morning, ma'am," a burly security guard greets me and opens the door as I get closer to the building.

Inside, a handful of other early birds are scattered across rows of chairs, many of which are empty. Another group stands in line at a kiosk. Signs point me in the direction of where I should go and what I should be doing.

Next thing I know, I'm in the line with the folks at the kiosk. After completing the electronic questionnaire, I take a number, and join the rest of the flock in the sparse rows and wait for my number to be called.

Several minutes pass before I'm called to a window.

"Window 12," the electronic voice blares throughout the room. I gather my things and head in the direction of my designated window.

Darby Coleman-Shields. My name has always had a nice ring to it. And the hyphen added a bit of pizazz. I felt connected to the Coleman surname, in hopes of connecting with a lineage that I never knew. Not anymore. Not with what I know now. Not with the pain it has caused me and probably the generations before me. Going forward it's Darby Shields. Period!

The agent smiles and looks over my card and driver's license before typing on her keyboard and completing the transaction. After a few minutes, she responds. "You'll have your new social security card in three to five weeks."

"This is the last time Coleman will be anywhere near *my* name." I chuckle with an unbridled attitude to the agent.

As I exit the office, I feel like singing. I feel like dancing.

That foul Coleman spirit no longer lingers over my last name.

CHAPTER 35

Rhythmic notes of smooth jazz flow from the small wireless speaker as I watch frost dissolve on the window of my home office. It's the Friday leading up to Christmas break. All's quiet, not a creature is stirring, and I'm ready for vacation to begin. Most of the staff and writers have already taken off to begin their holiday. I'm glad I'm working at home and starting the holiday break in a few hours. Sliding the hard copies of final edits for upcoming articles, I reflect on how productive I've been this morning, despite the fact that I'll be facing a showdown in a few hours.

We're scheduled to meet with Bishop Jefferson and my parents in a few hours. I'll be relieved to get it off my chest and finally confront my father.

Trying to visualize what the upcoming hours will bring causes a flutter in my chest, knowing that the moment of truth is less than a few hours away. I'm ready. I take a deep breath, then exhale with short releases. As I rub my hands against my legs, the dampness on my palms absorb into my yoga pants.

The rumbling of a truck outside grabs my attention. Hoping that it might be Quentin coming home early for lunch, I glance out the window. A brown van pulls up against the curb across the street.

The driver leaps out, carrying a large package, which he places on the doorstep, before hopping back into the truck and whisking away.

Rising from my desk, I pick up the five-pound hand weights on the floor, near the bookcase. This should center my mind as well as my core. It doesn't take long before the repetitive motions above my head begin to ease the tightness in my shoulders and neck. After turning up the music's volume, I move to the next set of exercises, which focus on my triceps

Moisture collects into small beads on my forehead and travels to my nose and chin. Raising the tumbler from the desk, I take a sip of the cool water and again ponder what the afternoon will look like. Lifting both arms outward, I turn up the volume on Alicia Keys and move on to the next set of reps. I hadn't intended to work up this much of a sweat. Laying the weights back in their place, I exit my office and head for the shower.

The fragrance of eucalyptus infused with the shower's steam penetrates my nostrils as I inhale and rub my shoulders. The newly installed speakers mounted inside the shower head project the syncopated notes. That's my Quentin. Always doing some type of home project. A couple of weeks ago, he'd spent Saturday morning making sure the vibe inside the shower stall was just right.

Rubbing my hands across my forehead and along my eyes, I remind myself to stay in control, anticipating that the discussion is going to become heated in the bishop's office.

The sudden figure outside of the shower door startles me.

"Quentin! I didn't hear you. You scared me half to death!"

"I'm sorry. I thought that you heard my footsteps on the tile, and I didn't know you had your eyes closed."

The shower head drips to a thin continuous stream while I spin the handle to the off position. Pushing the glass door open, I step out of the shower stall and reach for the towel. Quentin removes it from the hook first, then hands it to me.

"Thanks," I respond, wrapping the large towel around my body.

Quentin pulls me toward him and offers reassurance. "I know this has been stressful for you. Try not to think too much about how this is going to go down in the next hour. When the bishop starts the meeting, just let it flow."

"What do you plan to say to him?" I ask. "My biggest concern is that he'll set you off and who know's what will happen then." That worry fuels the next one. "It torments me that Robbie's confused, thinking that he's done something to cause my father to assault him. It's a wonder that we've gotten this far."

"Yeah, It's been a test of self-control, that's for sure," he adds. "I have my thoughts on what I'll say to him, but I think the best approach is to give him the opportunity to speak first. That will determine what happens next."

He turns and abruptly heads out of the dressing area while inquiring over his shoulder, "I'm going to go make a sandwich. Do you want one?"

"No. I don't have much of an appetite."

The December clouds have made way for what will be a showdown in just a few moments. The car pulls into the church's sparse parking lot.

My father's truck is nowhere in sight. A sense of bewilderment comes over me, knowing that my father's old army habit of being early at any place and on any occasion is still how he operates.

Quentin's eyes scan the parking lot as well. We exchange obscure glances—no words spoken, only the telepathy between us conveys that something feels off.

Same place. Different week. Quentin pushes the buzzer, and we wait to be let inside.

CHAPTER 36

The long drive lulls into late afternoon as we pull off the interstate and onto the narrow road heading toward Mount Charcot. I take in the beautiful scenery and try not to think about yesterday's disappointment. Waiting for my father to show up at Bishop Jefferson's office had my adrenaline going. He simply refuses to be held accountable.

The landscape shifts from the busyness of the highway to a careful pace leading up the mountain. Small patches of melting snow line the hillside, with the sun casting its warm glow on the damp rocks nestled against the hill. The four-hour drive feels worth the wait now that we are close to our destination.

As usual, Robbie is captivated by the view as we drive up the mountain. While the car sways in motion, he lays his video game in the seat next to him, directing his full attention out the window. Our cares and concerns seem to dwindle as we head farther up the summit and toward the enchanted surroundings of the resort.

Quentin's friend, who is in property development, clued us in about this place during the planning phase of this resort. The Christmas getaway to Mount Charcot has become our Shields family tradition for the past several years.

Just as in previous years, the trees lining both sides of the road toward the resort are adorned with holiday lights. Finally, we reach the resort and pull into the main parking lot to check into our villa. Quentin and Robbie wait in the car while I step inside the lobby to check us in. Inside, the vibe of a winter wonderland is on full display. The lobby is stunningly decorated with a makeshift pond, ice skaters in motion, and carolers adding to the charm. The ceiling-high Christmas tree is enhanced by its flocking and serves as the backdrop. Feeling as though I've been transported into a village scene, I lean with my back against the counter, taking in the stunning interior landscape.

"I'll be with you in a moment," the desk clerk acknowledges while he finishes checking in another guest.

I'm able to think about the days ahead. Robbie has come so far since he revealed the trauma he'd been suffering. But the driving force of truth I've uncovered hasn't diminished yet.

Yesterday, Quentin and I had sat and waited for my father in Bishop Jefferson's office for nearly an hour. The small talk between the three of us in the conference room seemed at first uncertain. As the minutes grew into half an hour, and finally an hour, it became apparent that my father was not coming.

My father, surprisingly, took the chicken way out. The man with all of his outward bravado and steely strength was a no-show.

Charlene had poked her head in the door after thirty minutes to say that she had left a message on my father's voicemail, but he hadn't returned her call. That was so unlike him, yet true to the nature of a bully.

I never would have suspected that my father would shrink. Having been prepared to confront him, I reflected about not being able to reveal to him all that I knew. At the moment I'm not sure how I feel. I'm just happy to be in a new setting.

"Yes, ma'am, can I help you?" the late twenty-something man at the check-in counter inquires.

"Hi. Darby and Quentin Shields, here to check in"

No more Darby Coleman-Shields. I smile to myself.

After checking my ID and handing me the keys to our villa, I head back outside and hop in the car. We drive further up the hill, passing other villas and more vacationers who are checking in for the Christmas week. A sense of relief emerges from my body as I take in the atmosphere and the events that I've left far behind.

The hush of the darkness torments me. I kick the covers off and turn on my side, facing Quentin's back. He stirs as though he senses my restlessness. His breathing rises, then ebbs in the stillness.

My agitation persists as I lie in the darkness, wondering—wondering what if? What if we'd had that meeting with Bishop and my father?

Through the small opening in the bedroom curtain, a stream of twilight brings enough light which guides me into the living area.

I sit up and swing my legs over the edge of the bed while noticing the bedside clock—4:00 a.m. My floral kimono robe lies at the foot of my bed. I grab it and wrap it around me. Slipping my feet into the shearling house slippers, I take a few steps to the door, closing it quietly behind me. Through the cracked bedroom door, on the other side of the living area, is Robbie deeply asleep.

It's just me. Alone. Alone with the understanding that being stood up by my father is his usual way of asserting that he's in control.

The cold night air seems to usher in the right perspective, as it occurs to me that my father is doing what he's always done. He's not one to be held accountable, so he's shutting me down. I don't get a voice, in the usual pattern of our family dynamics.

He's undoubtedly thinking that this whole thing will somehow get swept under the rug and all will be well. That's always been the way in which the Coleman clan has operated.

Still in the darkness, there's just enough light peeking through the sheers. The brilliant moon casts a streak through the room that relaxes my drowsiness and guides me. Stumbling in the dark, I navigate my way, finding relief in my solitary thoughts and the quiet throughout the two-bedroom villa.

The throw blanket is still lying across the sofa. The Scrabble board still sits on the coffee table where Robbie and I had left it in the middle of our game. When I'd returned from the kitchen with our hot chocolate, I'd found him asleep, sprawled across the sofa. After a while, Quentin had picked him up and carried him to bed.

A glass of chardonnay after dinner had left me with no reserves to hang on to, and after Robbie went to bed, I pretty much crashed on the sofa next to Quentin, with a Netflix movie streaming. My last memory was the sound of cars rumbling in an action drama. I don't remember at what point I had dragged myself to bed.

But now I'm alone, welcoming the opportunity to process yesterday's ghosting and what I should do next.

I toss the blanket across my lap as I sit down on the sofa. The quiet draws me to my next move. My laptop sits alongside the Scrabble board on the coffee table. Intuitively, I pick it up and begin drafting a letter to my father.

The more I type, the more intentional I become. Moving from my heart to my head, the emotions travel through my fingers. The tension in my neck begins to release as keyboard strokes are formed into words.

Dad,

You've backed out on two meetings, after what was YOUR idea to "get to the bottom of this and settle it" (you having sexually violated Robbie). Your ducking and hiding by refusing to meet with me is shameful and cowardly, at best.

I've come to discover the real reason you left Piperton as a young man of nineteen.

I will be at Hava Java's on New Year's Eve at 11:00 a.m. I hope you and Mom will be wise in your decision to meet Quentin and me there.

Your failure to show will leave me no choice but to reveal what I've learned about you to ALL my siblings and the entire family.

Darby

After proofreading the letter a few times, I save the file, and close the laptop. The blueish streams of early dawn light enter across the balcony and through the vertical blinds of the sliding glass door. As the weariness overtakes me, I pull the blanket upward to my chin. Then I curl my legs up on the sofa, rest my head on the arm, and close my eyes.

CHAPTER 37

His spindly legs look like they can hardly hold his body up. At the condiment bar, the elderly Black man adds a packet of sugar to his coffee, stirring it with an unsteady hand. There's something about that flannel blue shirt that he's wearing.

Where are they?

When I'd pulled into the parking lot of Hava Java, I'd noticed my father's white pickup truck. It's 10:50 a.m., so he must already be here—always ahead of schedule. One of his favorite sayings has been that you could set your watch according to his schedule. When he walked through the door in the evenings, we knew the time was five thirty without looking at the clock. His ability to be on time was always a source of pride. The residual of the proud military career.

Well it doesn't look like there'll be a ghosting today. Seems like the letter worked. The showdown will move forward. But where are they?

I take in the room, knowing that they're here somewhere. The place is brimming with the usual sprawl of Saturday morning minglers, head glued to a laptop here—a phone there. The line at the counter stretches into the sitting area, with folks waiting for their brew. The post-Christmas shopping crowd from the nearby outlet mall adds to the bustling overflow.

The few cushioned chairs in the sitting area of the coffeehouse are all taken and the tables are fully occupied. Except one.

At a lonely table far in the corner sits an elderly, fair-skinned Black woman with a cream-colored cardigan draped across her shoulders. The curls of her silver-colored hair are spun loosely on her head and seem to glisten from the pendant lighting hanging above. She's immersed in her usual morning ritual of reading her newspaper with a cup of coffee close by.

Though we've been estranged for a over a year, my eyes moisten upon recognizing the sweet-looking silhouette of my mom.

Where's my dad?

As customers breeze by, I scan the room again. I look again toward the condiment stand. The same feeble man I'd noticed before has finished stirring his coffee. He turns from the counter. Standing several feet from me, the frail guy looks up, as if he's trying to catch his bearings.

It's my dad!

His legs look like sticks trying to poke their way through his jeans, which hang from his waist.

My heart drops.

Our eyes meet and lock on to each other across the room.

I don't want to feel sorry for him. It's all foreign to me. I struggle to stay composed.

The dignified looking soldier who formerly held his head high and marched with long strides is unrecognizable. Gone is the imposing, larger-than-life figure. In its place is a decrepit old man who can barely walk.

I can't believe that the gaunt silhouette I'd looked past seconds ago is my father. His expression reveals that he's apparently stunned as well—frozen in motion, gawking at me.

Is that fear I see?

He shuffles toward me. The uncertainty in his expression changes. With one unsteady hand holding his coffee, he uses his other arm and reaches out. Grasping my shoulder, he tenderly pulls me close and embraces me.

Somehow, I manage to respond past the uneasiness. "Hi, Dad."

Though his voice is barely audible, he hesitates before assuming his customary posture. The scratchiness in his voice is unrecognizable, as he issues a mild directive. "Let's go sit over there with your ma." His head motions toward the small table in the corner. The dismal atmosphere proceeds ahead of us as he abruptly scuffles along in the direction of my mother. Once we're within her range, she notices us. She raises her head from her newspaper and adjusts her glasses resting on the tip of her nose. There's a hint of sadness in her expression as she softly greets me, "Morning, Darby." She reaches upward to embrace me.

Bending down, I press my face against hers, taking in the warmth of her cheek, "Hi, Mom." Her weight rests momentarily in my grasp, as anguish washes over both of us. I kiss her forehead before taking the empty seat next to her.

Yes, it's come to this.

Without warning, she assumes a different stance and becomes preoccupied with folding her paper.

The well-known authoritarian wastes no time in taking charge. Immediately he shifts position. With eyes as sharp as knives, Papa George leans forward in his chair and scowls, "Now, what's all this you talkin' bout in this letter you sent me?"

Oh, I've been waiting for this.

CHAPTER 38

Seconds pass, as both my mother and father direct their attention at their coffee cups. Beginning the exchange as controlled as I possibly can, the repetition of this scene in my mind plays again.

Stay calm. Don't take his bait. Stay the course.

"Dad, you and I both know that you sexually assaulted Robbie. I don't expect a confession from you, nor do I need one. The reason I'm able to sit in front of you today without strangling you is because I'm no longer traumatized. I never imagined you to be the person that you are. I never imagined that the moral character that you instilled in me would be lost in you."

I'm sure that my mother has clued him in since the clash she and I had in her hospital room. I expect that he's fully prepared for this confrontation.

He listens without interruption, then holds both hands up in a surrender position and looks towards the ceiling. "Father, if it's true, I hope, you'll strike me dead."

Oh, he's good. But I'm not in for the theatrics.

"Dad, I understand now why you left Piperton when you were barely twenty. You always told us that your Uncle Sam came calling.

Yeah, that was the joke, but that's not true. You were drafted, and you got out of town three months before *your son*, Gator, was born."

"My son?"

Wow. He acts like he has no clue who I'm talking about. If I hadn't known any better, I'd swear he was at a loss as to who Gator is. Even though my patience is already thin, I'm determined to stay steady. A visual passes through my mind like water flowing through a crack. I think about the certified letter that I mailed from Mount Charcot. And with the letter, the picture of Gator and me standing beneath the old oak tree outside our grandmother's house

"Yes, Gator. Your sister, Jerlinda's son. Uh, *your nephew*?" As I enunciate the words, the indignation swells in my tone.

"Huh? Wha...What are you saying?" The hesitation in his voice is matched only by the shock on his face.

"Your nephew!" His imaginary confusion has worn my patience down. "Your nephew Gator is *also your son*!" I pronounce the revelation with such conviction that my air of comeuppance lands like a clean blow to his jaw.

"Shh...shh. Y'all are too loud." Concerned about attracting attention, Mom looks nervously around the room. At this point, I don't give a damn.

"Here's the DNA report!" I unzip my purse, which has been in my lap, waiting precisely for this moment. "It shows that he and I share the same father. Um, that would be *you*, Dad." I slide the report across the table to him. He makes no movement toward it.

"And I've got your enlistment record—not a draft card—from the Department of the Army. Would you like to see that too?"

He stares at me as if he can't believe I'm speaking to him so harshly. He says nothing. His body stiffens. Seconds pass as they both lower their heads and direct their attention to their coffee cups.

Don't stop now.

Seeing that I've got him against the ropes, I go in for another punch. "It's dated March 8, 1965. And Gator was born three months later—June 15, 1965." Drawing the conclusion for him, I go in for the finish. "Seems like you hightailed it out of town three months before your son-nephew was born."

I expect him to posture with something resembling false indignation. But he doesn't. Realizing that he's immobilized from the punches I've landed, I savor the uninterrupted pause. He falls back in his chair, releasing a breath so intense that I can almost see its vapors in the air. He shifts his weight in his seat. His bottom lip quivers and his mouth uncontrollably drops open. His jaw trembles, although he's unable to release any words. It's as if his mouth is hinged open by invisible brackets, which he's unable to close shut.

Oh my God, what have I done? I think I've given him a heart attack.

His body is motionless, slumped against the back of his seat. Oh my God!

"Dad!" I call out to him.

Just as I'm about to scream for someone to call 911, my head spins in my mother's direction. Sitting calmly and watching our exchange, my mom swings into action in a startling, yet self-assured, manner. With her bony index finger in full motion, she points the appendage across the table toward him. With a smirk on her face, she hurls her own offense and comes in for the kill.

"She's saying *you raped* your sister, " she retorts while wagging her head indignantly. Her charge lands like a left jab to his nose in what appears to be *her* day of reckoning.

What the hell?

I'm baffled as I study him for a reaction. His normal tactics of denial and deflection don't look like they'll be making an appearance. Hoping to gain some understanding, I turn my attention to my mother. Now I'm even more puzzled by her smug expression. She sits perched upright, looking like the cat that ate the canary.

Un-friggin real!

He shakes his head back and forth, as if he's trying to snap out of it. With what looks like all the determination he can muster, he gathers himself and rises to his feet. Shaky, but still kicking, he manages to issue a well-worn command, "Let's go, Louvenia."

The order has been issued. The time of reckoning has passed.

I'm pleased that I've doused his facade with the ugly truth, but now I'm confused about what else is hiding beneath the surface of mom's insinuation. Did he rape somebody else? What else does she have on him?

Without making eye contact with either of us, she dutifully gathers her purse and sweater, then rises in habitual compliance. In an instant, she returns to the docile posture with which I'd been familiar all my life.

Amazing.

Wanting no further interaction with either of them, I leap from my seat and bolt for the door. The sounds of their shuffling footsteps are behind me.

Don't look back. Then it dawns on me—I've said this before.

This feels *so* familiar. All of the family drama that I finally got tired of, but didn't know how to escape from. Then one day I walked away and told myself *don't look back*. And that's when a new understanding opened up to me.

Every few seconds I glance in the rearview mirror, wondering if he's going to run me off the road. What just happened back at Hava Java? I take a few deep breaths, steady my sweating hands and tighten my grasp on the steering wheel while being keenly aware that he's probably gaining on me, like a wild maniac. The sparse flow of traffic moves steadily behind me. I search for his recognizable truck. None of the vehicles resemble his truck.

Bishop's words come to mind, "This is being brought into the light. People have been killed over matters such as this."

Yes, He's exposed and I have evidence. There's no telling what he might do in knowing that the covers have been pulled off—just as Bishop said.

Imagining that they're speeding toward me conjures images of growing up in the midst of my family's turmoil. Now that I've confronted the depth of my family's turbulence, the unresolved issues are being challenged for the first time. I could never have imagined this scenario. The melody of smooth jazz travels through the speakers, mixing with the cool breeze from the slightly open passenger's window. I take in deliberate breaths, then slowly exhale to match the rhythm of the music.

I imagine that he's in the middle of shaking some of the shock factor off. He's always had to have the last word and surely feels ambushed. No. He's not having that.

The breeze grows colder through the passenger window. It moves across my face and body, cooling down the rush I've had since taking flight from Hava Java. Speeding down the freeway, heading home, I can't get over the monkey wrench that my mom threw into the mix. Now it feels like I've only struck the tip of an iceberg, with the Gator discovery.

I can't get my mom's agitation out of my mind. What's she got on him? Given the facts that have just been revealed, her reaction is nothing short of weird. I don't know what to make of it. There was no sense of surprise from her. And her use of the word rape is mind-boggling—not to mention that sneer. I never said that my father raped his sister. My mother used the word rape—not me.

Thinking about the research I'd gathered leaves me believing that dad's sexual relationship with his sister, Jerlinda was consensual. It wasn't uncommon for large clans to believe in and practice incest. The research paper I'd found said that they viewed it as making the family unit stronger. It's a belief that was passed down from generation to generation. If the female family member became pregnant, only then did it bring shame upon the family. She'd be sent away to some distant relative. Or the family would strong-arm some poor soul into marrying her. I wonder if my dad came to realize the taboo of this practice once he left home to join the army when he was nineteen. He'd often said that he'd never been more than twenty miles outside of Piperton, until he was in the military.

The bitter cold whisks through the car, biting my cheeks, yet leaving me alert. I replay the events and reactions of moments ago, miles back at Hava Java. My stirring thoughts leave me to my father's laughter when growing up and how he'd tell a particular tale which left me mesmerized, yet bewildered. He would roar with laughter about some unsuspecting lad who had been coerced into having a shotgun wedding. It sounded like a regular occurrence that happened in the backwoods of Piperton. Fascinated by such a wild story, I never fully grasped whether the legend was fact or fiction.

"Dad, what's a shotgun wedding?" I'd inquire in total innocence.

He was always amused at my response as I clung to every word of the tale. My mom would usually be somewhere close by, quietly enjoying his stunt. They would silently communicate to one another, as their eyes telegraphed their unspoken language. On another occasion, I might inquire, "Did the girl's father *really* get his rifle and go after the guy?"

At this point, my father would howl with laughter and leave the room. His cackles would travel down the hall with him, diminishing only when he reached another part of the house. His entertainment was not complete without tapping my mom on the arm, at the inside joke that they shared. She'd grin in amusement and carry on with whatever she was doing. I was left with only a sense of being shut off. No explanation would follow after the laughter cleared, only the reinforced message of what I already knew—this was grown folks' business. Therefore, their private joke. You can ask all you want; you won't get an answer.

There must be something else that is lurking below the Coleman burial ground of secrecy. The inside jokes meant for adult consumption, as well as finding amusement in my childhood innocence, is the only reassurance I need. At this moment I'm still spooked by my mom's smirking posture and her use of the word "rape" trolling in the air.

Yeah, there's more there. Something she's held over him. For some unknown reason, I'm feeling confident that it'll reveal itself, just as I have been led in uncovering that my father impregnated his sister.

Feeling triumphant, yet disturbed, by my mother's reaction, the freeway exits speed by with the landscape of the highway along the way. I realize that within the next mile will be exit 34B, which leads to a strip mall that's occupied by my favorite shoe store. I pull off the freeway at the exit.

Slowing down and driving around the ramp, I navigate through the sparse parking lot and choose a space among a deserted row. Turning off the ignition, I maneuver the seat into a recline position, then exhale. If I hadn't experienced the past forty-five minutes, I couldn't have imagined this outcome. I'm at peace with this episode being over.

A half hour later, I finally pull into my driveway, feeling emotionally exhausted. On the side of the house, I hear the bouncing of a ball, along with Robbie's voice and the voices of a few neighborhood boys.

As I open the front door, the simmering smell of a spicy aroma invites me past the living room and into the kitchen where Quentin stands in front of the stove. He studies my face before inquiring, "How'd it go?"

"I did what I went there to do. I threw this evil darkness back in his face. I can't tell you the satisfaction I felt by letting him know that I'm aware of his lies, beginning with being drafted into the army and leaving Piperton. Honey, I was frightened for a moment because when I unleashed it on him, I thought he was having a heart attack."

Quentin moves a few feet toward the kitchen island and pulls out one of the bar stools. With his chin in his palm, he leans forward, captivated by my every word.

"Holding him accountable was completely unheard of when I was growing up." I had to find the word for myself to describe how it felt. And that word is … 'foreign.' Once I got started with the enormity of the lies he raised me with, the more I felt a heaviness release from me. It literally seemed as if I could see a big ton of garbage being thrown back into his lap."

"Good. Babe. I'm proud of you."

"So have you and Robbie been at home the entire time? I heard him on the side of the driveway playing basketball when I pulled up."

"Actually we haven't. Over an hour ago, I left to run some errands. Robbie was playing next door. As I pulled around the corner, I saw your dad and mom coming from the opposite direction, turning into the cul de sac. They didn't see me, but obviously they were going to our house." Quentin stands from the bar, retelling the ordeal. "I turned the car around to come back home, knowing that you hadn't got back yet. I was wondering what was up. As I pulled against the curb, your dad was walking up the walkway like a wild banshee. I got out of the car and stopped him before he got to the front door. He was pretty heated and told me we needed to settle this. When I ushered him back into his car, he sneered at me and told me that I needed to have your head examined. He was ranting that you're crazy when he drove off."

"Yeah. That sounds about right. Somebody always has to be crazy. And according to them, I'm it." I take a quick breath. "You'll never guess what happened when I confronted him."

"He probably came close to a heart attack."

"Yeah, I thought the same thing, but listen to this…My mom had the most smug reaction about Gator. She didn't appear surprised. She had a posturing that was like a comeuppance, as if she was pleased with me exposing this information."

"Really?"

"Yeah, she actually gloated and pointed her finger at him and said, 'She's saying you raped your sister.'" I got the feeling that she was low-key delighted with the news. Like she now had something to hold over *his* head. Her emphasis was on the word rape–which was a word I hadn't used–rather than any shock about Gator as his son."

"Yeah. Well one thing's for sure. This thing is bigger than Robbie, but he's all I care about."

"The entanglement is more than I would have imagined. All the secrets, lies, and cover-up."

The pot on the stove sizzles in the stillness, as I reimagine the high speed pursuit of earlier this morning.

CHAPTER 39

The burning glow of the fireplace warms the room, shaking off the chilliness. Like a dull hangover, New Year's Day and its festivities have come and gone, as if they've foretold shadows of winter doldrums. Quentin and Robbie have gone to visit Robbie's godparents. I'm glad to settle in with some alone time and leftover gumbo. As I prop the pillows against the sofa, this opportunity I have to be myself helps me to collect my thoughts and concentrate on being emotionally centered.

Reaching for the fuzzy sofa blanket and wrapping it around my shoulders, I reflect on Bishop Jefferson's sermon from this morning. In his usual style, his voice crescendoed when he reached the point he was emphasizing. "You've got to trust God enough to get your feet wet!" Hmph. At this point, I've been thrown into the deep end. I have no choice but to trust Him. There's no way I could have pieced together my father's past without God leading me. This is surreal.

"Alexa, play Darby's playlist, number one." Just as I finish the command, my phone rings. I'm startled by the caller ID, after managing to find my phone between the layers of pillows. *It's my mother. Why's she calling?*

"Hi, Mom."

"Darby, your Daddy's losing his mind!" The fear in her voice is real.

"What? What do you mean, Mom?" I'm hoping she'll mirror my tone by responding deliberately, with assurance.

The hysteria surrounding her is far from rehearsed. "I don't know what's wrong with him. You have to come right now."

"Tell me what's happening, Mom. Are you at home?"

"We just got home. We had just made it off our exit from the freeway." Between pants of breath, she manages to give some details. "All of a sudden your dad got disoriented and couldn't remember where he was." Her panting grows with intensity, now sounding like she's finished a sprint. "I had to tell him how to get home 'cause he didn't know the way to the house. Can you come now, Darby? Her plea grows in between breaths. "It's an emergency!"

A flashing thought tries to overtake me—one of speeding down the freeway to get to my parents' house located thirty miles away.

Get her to think rationally, with confidence.

"Mom!" The silence of a few seconds shifts in my favor. "If it's an emergency, you need to get him to the hospital—now!"

"Ah ... oh. Okay."

"Mom, you can do this. Everything's going to be okay." Praying as I'm speaking with her, I silently ask that my words will soothe and empower her.

"Okay."

Simple instructions. Tell her more.

"Don't wait on me! I'm thirty minutes away!" I add, firmly, "Just get him to the hospital. And call me if and when they admit him."

"Okay," she murmurs.

I glance up at the clock on the wall. The ticking is all that can be heard along with the hum of the gas fireplace. It's two thirty in the afternoon. I wonder what I should do. Somehow, I don't feel as though I need to do anything at all. I stay seated on the sofa in the stillness. The backyard, the tinkling of the wind chimes blend with the whirl of the wind.

Wow, it was only a few days ago. It was New Year's Eve when Dad had barreled up my driveway, after leaving Hava Java. Quentin had described the confrontation to me that day.

From the kitchen, the timer from the microwave beeps, reminding me of my deliberate attempts at staying emotionally centered.

Now, I can't help but reflect on Mom's words. "He's losing his mind."

After finishing off the leftover gumbo, I once again wrap the blanket around myself. Kicking off my house slippers, I curl up on the sofa and relax my head against the pile of pillows. Snuggled like a cocoon, I fall into a deep sleep.

I'm spooked by the glaring chime of the phone, which awakens me. The gas fire still hums, casting a soft glow on the evening shadows in the family room. The whirling of the wind has stopped. I look up at the clock on the wall. 7:00 p.m.

"Hi, Mom?"

"Hi. Your dad's been admitted, down here at Newton Hospital." She sounds tired, yet there's a sharp contrast in her voice from hours ago. Her voice sounds as light as fog lifting from the surface, as she adds, "He's had a stroke. He can't speak or move very much. They are running more tests."

"Thanks for calling, Mom."

"I'll let you know when I have further details."

"Okay." As I tap the phone off, the words in my father's letter come to mind." It's weighing heavily on me."

CHAPTER 40

"I'm going to use the ozone steamer on you for about fifteen minutes before your facial." Imani explains the next step of the facial treatment as the spinning wheels glide the machine from the corner where it's been standing. She maneuvers the arm of the instrument close to my face before it begins the process of loosening my pores with pulses of steam. The steam along with the scent of eucalyptus oil penetrates the room.

Moments later she removes moist towels from the warmer where they've been left steaming. She tightly wraps my feet like a bundled baby. The soothing sensation cradles me. As I lie facing the ceiling, the soothing sensation of the treatment and soft music leaves me relaxed and nearly dozing off.

Hydrate. Hydrate. Hydrate.

I imagine the toxins having no choice but to leave my body, like vapors dissolving in the air. The stuffiness I'd felt earlier in my sinuses begins to dissipate, leaving me with an overwhelming urge to exhale. The tension in my neck welcomes the relief as Imani's fingers gently apply pressure to my muscles along my neck and back.

"You can just lie here and relax for another twenty minutes."

Imani steps towards the door, closing it behind her while I lie in the stillness.

Ding.

The ring of the timer moves me from my peaceful state, indicating that my spa day has come to an end.

The dim light comes into focus as I remove the moistened eye pads. I lay on the treatment cot, indulging myself for a few more seconds. Reluctantly I sit up, reach for the terry cloth robe hanging on the hook and head for the locker room.

"How was everything?" Imani sits waiting for me at the reception desk.

"Wonderful. I feel like a slug barely able to move."

"Oh good. I'm glad." Turning to the elevated counter behind her, she reaches for a paper tote bag. "I got your message that you were out of these."

"Thanks. I almost forgot."

After swiping my card, she hands me the bag of skincare products.

"I'll give you a call in a few weeks."

The bell dangling over the door ushers me from the spa's blissful vibe and into the brisk air outside. The overcast day has fallen into the early evening. I get into my car and notice a fine mist has settled on the car's windshield, as if waiting to hasten the path downward. I pull the seatbelt across my lap, then reach for my phone to check my email.

What on earth could *she* want?

Darby,

I have legal authority over the health care matters of our parents. They are in need of and have twenty-four-hour care. As allowed by the legal authority given to me, I am providing you with the guidelines for visiting our parents:

All visitations will be communicated to me forty-eight hours prior to visiting our parents.

The twenty-four-hour caregivers are in agreement with the above and will inform me of any lack of compliance. I will respond with the appropriate legal measures.

I am open to meeting with you should you wish to know how you can help in the care of our parents. No response will be an indication of your agreement to the above. I appreciate your cooperation in this matter.

Maxine

I stare out the window and into the dusk feeling as though I'm in a trance. Paige's image illuminates on the screen as the phone chimes.

"Hey, Paige."

"Hey, you!" Her cheerful voice brings me back to the moment. "What are you up to on such a dreary Saturday?"

"Oh, I'm just hanging out and pampering myself. I'm leaving Serenity Day Spa."

"Oh-h-h, and what treatment did you indulge in?" Paige perks up at the mention of one of our favorite spots.

"I needed some exfoliating. I got a deep cleansing facial and a massage. Believe me, I needed it. Imani's running a special through next week."

"I know what you mean. A little self-care never hurts. And with everything that's been going on with you, it's good to hear that you've taken some time for yourself."

"Yeah. What are you up to? Do you want to go grab a quick dinner?"

"Well, speaking of spa treatments…" Paige laughs as if I've tickled her unexpectedly. "I've got a full mask on, and my hair is wrapped in a hot treatment. I doubt that I'll be going *anywhere* this evening. Her giggles have me laughing along with her. "Why don't you come over and keep me company? And there's something I want to share with you."

"Okay. I should be there in fifteen minutes or so. And I've got something I want to show you. Talk about working my nerves."

"Whoa, now you've got me curious." Paige pauses as her voice takes on a tone mixed with curiosity and concern. "You sound a little worked up. Everything okay?"

"Yeah. Just the usual stuff. Maxine rearing her controlling head."

"It's funny that you mention Maxine." She takes a deep breath before continuing. "It's like your ears must have been burning."

"What do you mean?" I brace myself.

"It's nothing for you to be concerned about. I just wanted to give you a heads-up, so come on over and I'll fill you in." Paige's reassurance eases my concern.

"Okay. I could use a glass of wine."

"Girl, I got you. You know I always have some Cabernet. See you soon."

The wind begins to howl as the mist outside turns into steady streams.

Cautiously, I pull away from the curb and into the street, heading for Paige's house.

Paige pauses, which allows me to begin processing wherever she's leading. "My mother-in-law gave me a call yesterday about a phone call that came in at the church office. She still works as the church administrator at New Jerusalem."

She places a dish of seedless grapes on the counter. On the charcuterie board is an assortment of appetizers. "That's right. Ms. Edna is still holding down the fort over there." She chuckles. She takes a sip of wine, then hesitates. "She felt so troubled when she got Maxine's phone call. She said she wrestled with whether or not she should tell me, knowing that I would warn you. But on the other hand, she felt that Maxine was plotting and scheming and thought that she should intervene."

"Okay. I'm all ears." After taking a sip of Cabernet, I hold on for the unexpected.

"Ms. Edna said that Maxine had an outlandish request." Paige takes a bite of her cracker. "She asked if there were any psychologists among the parishioners whom she could recommend, because she wanted to have you declared mentally insane."

I grab the napkin next to my appetizer plate. The sudden move prevents the wine from spewing across the room, but a droplet dribbles down my chin. I manage to catch it with my napkin before it lands on my shirt.

Paige's attempt at keeping a straight face is lost now that I've come unglued. The two of us barrel together in uncontrolled laughter.

"Girl, are you kidding? She actually wanted a reference to a psychologist, in order to declare me insane? This is too loony to believe. I couldn't fathom such a story if it hadn't come from you."

Paige raises her hand in the swearing-in motion. "Dar, I couldn't believe it myself. This is so far-out that I couldn't make it up if I'd tried. Ms. Edna was shaken by such an outlandish request. She was reluctant to convey something so ridiculous. But she also knows we're close and wants you to know that she has your back and to be careful."

"I just don't get where Maxine's head is. Why is she planting a wild conspiracy against me?" I reach for my phone inside my purse where it lies on the stool next to me. Paige pops an olive in her mouth as she contemplates Maxine's bizarre request. I scroll to the email I received from Maxine only an hour before and begin reading it to Paige.

"I don't believe this? What's she afraid of?" Paige's gaze is fixated on the phone, then back at me. "Or better yet, what's she hiding? I get the feeling that for some reason, she's trying to isolate them."

"Yeah, that's the sense I'm getting. But it's clear that she's paranoid," I reply. I grew up in a household that was in a total state of confusion. You never knew when either Papa George or Maxine was going to pop off. For that reason, I could usually be found curled up in my room, out of the line of fire. The 'she's crazy' approach is so old. I would think she could come up with something more original."

Paige listens empathetically, "Sounds like growing up, you figured out a survival strategy from the shenanigans."

"Hmm..." Without prompting, I have an urge to unleash more details. "For example, if one person was in the kitchen and maybe I heard someone else go in there, you could bet that all hell was going to break loose. You could count on it, and I could never figure it out. As I got older, I realized that oftentimes the commotion was between Maxine and my dad."

"From what you've shared with me in the past, somehow I'm not surprised to hear that," Paige responds.

CHAPTER 41

Newly submitted articles sit in my email file, awaiting approval for the next edition of *Dynamic Parent*. I sense a presence in my office as I scan the thread of messages. I look up to see Gavin grinning in the doorway.

"How's my favorite Vanguard executive editor?" he whispers. Today he's got a sophisticated-casual vibe going on, while sporting a black turtleneck, layered beneath a plaid jacket. As usual, Gavin's attire shows that he appreciates the pleasure of high quality menswear. Where someone else might see gray pants, not Gavin. To him they are flannel pants, to be worn only during the appropriate season.

"When did you get in town and what in the world for?" I tease. Turning my attention away from the computer, I feel the tension I've been carrying slip away as a smile escapes my lips. Gavin reaches out for a hug as I extend a greeting. "Happy New Year. I haven't seen you since the Amy Awards. How were your holidays?"

Gavin moves toward the chair facing my desk. "They were fabulous." He places his water bottle on the desk before flopping down in the chair. "I went to Italy. Got these new kicks over there." He crosses his legs to better show off a pair of argyle socks and Italian-leather loafers. "Stayed two weeks, and just got back a couple of days ago. It's the first time I spent the holidays outside the US, and I tell you it won't be my last," he pronounces, still full of excitement.

"Wonderful! All of the publications must have been keeping you on your toes, since I haven't seen you in a while. And whose lives around Vanguard have you been making miserable lately?" I tease as I take a sip of green tea.

"Oh, I see you haven't lost your touch, Darbs." He chuckles. "You never fail to amuse me. Let's go grab some lunch."

"I'd love to, Gavin, but I'm going to have to pass."

"What? Working so hard this early in the New Year?" he smirks. "You're the one who always warns *me* to pace myself."

"Yeah. I know. I'm not eating today. I'm on a fast."

"Oh wow, Darbs. That sounds like a drastic way to lose a few pounds," his startled look conveys genuine concern. He crosses his legs, then leans forward. "You've always been so health conscious, " he responds with bewilderment.

"Thanks, Gav. It has nothing to do with dieting. I'm on a spiritual fast. Some Christians do a fast at the beginning of the year. The first part of the year is dedicated to God. You're going to be in town for the rest of the week, right? Let's do it on Friday, okay?"

"That'll work, my friend," Gavin responds before rising from his chair and heading toward the door.

"See ya, Gav."

My head feels light and my stomach feels queasy, as I turn my attention back to the monitor. I scroll down and scan the subject lines of the messages in the thread. There doesn't seem to be anything urgent. Just the usual stuff. It's as if folks are still sleeping from the holiday. Knowing that it'll pick up in a matter of days, I relish the slower pace and take a deep breath. I turn my attention to a spreadsheet for the department's quarterly budget.

My head still feels light, which is not unusual during a fast. This is my third day with liquids only, so I'm glad I'm almost through it. I'd remember reading in the Bible about the characters who gained mental clarity by fasting and thanking God for the new year. Whew! This time I'm really feeling the effects. This is no joke.

The fasting coach at church had advised us to stay hydrated and drink more than the usual eight to ten glasses of water.

I head down the hall to get some water, knowing that sometimes the body can trick itself, when in fact it's really thirsty instead of hungry. I'm feeling more lightheaded today than usual. I'll guzzle some water and see if that helps.

The aroma of freshly brewed coffee permeates the hall and gets stronger as I approach the break room. The office is sparsely filled—an open door here, another closed farther up the hall. It looks like folks have taken an extended vacation, while others may have decided to work from home.

I enter the empty break room, where two tables sit empty—unusual for a late Monday morning. On one of the tables, the January print edition of *Dynamic Parent* lies along with a few of Vanguard's other publications.

I take a bottle of water from the refrigerator and head back to my office.

Back at my desk, I sit back and return to the spreadsheet I'd left. Trying to center myself in my chair, I pause and decide to take my mind off work with a few stretches. I spin my chair around to face the window, looking into the near-empty offices of buildings in my view. I rotate my shoulders back and forth, then stretch my neck for several seconds, left then right. I complete another set with the same repetitions. Much better. I turn back around and face the computer screen. 12:45.

This is not helping. Oh, who am I kidding? I just can't concentrate today.

I close my laptop and open the bottom drawer of my desk. I pull out my briefcase and place my laptop inside. After locking my door, I head to the elevator, leaving the deserted office behind.

Once I'm in my car, I search my briefcase's outer compartment for the parking garage's passkey. The gate lifts as I hold the electronic key up so that it can be scanned by the card reader.

As I'm pulling out of the parking garage, I hear a faint whisper. Not an audible voice, but a whisper that's soft and inviting. *Go see your parents.*

What in the world? The lightheadedness I'd felt earlier has reappeared. I feel so off. The car behind me taps his horn. Trying to pull myself together, I pull out of the garage. All I can do is wonder. What's wrong with me? I leave the garage and watch for an opening in the traffic. I move with the flow of traffic, until a block away, I reach a stoplight.

Go see your parents. Now.

Without warning, a vision of Maxine's baby picture moves leisurely in front of me. It's the picture that sat on Mom's dresser the entire time I was growing up. In the photo, my mom is holding Maxine. For some haunting reason, my focus is on Maxine's facial features. She had the most adorable cheeks and pronounced lips. In the studio portrait, Maxine looks to be about six months old. She has on a white outfit, with matching bloomers and a lacy bonnet. She looks expressionless as she stares into the camera.

I'd passed this picture many times, where it stood as an immortal marker on my mother's dressing table. Years came and went, but this photo somehow came to symbolize something never-ending. I'm not quite sure what. Every time I'd go into my parents' bedroom I'd pass the picture.

The photo stays in my mind. My mother looks stunning while holding Maxine up next to her. With her bangs swept to the side, Mom's classic hairstyle matches the timelessness of the picture.

What always struck me about the photo was how sullen my mom looked as she held her only child at the time. I'd always wondered why.

My nagging question is why this illusion is appearing to me without any thought of it in recent years. It's as though it has appeared like a mirage in the middle of a desert.

Seconds later, the light turns red. As I pull off, a sensation overcomes me, making me feel a strange sort of attachment in a very subtle way.

The motor hums and the gears shift as the sound of the car's engine accelerates. I'm relieved that it's early afternoon and the traffic is light as I head home. I'll be able to focus better in my home office and get a jump start on the budget adjustments before next week's meeting with the finance team. My speed picks up as I move with the flow of the traffic.

I don't understand why, but I'm feeling a little spaced out. Unexpectedly, I feel the urge to blink again. It feels like I'm gradually being pulled like a paperclip to a magnet—a gentle strength I can't resist.

Shaking my head in hopes of restoring my equilibrium, I glance in my rearview mirror. The cars are quite a distance from me. I click on the turn signal, and pull over to the side of the road, away from the traffic behind me in the distance.

As my car comes to a standstill, the image appears again. It's the same baby picture of Maxine. This time the photo is enlarged, with Maxine as its focus. My mother has been cropped out. It accentuates Maxine's chubby cheeks and pouty lips in a way that

I'd never noticed. Then a second photo appears of a familiar figure who smiles confidently into the camera. The new photo travels from left to right until it lines up next to the baby picture of Maxine, which has moved right to left. The two photos meet, standing side by side for brief seconds. Then they both fade away, like an optical illusion.

This is crazy. I'm not hungry. And I don't feel lightheaded at the moment. I blink my eyes again. And again. I shake my head repeatedly.

Go see your parents.

It's pulling me again, like a reckoning, yet calm, force.

Bishop's counsel comes as a passing thought: "Don't get ahead of the Holy Spirit."

The Holy Spirit. So *this* is what has been guiding me. Through discoveries, revelations, and the decoding of weird behaviors and their hidden meanings. And the sessions with Dr. Floyd felt like a supernatural guide which was leading me to truth.

I cautiously pull back into traffic. With no understanding as to why, I pass my own exit and head in the direction of my parents' house.

I ask myself why I'm going. I don't have an answer. Yet, as I proceed along the highway, I sense the rolling hills acting as a barricade against an invisible force. I ring the doorbell. She answers.

Her eyes communicate that she's worn out, yet glad to see me. She gently reaches out. We embrace. I step inside and head towards the kitchen. There, I find my father with his head tucked deeply inside a lower cabinet in search of something. A pot on the stove boils so fiercely that the kitchen window is fogged. He turns to see me and my mother standing several feet from him, with a look of fear mixed with shame.

"Dad, For all of your wickedness—for my son's childhood that you've stolen…I… I…"

What's happening? Where are my words?

"I forgive you." The dam has burst inside me, as the tears stream down.

"And Mom, for you being his accomplice—for you luring Robbie here to spend the night, and for whispering, 'don't tell,' in his ear, I forgive you too."

With that, I turn and walk out the door. All of two minutes have passed.

I feel a sense of astonishment, as if I've given myself an unexpected present. I feel like I've released myself off an unseen hook.

As I drive home, the hills have dropped their barricade and seem as if they're smiling. Through my tears, and for some odd reason, I'm smiling too.

CHAPTER 42

"I miss you, Darby," my mom says. "It's been so long, and me and your dad aren't doing so well." Her voice is weaker than I remember it being since the showdown at Hava Java a couple of years ago.

"I miss you too, mom."

"Your dad's having cataract surgery tomorrow. He'll be gone for most of the day."

I know in an instant that this is coded language for "the coast is clear."

"Oh, I'm sure he'll be fine." My quick thinking leaves memories of how she set me up for an ambush by Maxine some time ago. Even though the frailty in her voice pulls at my heartstrings, a vague response is all I give.

At that time, Maxine had been there for a visit. She'd gone off on me—for some reason that I can't recall—just like she did at Cafe Noir. It took me some time to realize that my parents use her as the family's attack dog in an attempt to get me in line. Since they can't reel me in, they've unleashed the pit bull. I won't have anything to do with them. All part of the family's sick pretense that all is well within the Coleman clan.

And now I know the reasons for the pretense.

It's taken Robbie being molested for me to understand the collusion and shared secrets of my father being a pedophile. Along with my mother's and sisters' allegiance to him.

Hours later, I put my ear to the door and listen for sounds coming from inside. All's quiet in the moments after tapping on my parents' front door. Haven't heard a peep from my parents, Maxine, or Gloria. Other than Maxine's forty-eight-hour notice, there's been no word out of them.

An unfamiliar woman pulls back one of the window's panels halfway and peeks through. Surprisingly, she appears to be not much younger than my mom and dad—maybe in her early '70s. She looks to be of average height, Filipino, with grayish-brown hair combed neatly into a bun resting at the nape of her neck. There's a stern presence about her, which is heightened by the glasses sitting on the tip of her nose. She manages to peer above them while giving me the once-over. In a matter of seconds, it feels as though I've received a thorough inspection.

"Yes?" she cautiously addresses me.

Well, *this* is uncomfortable.

"Hi. I'm Darby, George and Louvenia's daughter." While smiling, I pour a bit of sweetener on my tone, though it does little to disarm her.

There's now a standoff between her and me. She hesitates, and after several seconds, she partially opens the door, though she doesn't welcome me in. Her body acts as a barricade between me and the entrance.

"Excuse me," I move closer to the entrance, and step onto the threshold. "Um, Maxine didn't tell me that you would be coming. I don't think you have permission to…"

She moves to the side as I brush past her. I make my way through the doorway and step into the entrance.

I don't have time for this nonsense.

Moving past her and beyond the entrance, I enter the hallway and flip the light switch on. The formerly dark passageway leads me into the living area. Behind me, her cadence picks up as her footsteps tap against the hardwood floor. Steadily, she's on my heels as if she's been anointed warden over George and Louvenia's house.

Even though she hasn't introduced herself, I take the high road, and hope she picks up on my implication that she's rude. "Excuse me. What'd you say *your* name was?" The civility has left my voice, and I'm no longer smiling. Spinning around to face her, I wonder if she gets my signal that she's as annoying as a buzzing fly.

"Oh! Analyn," she replies meekly. Abruptly, she turns in the opposite direction and scurries back toward the entrance and up the stairs.

Exhale.

Leave it to Maxine to find a caregiver much like herself—annoying *and* a grump.

Continuing down the hall, I take notice of the hallway runner, which looks just as I remember, though the reds and greens in the pattern don't seem as vivid. Otherwise, the house is still familiar and inviting. Everything is in its place, just as it always has been. The brown leather sofa sits against the wall with a distressed look. Its wrinkles signal maturity, having aged well along with all the other furnishings. Above the mantle hangs an oil painting of field hands surrounding a horse and carriage. Its muted blues and grays are an accent to the otherwise neutral room.

The clock chimes along the wall, as though it's announcing my entrance. Two hanging ferns sway gently in the breeze from the ceiling fan. The broad leaves of the ficus plant cast a gentle shadow across the lounge chair nestled in the corner.

Trooper lifts his head from his cot against the door. He rises, then stretches from his midmorning nap. He nudges against my legs—his usual gesture to be petted. He sniffs the air in anticipation as he looks upward at the pink bakery box in my hands.

And wouldn't you know it. My parents are sitting inside the sunporch. Mom has her newspaper in its usual position in front of her, while Papa George sits half asleep next to her. Not surprisingly he's without his hearing aids. His favorite green wool jacket is wrapped around his shoulders, making its entrance just as it does at this time every year—early winter. It's always been one of his favorites, with antelopes and pinecones spun throughout the garment. He once told me he loves it so much because of the memories of their cruise to Alaska years ago, in the fall of their lives. The jacket drapes his shoulders on top of his flannel pajamas. His legs are stretched out on the ottoman in front of him, with a light throw tossed across his feet. I've never known him to be bundled up in layers while he's inside the house. This languid sighting of the two of them causes the reality of it all to sink in.

With the morning rays casting its light on them, the scene speaks for itself. If it could spin a tale, it would spin a story of how the years have woven them together. Dad—though half asleep with his mouth open—seems content snuggled next to Mom as she reads the paper. Knitted together like a handmade garment, they complement each other, even now. Even though he can barely hear, I'm sure she's been reading articles aloud to him—whether he is interested or not.

Together the two of them look as though life has bestowed all the grace it has to offer. It would be unimaginable to think otherwise. I can't imagine all of the good or all of the bad. It's probably best that I don't know. Their ruckuses were left for interpretation—left for whomever to fill in, based on their interactions and my imagination.

Mom looks up and notices me standing in the doorway. She stops reading the paper mid-sentence, while the corners of her mouth turn upward. "Well, hi, Mom. I thought Papa George was having cataract surgery today."

"Um… it got rescheduled." Her sheepish look gives her away.

"Yeah, right." I turn to leave, refusing to be part of the obvious setup.

Papa George opens his eyes, perhaps prompted by the ceasing of the flow of Mom's voice. He looks at her with a bewildered expression. He notices she's no longer looking at the newspaper. His eyes then follow the direction of hers. His body stiffens. "You still been vilifying my name?" He stabs me with his bloodshot eyes.

Trooper nuzzles his head on the edge of the sofa's cushion. "C'mon, boy." My mother pets his head before placing him in her lap.

"Yeah. Whatcha got there?" She nods her head with interest, toward the box I'd placed on the end table.

"I stopped at Sweet Camelia's and brought you some scones."

"Well, thanks, Babycakes." Her gentle voice is sincere with appreciation. "Have you talked to Maxine?"

"No. I haven't." I head in the direction of the door. "Love you, Mom."

"Well, y'all should keep up with each other. You should call her. My father always taught me and my siblings to keep up with each other, and you all should do the same."

She's never going to let up.

"Are you Darby?" A tall Latino police officer interrupts as he stands in the doorway of the sunporch. A bit portly around the middle, he appears to be in his early '50s. Other than his uniform, he appears nonthreatening enough. But why is he here? Who let him in, and what does he want with me?

He skims over the sunporch, briefly resting his eyes on Mom and Dad. Then he motions with his index finger, a gesture I take to mean come here.

What the hell?

With reluctance and a bit of fear in my heart, I take minimal steps toward the officer, into the adjoining living area, where he closes the glass-paned door behind me, leaving Mom and Dad remaining on the sunporch.

"I'm Officer Cortez. We got a call from your sister, Maxine, saying you're not supposed to be here." His voice is slightly above a whisper and, again, doesn't feel threatening.

"What?"

"Yes. She says that she has power of attorney and that you're supposed to give her forty-eight-hours notice in order to visit your parents."

Analyn enters the room, holding a laminated document, which she hands to Officer Cortez.

He looks it over, turns it from front to back, then after only a few seconds, he turns to me. "You know, she's on her way down here right now."

Analyn stands several feet away, looking smug while watching the exchange between Officer Cortez and me.

Without warning, my dad opens the sunporch's door and enters. Sheepishly he looks at Officer Cortez. He heads to the kitchen, clearly out of the line of fire. He speaks to no one in particular, though he makes a bold pronouncement. "Ain't nothing going on round here." I notice that he makes no eye contact with Officer Cortez or anyone else. He seemingly is putting on a display of exercising authority as the homeowner, although it's clear he has very little authority over his own residence—or himself, for that matter.

Papa George sticks his chest out, and makes a feeble attempt to strut several feet over to the kitchen, out of the line of any possible confrontation. Though he's made a statement, Officer Cortez doesn't acknowledge him, as Papa George strategically walks past the officer and exits, stage left.

I take in Pap George's movements as he shuffles several feet into the kitchen. He straggles his feet along the way, stopping only when he's reached his destination to the kitchen counter, which he uses to lean against for support. He's still aware that as a Black man, having a discussion in his own living room with the police carries a high risk of things going sideways without a moment's notice.

Watching his posture dart out of sight and away from any discussion with the police officer leaves me imagining his posture during his upbringing in Piperton. Through the years, he talked about the prevailing stance of having no confrontation with police under any circumstance. Today, and I'm sure for my benefit, he wants things to appear as if he's in control.

Yeah, right.

Glancing over to the kitchen, I see that Papa George is now preoccupied, making himself a snack. The quick shift of his posturing, which is now a subservient stance, has thrown me for a loop, but only for a minute.

As I watch him in the kitchen, a young officer quietly walks through the back door. He stands at the door's threshold, surveying the scene. He's of a slight build and looks to be only a few years younger than me, maybe early '30s. His strawberry blond hair is cut in a crew style and looks to be freshly cut. His eyes graze over Papa George, still at the kitchen counter, head down, immersed in his task. For only a brief second, a foggy shadow appears and surrounds my father. It's as though the spirit of oppression has emerged, which now overshadows his existence. He's there, making a sandwich, but he is fully aware to stay in the shadowy existence in which he's encapsulated. His posturing speaks volumes of all that was familiar throughout his lineage.

Through the open kitchen, the young, blond officer stares intently at me while witnessing the interaction between Officer Cortez and me. With his billy club in one hand, he loudly pats the open palm of the other hand, resulting in smacking noises, which travel through the adjoining rooms.

I've gathered that Officer Cortez is the senior officer. He notices the young, blond cop in the doorway, but does not address him or bring him into our discussion.

"You know she's on her way down here," Officer Cortez repeats.

"No. I had no idea."

"Look, I suggest you take this up in civil court," he advises in a way that clearly suggests this is a family issue that doesn't warrant police intervention.

By this point, Papa George has finished his drawn-out task of making a sandwich. He moves slowly from the kitchen, with his plate in his hand, and steps into the family room. Headed in the direction of the sunroom, he makes his way around the two of us, appearing to loiter inconspicuously in an attempt to hear glimpses of the conversation between the authority figure and me. He passes behind the two of us in a way that seems to suggest he'll catch the plague if he gets in too close proximity to this commanding figure who represents a threat—although this particular officer genuinely seems to be trying to de-escalate a family squabble.

Ms. Louvenia ambles from the sunporch, like a cat who has awakened from her nap. She stands a few feet from us, next to Papa George, clearly baffled as she looks on.

Wide-eyed and innocent, she asks, "What's going on?"

My jaw tightens. I can almost see vapors, since it feels like I'm pushing my breath from my chest and through my nostrils. "Nothing, Mom!"

My swift retort is matched by a spin on my heels. Whirling away from the three of them, I pass Analyn, who is still watching the events play out from the kitchen. I imagine she'll give a play-by-play briefing to Maxine.

The young, blond cop stands uninterrupted at the threshold on the other side of the kitchen. The few moments that have passed seem like surreal seconds in a never-ending saga of wondering what Maxine will concoct next.

My anger moves ahead of me, clearing a path. I follow it, not knowing where it will lead. I head in the direction of the kitchen where the young cop stands in all his blue authority. As I come upon him, he moves ever so slightly to the side, as if I've brushed him away.

The sound of my footsteps no longer click against the kitchen tile. I've passed the young cop and head towards the formal dining room. Behind me, the smacking of the cop's club against his palm is only a foot or two behind me, coming closer and closer on my heels.

As I enter the dining room, he's still in pursuit—just behind me—striking his club even louder into the palm of his hand–a gesture, no doubt, meant to intimidate me.

In the dining room, I stand in front of my mother's curio cabinet. Inside of it, several Lladro figurines are on display. The porcelain figurine of a Black bride and groom, which was the fiftieth wedding anniversary gift I gave to her, stands on one of the shelves. She had cooed over it, saying it would be an heirloom that she hoped I'd pass on to Robbie or his wife, someday.

"Hey!" the young cop warns.

I ignore him, snatching the magnetic door of the cabinet open. I reach inside for the cherished statue and take it from the cabinet.

"Don't take anything from the house!" he growls.

Somehow his bark does nothing to sway me. My face is hot. My jaw is tight. And my fists are clenched.

Without hesitation, I spin around to challenge him, carrying a strength I didn't know I possessed. I hadn't recognized it before, but his face appears to be closer to the color of his strawberry blond hair—slightly crimson.

"I. Will. Take. What is *mine.*" The snarl spews from my mouth, as if I've brandished a lethal weapon. The young cop bats his eyes in disbelief. He freezes as I bolt past him, out of the living room, and toward the entrance.

The pattern of my footsteps lands quickly and steadily against the entryway's tiles. The living room's carpet is no longer beneath my feet as I dart in the direction of the front door. I'm not sure where the cop is. He may still be right behind me. Maybe he's still standing in the living room.

My heart beats louder. And louder. I open the door and rush through. The late-morning gust of air welcomes me.

And carries me.

Down the driveway, a sense of reassurance kicks in when I see my car. Knowing that I'm about to jump in and escape this nightmare gives me a few seconds of relief.

As I glance down the street, I take in the stillness of the neighborhood. The late-morning clouds still loom overhead, as if their plans don't include leaving.

Two police vehicles are parked against the curb. One has its lights on, which seem to rotate in slow motion, and is parked in the wrong direction, facing the other police car against the curb.

The blue lights spin. And spin. Through the car's open window, the sound of crackling and static emits from the police radio. The dispatcher's voice is filled with inflections and codes.

The implication that a crime is being committed is surreal.

Is this for me? Was all of this because of me? My heart beats louder with each step I take. The anger and fear pound against my temples.

I don't believe this. Maxine not only called the police, but she obviously made it sound like an axe murderer was at my parents' house. I could have been seriously hurt!

My hands tremble as I get into the car and manage to put the key in the ignition. Every pant of my breath releases disbelief from my chest and through my nostrils. The wheels screech once I back out of the driveway and head down the street. After a few miles, my chest begins to feel lighter. And lighter.

Exhale.

Bit by bit, I catch my bearings and gradually do a sanity check. What just happened? It was real, but it felt like something out of a horror movie. It's as though today marks the beginning of something else. As though I'm moving towards another layer of something unfamiliar.

CHAPTER 43

My hand fumbles along the night table, as I try to distinguish the TV remote from my mobile phone. The display reads 5:45 a.m. I don't recognize the number. It says, however, that the call is coming from Arkansas. Who in the world is calling me this early.

Quentin stirs on his side, but otherwise shows no sign that the blaring noise has disturbed his sleep.

"Hello?" I whisper in the darkness.

"Hello, is this Darby Shields?" The wispy voice is hardly audible. My curiosity gathers.

"Yes. Who's calling?" I manage through my grogginess.

"This is Mrs. Archer from Banton University."

Her introduction means nothing to me, which is communicated by my silence.

"In the admissions and records department." Her volume goes up a few notches. "I spoke with you a few weeks ago about your mother's transcripts?" She waits for my response.

"Ohhh. Hello, Mrs. Archer. Thanks for getting back to me!" Her aged voice clues me in that she's missed a step in realizing the difference in our time zones. "Can you hold on just a second?" I ask. "It's close to six o'clock here."

"Sure. That will be fine."

That visual of a sweet old lady with gray hair, diligently working in the records department for decades comes to mind. Her southern dialect and charming tone has me imagining her as a fixture at the historical Black college. Apparently, it didn't occur to her of the difference between our time zones.

I hop out of bed and grab my robe. I stagger down the hall, past Robbie's partially open door. The streetlight beams through the window's partially open shutters. It casts a peaceful glow across his face as he sleeps. He looks as if his life has been unaffected. Just as it should be. As if evil had never touched his sweet flesh.

But it has.

In those few seconds, my world is untouched. The reality, however, is that I never imagined wickedness could be so close—hell-bent on destroying the good along its path. Though it hadn't occurred to me before, I've come to understand that evil has a beginning, and it has an end. Curses were made to be broken.

Somehow, I'm part of evil's ending.

I ease into my office at the end of the hall, where I switch on the LED lamp on my desk. It emits a light that eases the room awake. "Thanks for getting back to me, Mrs. Archer," I say as I sit down on the loveseat.

"Well, like I had told you when we talked the other day, there is no record of Louvenia Jackson at Banton University. But when I had some time, I went across campus to the records room where the older archives are kept." She takes a breath before continuing. "I searched through the microfiche of Sims Negro Teachers School. I had to go back many, many years," she declares, matter-of-factly.

"Oh, I sure do appreciate you going out of your way, ma'am," I acknowledge before she resumes. As anxious as I am for her to spit out what she's found, I'm over the moon by her willingness to investigate.

"Now, you said the year was 1965?" Mrs. Archer pauses, which feels like things are about to take a turn.

Without hesitation, I answer, "Yes, m'am. 1965, or perhaps within a couple of years."

"No. I don't have Louvenia Jackson's transcripts." Her declaration ends on a downward note.

The disappointment hits me. I was sure that I was on to something. Something hadn't felt right in my mother's biography that she had written years ago for her anniversary.

"But I did find something else," Mrs. Archer resumes unexpectedly. "What I have is a note written by your mother to Mr. Sims. He was the headmaster at Simm's College." I listen intently at her discourse of the history of the school. "Before it was Simm's College, it was founded as Simm's Teacher's College for Negroes in the early 1940s."

I hear the sound of papers being shuffled during her slight pause. "Simm's later merged with Banton University, which is now a Historical Black College. It doesn't look like your mother was a student at Banton."

"Oh, I see." The sense of doom surfaces in the pit of my stomach.

"Would you like me to read what I *do* have?" Mrs. Archer asks.

"Yes, I'd appreciate that." Wondering what information she has, I lean back on the sofa, anxious to hear what it is she's about to tell me.

Mrs. Archer begins reading. "It's dated September 20, 1964. It reads, Dear Registrar's Office, I won't be able to attend school on account of illness. I would like to receive my enrollment fee at once."

I picture my mother writing, as I'd always seen her at the kitchen table with the task of writing checks and handling the household bills.

"The money is very much needed. My date of registration is September 7th. My withdrawal is September 15th. Please let me hear from you at once. Sincerely, Louvenia Jackson," Mrs. Archer concludes the letter.

The chilling manifestation of what's been uncovered moves from my spine to my head. "So, you mean she was only in school for eight days?"

"That's what it looks like. As I said, there's no transcript, because she didn't complete the first semester," Mrs. Archer explains. "The only other document is the freshman application." The rustling sound of papers comes across again. "Oh, here's another brief note."

"Can you please read that one as well?" I ask.

"Surely. It's dated December 1, 1966. And it reads, Dear Registrar, I received a letter from Mrs. Monroe (secretary/treasurer), stating that if you would indicate the amount of refund that I am due, she would be in a position to make a refund check. I am asking if you will please do this immediately. I am very much in need of the money. Yours sincerely, Louvenia B. Jackson."

I'm without words, but a few manage to gather in my throat and faintly release. "Can you please send everything you have so that I can have it for my family's records?"

"Of course. It's the same address as the one on your request?"

"Yes, ma'am. Thanks for all your trouble."

"Not at all," Mrs. Archer responds politely before hanging up.

I stare blankly into space. Mom never mentioned that she was in college—even if it *was* only for a few days. Attending college would have been such a big deal for her. Small town country girl. I would have heard about it at some point in my life. I start doing the mental calculations. She would have been nineteen in 1966. If she had gotten sick and had to drop out, the story would have taken its place alongside the other legendary ones.

She always wanted to be a teacher, though. Funny how she never answered when I would ask what stopped her from becoming one. Her version of that particular period of her life always began and ended with being stationed in Germany, shortly after marrying my dad.

In the muted lighting, I tap the off button on the phone. I sit, pondering over the new information like an unsuspecting spider being lifted from her web. Somehow, I know that this new disclosure unravels another thread that has been spun into the Coleman family lore.

CHAPTER 44

Seated across the dining table from me, he's dressed in his favorite chambray shirt. He focuses his attention on his steak and collard greens. His dinner seems to offer him a welcome distraction from looking me in the eye.

I know this stance. I learned it well when I was growing up. It's what we did. Sweep things under the rug and forget about them. This is his way of pretending that the confrontation at Hava Java never happened..

But it did. And I don't pretend.

Although he appears engrossed in his meal, I can read through the pretense. He's uncomfortable because he doesn't know what to expect. He's not in control. I'm not convinced that his stroke caused a memory lapse. But I won't be surprised if that's the angle he'll try to play.

Of all the things he could choose to ask, I'm not surprised he chose small talk about church. For him? Any old talk will do. Not today. His face remains buried in his plate, signaling to me the importance of his unhindered ritual. The only sounds are the ones coming from his mouth as he consumes his dinner.

Trooper, as usual, lies close by on his cot in the corner, content and unconcerned.

He looks pointedly at me for just a few seconds, like a boxer anticipating his opponent's next punch.

The atmosphere is surreal. I'm clear about what I intend to accomplish. There will be no sweeping under the rug. Once again, the truth has been exposed, as if it's been calling me by name. The air in the room is thick, yet steady.

My mom inches nervously from the kitchen, toward the dining table. She takes her position, standing as an ally behind Papa George, ready to back him up, as usual, with more layers of lies. It's as if telepathy has played its role and called her in as reinforcement. She's unaware that this time it's *her* whose past has been summoned from decades of deceit.

This is good. My strategy seems to be working with little effort on my own. Keep them tied together to the foundation of their lies. It's what they've always done.

I take in their dynamics and let them simmer. Why didn't I see this before? Their shenanigans have existed my entire life. No need to decipher. It's just one big cesspool of lies. The entanglement, however, is about to be laid at *her* feet.

"Want some cake? I baked it this morning." The harmless question drips from her lips, like the sweet icing poured on top of the German chocolate cake that sits in full display on the kitchen counter.

"No," I respond bluntly. A chill passes through me, causing an unseen shift in the surroundings.

I'm not here for a tea party. I'm done with the chitchat.

I reach into my purse and pull out the first document.

"Whatcha got there?" Papa George raises his eyes from his plate while focusing on my every move. His question is like kindling being added to a fire.

Like clockwork, my mom takes her cue and changes the subject. "Oh, Dar-Bee, I'm so glad you came by today," she interrupts with a faint smile on her lips. "Cause I sho' been praying." Changing the subject has always been a Coleman tactic. She comes from behind the chair where she's been standing guard over my father. She takes the seat next to him.

Wonderful. Now she's sitting next to me. I direct my attention toward her and away from him.

"You've been praying?" The reservation in my voice seems to unsettle her. "What exactly have you been praying about?"

She stammers before answering, "That...that we'd get things settled."

"Oh, they're settled," I say firmly. "I've got something to show you," I gently add. "Oh, but before I do," I caution. "Sometimes secrets take forever to reveal themselves, but if they're supposed to, then that's exactly what happens. The truth will come out." I begin unfolding the documents in my hand.

Papa George stops chewing. A small leaf of greens hangs from the fork that he's holding and was about to bring to his mouth before he heard my comments.

The rustling of my papers is now the only sound at the table.

"What?" My mom mumbles as her jaws loosens. "What secrets?" she asks.

Silence.

If the distress on their faces is an indication of what they are feeling, then the torment must be tearing them apart.

I hadn't expected this. They're having a hard time dealing with my calm approach.

"I have a very old document from Sim's College for Negro Women. It's your application."

Papa George tries a diversion tactic. He mumbles, "Did 'y'all get your…?"

I ignore him by keeping my gaze fixed on Mom. "You always wanted to be a teacher, Mom. Here's your application from 1966."

She's disarmed. Not knowing what to say, she simply agrees. "Yeah, well, what … what do you mean?" Her eyes blink. Rapidly. By the look on her face, she's petrified.

"And you would have been a wonderful teacher," I add without restraint. "But something happened, and your dream faded away."

Papa George says nothing. She looks hopelessly across the table, gazing toward the window, then back at me.

There it is. That indignant look. The *"we're no longer talking about this"* look that I grew up with, especially when I ventured on to an unknown landmine with a harmless inquiry.

But we *are* talking about it. Now.

"This is your letter, Mom. From 1966. Here, let me read it to you." Each of my words are steady and deliberate as I begin plowing through the letter. "Dear Mr. Sims, Since I won't be able to attend school, on account of illness, I would like to receive my enrollment fee back at once. The money is very much needed."

She says nothing. The room feels like a raging fire with no place to run for cover.

I take in the moment, listening to their deep sighs.

"The date of registration is September 9, 1966. I conclude by reading the last line, "Please let me hear from you."

"1966? No. No-o-o."

She sounds delirious.

"Yes. 1966. And that's your beautiful handwriting and signature right there." I tap on the elegant cursive writing on the paper. "Here, take a look," I reply while delicately pushing the letter across the table toward her.

"Where'd you get this?" she asks, her voice cracking.

Her repetitiveness starts to wear on me. My face grows warm. "They sent it to me. They have it on record at Sim's College." Pausing intentionally, I repeat the sentence, enunciating each word. "They. Sent. It. To. Me."

"But *how come?*" she shrieks. She's caught in a loop, asking the same question but uttered in a different way. With each inquiry, the wailing in her voice heightens until it reaches a crescendo. Then it turns into a full-blown rage.

I almost feel sorry for her. Almost.

"Because I asked for it! It's the truth. And the truth will set you free!" The words leap from my mouth unexpectedly. Without warning, *her* anger has fueled *mine*.

Knowing that the job is not finished, I close the loop by stating the obvious. "You couldn't finish your first year of college because you were pregnant with Maxine." I take a deep breath and reload. "And so you dropped out of school, and went to live with your older brother and his wife."

A nervous giggle escapes her.

I take a pause to allow them to reflect on the truth that I've pieced together. "And that's where you had Maxine," I add delicately. "She was born in your brother's house. And *then* you met Dad."

With no defense, my mother glares out the window in front of her. She side-eyes me with a look of dejected venom.

At this point, I decide to tie up the loose ends. "And that's been the basis for how you all have operated—you keep my secrets, and I'll keep yours." Although I feel a bit of sympathy toward her, my gut tells me that this is not the time to take pity—on either of them. Their wicked entanglement of deception has been a breeding ground my entire life. It has caused Robbie so much pain and suffering. Heaven forbid, who knows what other grandchild is a victim of this sexual predator, who happens to be my father?

Yeah, they look feeble and frail, but I refuse to feel sorry for them. Not a bit.

Across the table my father shifts his weight. The back of his chair creaks in response. Here it comes. He's going to come to her defense, although I can't imagine what he could possibly conjure up. Their world is shattering right in front of them, after forty-five years of building layers of lies.

The unseen force which has been operating through cover-up and deception is dismantled. I feel its crippling presence crumbling throughout the room.

My mother's gaze turns from the window and is laser focused on me, as if she's seeing me for the first time. The disbelief spews from her pores.

I turn, directly facing her. "That's it, Mom. And there's the official stamp from the registrar's office with the amount refunded to you," I conclude by tapping the registrar's stamp, dated September, 1966.

"How'd you get that?" she asks.

Ugh. The reel has wound up again, leaving me wondering if there has been some lapse in comprehension. Each word grows angrier and the questioning gets louder. She starts to become vexed, reminding me of the day in the hospital, when I caught her off guard while watching *Wheel of Fortune.*

"How come they sent it to *you,* though?" The spiral persists as before, in the same loopy questioning.

"Because I *asked* for it!" I yell, fully aware that she still expects an explanation. A full accounting of what led me, how it led me, and why it led me.

How dare I not explain myself? The family pecking order tries to churn into motion, with its well-oiled spin. I imagine the sound of screeching like never before.

I ignore her questioning and brush it aside, like the buzz of an annoying fly. "Take a look at it, Mom. It's. All. Right. There!" My finger stabs the page as my words penetrate the decades of family lies and cover-ups. "You were only there for about a week! You had to drop out because you realized that you were pregnant with Maxine!" I leave it at that, although I wonder who Maxine's biological father is.

This explains it all. And Maxine's known all along.

But who is her biological father? Why has this been a secret my entire life?

"Wait now," she utters. Her daze has her holding both sides of her head, which she shakes, as if a convincing lie will be spun from it. I turn my attention to my dad, who still sits dumbfounded with his mouth open. Moments earlier the fork could be heard clinking as it dropped from his clutched palm and onto his plate.

Sensing that I'm finished with Mom, his eyes grow big. It's as if he wants to hold on to something; however, there are no physical reinforcements for him to grip. No rails. No support. Only his chair which has no arms. From the look on his face, a chair with arms might not be enough to hold him up, anyway.

"I don't believe this shee-it," he mumbles in sheer disbelief. His eyes are still fixated on his plate. His body shrinks in a trance-like state.

I push back from the table, then walk around and stand beside him. I place my hand on his shoulder. "Oh, Dad, by the way, here's another picture of Gator." Sensing the need to reinforce the truth, I add, "You know, your *son*?" I let the mock inquiry sink in. "Here's another copy of the picture I gave you at Hava Java. It was taken in Grandma's front yard in Piperton.

The thickness in the room is still. There are no words left for either of them to speak.

As if by intuition, the phone in the kitchen rings, breaking the shreds of deception that have been built over the decades.

"Hello? Hello?" My mom frantically answers, as if she's pleading for help.

My dad still sits at the table, petrified, head hanging.

"And Dad?" I say gently. "It's time for you to come out from hiding and reveal what was done to you. The shame that *you* were sexually abused as a boy."

Did I really say that?

Everything goes still.

I can't explain why, but this revelation has only come to me in this moment, and my gut is telling me I'm right.

The foul aura has fled the room. A hush has entered. I didn't notice that Mom had hung up the phone.

My dad lifts his head, as if he's coming out of a drunken stupor. "Thank you for that." His voice breaks after clearing his throat.

I don't believe what I'm hearing. Is he really acknowledging what happened to him? That he was molested?

My keys lie on the kitchen table, where I first left them. Although I haven't even been here for half an hour, it feels like an eternity. I feel emotionally drained, which is my cue. I grab my purse that's hanging on the chair where I was seated only moments ago and leave.

As I start my car in the driveway, I look up to see that my mom has followed me outside. She's standing on the walkway, sniffling while the back of her hand wipes the moisture from her eyes. She looks like she's figuratively been dragged across a room. She sheepishly hobbles toward the car. I feel for her, yet I don't. There's nothing else for me to say. Even though I don't want to deal with her, I let the window down a few inches, wondering what on earth she might say to add to today's drama.

She struggles for words, which are hardly above a whisper. "How did you know that your daddy's not..." her voice is barely audible, "Maxine's father?"

This time she's the one asking a forbidden question. Her tears flow freely as the seconds pass. Fully aware that the tables have turned. I offer her a blank stare. She asks again. "How did you know that your dad isn't...?" Though she's clearly weakened by today's revelation, somehow, she's determined to press on. She abruptly stops her questioning and inches closer to the car, clearly expecting me to engage her. She persists, "Who, who...told you that?" I feel sorry for her. Just a bit.

Ohhh, hell no! I can feel it coming. I won't go back into the muck and mire by getting into a debate that will go nowhere. She's asking only with the motive of challenging whatever I'll say. They've never been ones to be held accountable—and surely not by their youngest kid.

"Step away from the car, Mom," I gently coax.

She takes a few feet back as I put the car in reverse.

I'm emotionally exhausted—which has fueled my rage. Glimpses of her whispering in Robbie's ear flash before me. She really thought he'd keep their secret and never tell anyone. The sinister layers of she and my father's ways seem to have no end.

The fact that shreds of truth came out of them today is more than I could have imagined. My heart is pounding. I'm saddened, yet relieved that the jig is up. Their secret pact, *You keep my secret, I'll keep yours* has been dealt a serious blow.

This was the foundation upon which they built their union. My dad used her secret as leverage for his own. He used her as an accomplice. He did whatever he wanted to do, which included molesting Robbie and other family members. Apparently, she felt that there was nothing she could do about it.

My premonition has surfaced right before my very eyes, along with the reminder of Dr. Floyd's gentle explanation, "She's an accomplice *and* a victim"

Robbie's too young now to understand the larger story. The story of the foundation being laid from his grandparents' secrets. The story of how a generational curse moved through their deception.

I wonder how the story will play out as part of his healing journey.

I'm hopeful.

As the car backs out of the driveway, the unfinished piece of the question lingers. Who is Maxine's biological father?

I glance into the rearview mirror and watch my mom looking lost and alone in the driveway. With her hand clasped to her mouth, she stands there, sobbing uncontrollably.

CHAPTER 45

W hy doesn't anyone pick up? Moments ago I listened to Jackson's message, saying he had been trying to reach Mom and Dad for days. He'd left several voice messages but had not received a return call.

I hang up and dial Jackson's number.

Trying not to sound frantic, I pose the question. "Hey, It's Darby. I was wondering if by any chance you've heard from my parents?"

"No, I haven't. But I thought of something since I spoke with you a few days ago." His response carries the signal that he's aware of the family dynamics and thought of something that may be meaningful.

"Really?"

"Yeah, when I called, the caregiver answered the phone. I asked for Aunt Louvenia, and she screened the call, asking who I was. I told her that I was her nephew, Jackson." He pauses to gather his thoughts. "A few minutes later, Aunt Louvenia came on the line. She sounded hesitant, like she couldn't talk freely. I got the sense that the caregiver was on the other end, listening in."

"Maxine is on a power trip, since she has power of attorney. I realized this after the incident on New Year's Eve, when the police were called during my visit at my parents' house. One of the things I really took note of was how Analyn, the caregiver, was being used to enforce Maxine's bad behavior." As I'm conveying this to Jackson, another thought crosses my mind, which adds more fuel to the fire. "I just thought of something Maxine had warned me, 'If you have anything to say to Mom or Dad, you have to come through me.' It's starting to add up. She's been planning to isolate my mother for some time."

"Yeah, that doesn't surprise me about Maxine," Jackson chuckles. My silence seems to hint that I'm worried. "I know there's probably a reasonable explanation to what looks like the shenanigans," he consoles.

"I'm trying not to be alarmed. It's not like my mother to go weeks without calling me, especially since my father had another stroke and has been in a rehab for a few months. I'll let you know when I hear anything and when this situation all pans out."

I turn off the phone and place it back into the zippered pocket of my jacket. Continuing on my brisk walk, I'm greeted by joggers along the trail while I reflect on the occurrences of the past few weeks. Small flocks, as well as larger ones, are scattered among the sparse trail, but not a single goose operates solo. What a contrast to the family that I've grown up in. It always felt that the flock was in full operation only when there was a common cause. Oftentimes, I was the common cause. Maxine and Gloria had an amazing way of aligning together if there was an issue in which they needed to be a larger force against me.

I proceed around the trail, nearly a mile before I reach my house.

Quentin lowers the volume on the remote as I place the take-out bag on the counter. He turns his attention away from the football game and turns toward me. "How was dinner with your friends?"

"We had a good time. I guess you could call it the prelude to the bridal shower for Camille. There's only a few weeks before the real one, and Paige and I still have some planning to do."

He turns to me with concern in his voice. "Your mom called a couple of hours ago."

I step out of the kitchen, where I've placed his take-out order on the counter. Walking over to the sofa, I sit next to him while trying to keep my mind from rushing.

"What did she say?"

"She said she's at a place in Porto called Assured Assisted Living. She was able to get the information from a brochure that was lying on her dining room table. She doesn't remember how she got there, but she gave me the address and the phone number she was calling from." Quentin pauses, waiting for me to process what he's said. "She says she's fine. While she was on the phone, I could hear a door opening and someone saying to her that it was time for dinner. Your mom sounded pleasant, just confused as to why you hadn't come to get her. I wrote down the number and address and told her you'd call her when you got home."

"Okay, thanks." I pick up the mail on the kitchen counter and am amazed to see an envelope with Gloria's handwriting and return address.

> *Darby,*
>
> *It is not a good idea for you to visit our parents until you make a formal apology to clear the air. This will allow us all to be on the same page and maybe understand your motives. Your behavior is not having a good effect on our aged parents After all the ugly things you have said about our father, It is not OK.*
>
> *If you want to reconcile, then please consider making an honest, open, and recognizable apology that we can*

all understand. There are some things only you can come to terms with.

The relatives in Piperton are aware of the scandalous stories that you've made up about our father. They think that you are crazy. We apologized to them on your behalf.

We still can move forward though. You need to apologize for all the lies and chaos you have caused our family. It is time for you to come clean.

Gloria and Maxine

Oh bro—ther. I place the letter on the counter and head down the hall for a bubble bath.

CHAPTER 46

September 2011, Denton, California

The senior residents sit in their wheelchairs, which are pushed up against the walls of the corridor. It seems to beat the alternative of lying in bed all day. The distinct look of a blank stare is what they have in common. It's chilling to think that this reprieve from the confines of their room might be the highlight of their day. The smell of impending death looms heavily. Their dismal expressions along with their overall helplessness has reeled me in.

The drab-looking veteran's home is where Papa George is recovering from another stroke. But there's no hope for his Alzheimer's.

As I head down the long stretch of the corridor, my eyes rest on him. He sits among his new compadres, with his shoulders slumped, looking fearful and lonely. The towering man I'd known with the looming silhouette is a distant memory. I had never imagined that he could become even more frail since the showdown at Hava Java three years ago. But here he is, looking fearful and lonely in his wheelchair.

Hopelessness comes upon me, like an unexpected wave.

His eyes drift upward, conveying that he wants to ask for help, but one attendant after the other swiftly walks past him and the others.

Wow, he can't talk.

I wonder about the state of his mind. As each attendant passes, my father's forlorn look conveys that he wants to ask for help or at least inquire about something, but somehow he can't form the words.

The distinctly proud man no longer exists.

He tries hard to operate his new form of transportation but hasn't realized that the brakes are in the locked position. His body makes short jerking movements, forward then back. It's as if he thinks these movements, along with his sheer determination, will somehow force the wheelchair into motion.

Something stirs inside me as I gaze down the hall.

I don't want to feel sorry for him.

Never have I seen my father—once known for having an imposing persona—appear so weak.

All of a sudden, it feels as though there's an imaginary substance oozing from my chest. There's no tangible matter, but I feel the unmistakable form of something that I don't recognize or have words for. I stand there, looking intently down the corridor at my father.

The imaginary oozing in my chest continues to flow. It lands on the floor.

How strange.

It feels as though a foreign residue is leaving my body, directly from my heart. In that moment, I realize that's exactly what it is—the unsuspecting residue of unforgivingness is melting from my heart.

In the years since our meeting at Hava Java, I've realized that I don't want my life to become overburdened with bitterness and affect me physically and other parts of my life. The deliberate steps of literally talking to myself and saying, "I forgive him" have been my first feeble attempt at forgiveness. This has gone on for a few years.

My heart aches. I walk several steps and lean over his frail, slumped body. With as much jubilance as I can offer, I smile and say, "Hey, do you need some help?"

He looks up with surprise and relief. If he'd had the energy, he would have leaped into my arms. His face brightens as he struggles to form words. With determination comes a soft, melodic sound, "Darrrrbeee." He sits up in his wheelchair, like an eager child peering out of a car window.

"Lean back." I place one hand on his shoulder, grab the handles, and push him down the hallway—all while fighting back tears.

Once in his room, the limitations of his condition become more apparent. He makes several attempts to lift his body from the wheelchair to the bed as he points to it and mumbles. I'm aware that this new form of communication is the best he can do and is unlikely to improve.

"Hang on, Dad," I say as I locate the button to call the attendant.

The attendant arrives shortly after with dinner. He lifts Papa George, then props the pillows behind him. After he's made sure Papa George is comfortable, he slides the dinner tray in front of him.

"Th… thank you," Papa George mumbles.

I'm at a loss at what I've just heard from my father. I can't remember seeing my father so contrite. His acknowledgment of the attendant was not just done in passing. I actually felt it from his heart—as if he was sincerely grateful for the gesture that he may have previously felt was due to him. With an aching heart, I pull up the empty chair next to him.

I can't do this.

I feel an unseen presence next to me, as an encouraging voice whispers, "Yes, you can. You can do it."

I reach for the fork, expecting that he's opening his mouth to be fed. Instead a bewildered expression precedes the murmuring that he manages to force from his lips.

"I … I n-n-never k-knew, you l-l-loved me so much."

CHAPTER 47

"Oh, I see that you're George Coleman's daughter."

"Yes." The front desk attendant watches me sign the book while he introduces himself. "I'm Jason, the activity director."

"Nice meeting you, Jason."

He offers a comforting smile while as he sits behind the front desk, watching as I sign in.

"I played a card game with your father this morning. Nice guy. He was pretty clearheaded and engaging. I like to drill the newer residents to see what they remember about their previous home and their life. He told me that he likes to garden and that he has two daughters and two sons.

What? Who's my father counting as his children? Is he lucid? He left out a daughter, but which one? Was it Maxine or was it Gloria. My thoughts race. And two sons? Seems like he remembers the DNA fiasco and Gator, his nephew/son, but I wonder if he really believes he has another son? And which are the two daughters he's counting?

"Did he mention the names of his children?" "

"Nah, just that one of his daughters lives in Los Vientos."

"Oh. That's me."

Jason reaches across the counter, and hands me a large envelope, as he rolls his eyes. "Um, this is from your sister Maxine." He steps away from the reception area, then proceeds down the hall, presumably to attend to a resident.

To: Pleasant Shores Skilled Nursing
From: Maxine Coleman-Brown
RE: George Coleman

Please be so kind as to place in any of George's medical and/or administrative files.

This will establish and document our family's concern for Darby's mental instability and unsupervised off-site visitation with George.

Since I maintain the power of attorney for health care, please do not provide any health or personal information to Darby Shields regarding my father.

Please let me know if you have need of further information.

Maxine Coleman-Brown

After reading the letter, I head down the hall to see my father. Document my mental instability? Geeze. No surprise there. It's the usual campaign of tagging a family member as crazy, in an attempt to intimidate and control. It has its own elevated twist in my family. I guess I'm supposed to shudder at reading this letter. Why did she feel so threatened that she called the police on me when I was at my parents' house. As usual, it feels like an attempt to cover up something. I wonder what Maxine's up to now.

CHAPTER 48

"Hi-i-i! Oh, Tasha, I'm *so* glad you could come!" Maxine's squeal rings throughout the vestibule, greeting mourners as they arrive. One would think that she's at a citywide gala instead of Papa George's funeral.

Gloria follows Maxine's lead with uncontrollable glee as she bounces from one sympathizer to another. Her faux greeting, "Heya, girl," echoes throughout the foyer, followed by her nervous giggle. She dashes from one person to another, acknowledging their presence. Lost in Gloria's exuberance is the opportunity for the person to convey his or her condolences.

Two of Papa George's sisters and a brother have traveled from Piperton. They wait on the steps for the procession to form while standing several feet from Mom and me. I'm not able to identify who's who, and they don't appear anxious to greet me.

"Louvenia, how you holding up, baby?" my father's sister asks, after approaching my mother.

My mother pauses, loosens her arm from mine, before she responds, "Oh, I'm not so sure." She reaches out to my aunt, and the two embrace.

"Hi there, Darby," my aunt forces an unavoidable greeting. The chill of her tone coincides with the overcast morning.

Jackson had informed me that I've been labeled a troublemaker by the Piperton clan. The news of my father being both Gator's father and uncle had spread across the small town, faster than a lingering plague.

"She should have let sleeping dogs lie," I was told, is the mindset of the kinfolk in Piperton. A town whose population is mostly Colemans.

I wonder how Gator's taking our father's death.

The funeral director appears and guides Maxine and Gloria from the entry and onto the church's front steps. The two gather their entourage, dashing from the foyer to the front steps, where they join the procession. In their animation, they offer air kisses as they pass our mother standing at the front of the line.

The mourners stand as the family is escorted into the church.

My mother's sobbing is the only audible emotion that can be heard. It's as if she's the proverbial church mouse that has commanded the hush throughout the sanctuary.

"He served with distinction here at New Jerusalem Church. He was a deacon who could be counted on to visit the sick and shut-ins!" The pastor's praise of my dad is met with silent nods of approval. "He was a cherished member of *this* congregation and was a civic-minded individual who was also proud to serve his country!"

The ripples of his destruction feel like the aftermath of a structural shift. Part of his legacy is like a lingering residue that needs cleaning up.

My mother's sobs subside, causing my untamed thoughts to slip into the atmosphere, like steam from a pot. Those thoughts settle upon Robbie.

When I'd pulled out of the driveway nearly an hour ago, he and Quentin were in the front yard, playing with Rocco. Robbie's laughter echoed throughout the street as Rocco fetched the frisbee and playfully dashed back to him. It's been nothing short of amazing, seeing the resilience he's shown in the two years since he revealed the molestation. He has flourished as if evil had never laid a hand on him.

As much as I struggled to see my father in his final days, Robbie showed no emotion earlier this week when I told him that Papa George had passed away. His progress is has been wonderful, but at times I wonder how he'll cope when he's an adult.

The pastor pays tribute to George Coleman, and pours accolades upon his memory. Members of various committees and auxiliaries are seated together—a nod to their time of serving with him throughout the years. Their occasional amen or hmm-mm is the appropriate response when the pastor enunciates a point with which the individual agrees. Their jubilant response to the pastor's words causes me to drift back into the moment.

My mom clasps her delicate hand in mine. The brim of her black hat partially shields her eyes. She dabs them with the tissue she's been holding in her other hand. Her loud sobs blend with the pastor's words and compete with his eulogy.

Maxine and her family are seated in the row behind us. And behind Maxine, Gloria sits along with her husband and two sons.

No weeping.

No sighs.

Only the sounds of squirming as bodies shift in their seats.

"The next few minutes will be a quiet time in which you can silently reflect and read the obituary of our brother, George Coleman," Reverend Bello announces. Then he takes his seat behind the podium. After a while he looks out on the congregation and nods toward Gloria, signaling that the silent moment is over.

She steps up to the microphone. "Good morning, church. I'm George Coleman's daughter, Gloria," she says enthusiastically. "I'd like to celebrate his life by singing a song that he loved so dearly."

This is weird. When did she take up public singing?

She steadies herself at the mic, looks upward, toward the ceiling, while the pianist plays the introductory stanzas.

My mother's weeping gradually fades. Her expression changes as she looks at the stage with mild curiosity. I'm curious too. What bug has bitten Gloria to bring her to this moment? And what's the song that she's going to sing?

The pianist nods to Gloria, and she proudly takes her cue.

She goes into a rendition of "Swing Low, Sweet Chariot," unlike anything I've ever heard. Her voice deepens, going lower and lower, as she's swept up with the music and its melody. Her accompanist sheepishly looks up from playing—as if the runaway train that is Gloria can't be stopped. After a few verses, it's clear that Gloria is headed to an unknown destination.

"If I get there before you do," she belts out. She steps down from the stage and into the aisle. With each stride, she gets more revved up. "C'mon church! This is a celebration!" She throws her arms forward in full-performance mode. "Tell my friends Imma comin too." Gloria convincingly calls out the rhythmic phrase. Her mission to engage the audience is in full force,

"Comin' for to carry me home," the congregation manages to chant.

"Sing, girl!" A sympathizer encourages.

Gloria sings the last verse, solo. At this point she's fully immersed in the lyrics as she strolls backward towards the stage. She stands in front of the congregation on the opposite side of the church. Her head is held high as she sings to the heavens above.

She takes another few steps backward. Unknowingly, her backside brushes against Papa George's casket.

The flag which is draped across it slides to the floor. A few gasps can be heard. Across the aisle, a dutiful sympathizer in the front row rushes to pick it up. He quickly hangs the flag across the casket, then scurries to his seat several feet away from the mishap.

Gloria notices none of it. "But still my soul feels heavenly bound." She's still in that faraway place. The performance concludes as she stands on the stage, chin to ceiling, with outstretched arms.

"Coming for to...carry me ho-o-o-me!"

The final phrase is enunciated so forcefully that it seems that Gloria is planning on an excursion herself.

"Thank you, Gloria." Reverend Bello smiles as he stands and reaches for the mic. The congregation responds with muffled "Amens."

With her chest out and looking self-satisfied, Gloria takes her seat.

Reverend Bello concludes his praise of my father's well-lived life before pronouncing the benediction. My mother begins to cry again. This time a whimper seems to be all she can muster.

Two pallbearers begin the procession as the other two roll the casket behind them. An usher appears at the end of the row. She extends her arm, signaling to my mother to take her place behind the casket. I take my mother's arm as she dabs her face and steadies herself on her feet. The two of us proceed down the aisle behind the attendants. Mourners offer a faint smile or a conventional nod.

Reverend Bello stands at the exit, shaking hands as parishioners gather outside, mingling in small clusters. "Nice tribute to your father, Gloria." He pauses as he notices my mom and me linked together at the arm and coming out the door, just behind Gloria. He glances at Gloria, then back at me. "Are you two related?" he asks. His tone and furrowed brow feels slightly short of a cross-examination. Gloria seems uneasy that he's studying the two of us, seemingly looking for a resemblance.

"I'm Darby, George Coleman's youngest daughter," I answer.

The confusion lingers on his face before anything else is spoken. Gloria—now clearly agitated—darts away from the three of us and out the door, toward the clusters of folks mingling on the walkway and away from the awkwardness that has arisen.

"Heya, Girl!" Her faux greeting is a noticeable part of the backdrop.

"Here you go, Miss Louvenia," the hostess says as she lays the plate of steaming food in front of her. The weight of the morning has led into the afternoon of the traditional repast that has been set up in the church's hall.

"Try to eat something, Mom, even if you're not hungry."

She lifts her fork and takes a few bites of baked chicken, followed by green beans.

The mood of the sympathizers is lighter, with a buzz throughout the room. Much of the banter focuses on favorite memories of George Coleman and times shared with him. Many of the stories are unfamiliar.

An elderly Black man comes to the mic. "I just want to say a few words about how much George Coleman meant to me. He mentored me and many Black veterans who were making the transition into civilian life right after Vietnam. It was a real rough patch for me and my family. I owe much gratitude to him." He turns toward my mom. "Thank you, Miss Louvenia, for allowing him all the time that he took from *your* family to help me get on my feet. You be sure to call us if you ever need anything."

Miss Louvenia nods with a faint smile.

The acknowledgements continue for the next few moments before an unfamiliar woman approaches our table. She offers a comforting smile before asking, "Are you Darby?"

"Yes, I am."

"I'm Caroline, the office administrator at New Jerusalem Church. Your father left this in one of the classrooms upstairs." She extends a faded-covered Bible to me. "He always had it with him," she says before walking away.

Why is she giving this to me? I open the cover and turn to the inside page.

> Presented to: *Darby Coleman*
> *On this day of your baptism.*

I'd forgotten all about this Bible. He carried it all this time? I push back the lump in my throat.

CHAPTER 49

The repast winds down while mourners pay their final farewells and condolences. The mood has grown lighter as the afternoon has worn on. Except for a few stragglers, the crowd has thinned out. The fortunate few are being offered to-go boxes by the caterer as he and his team disassemble warming tables and other equipment.

My mom is several feet away, still seated at her table, nursing a slice of lemon cake and a cup of coffee, which I'm sure is lukewarm. I notice three ladies have surrounded her and are deep in conversation. Mom smiles at the group, fully enjoying the fellowship. The four of them chat like friends who haven't seen each other in a while. And I'm sure they haven't. She was fully devoted to Papa George and hardly went out during the final months of his illness.

"Now, Louvenia, I'm going to call you before too long. We're going to get together and play Bid Whist with Viola and them like we used to," I hear one of the ladies say.

I feel better knowing that Mom's mood is somewhat lighter since this morning. I can sense it from across the room. She nods her head in response and manages a short laugh. She reaches over to the empty chair where her handbag lies. Her "pocketbook" is what she's always called it. She opens it and pulls out a pack of gum. Yes, of course, gum, Kleenex, and feminine hygiene items— the staples every woman should carry in her handbag. That's what she taught me. Ever since I was a young girl, I knew if I wanted a piece of gum, she had a pack. Watching her takes me back to my earliest memories of recognizing her love for Double Mint gum—which she was never without.

Any type of gum wouldn't do. No way. Back then I didn't have a name for the brand. I just called it the green gum because there was no mistaking that bright green wrapper.

A smile comes across my face as I think about the surplus she used to have stocked away and the memories of going into her bedroom and finding her stash.

What has been tucked away in my subconscious has now resurfaced.

The jasmine scent of my mother's perfume enticed me into her bedroom. Her exit was always my cue to drift cautiously from the shadows, down the hallway, and into her room. I was delighted that no one else was there. The white chenille bedspread was as soft as I imagined floating clouds to be. I loved to lay on it, running my fingers along its delicate fringes. The atmosphere in the room was as pleasant and as charming as she was in her early '30s, at the time.

The room held the allure of forbidden territory, especially for a young girl of four. Although I was sure to be chastised if found wandering there, I couldn't resist. I was enticed by the captivating space of my mother.

Her iconic scent was the required accessory that displayed her femininity. Playing with her perfume was an absolute joy. Rarely would she head to church or any other special occasion without it. Mom's appealing tastes and mannerisms matched her outward appearance. She never left the house without looking "put together." Although acceptable at the time, she wouldn't dream of shopping for groceries at the army base exchange with curlers in her hair, covered by a headscarf. Her sense of dignity and aesthetics wouldn't allow it. I often took her presence in, aware of the subtle distinction between her and some of my classmates' mothers, both black and white.

I especially loved playing dress up with the contents of Mom's bureau drawer. That's where the treasures were. Mom had the prettiest things. I would search through its contents, adorning myself with the same things she wore: necklaces, brooches, and—oh—those white gloves. Never disappointed in the contents, I was delighted to also find the green gum among her things, as usual.

I often recalled seeing an obscure black-and-white photo hidden beneath the brooches, earrings, and green gum. A handsome man in an army uniform would stare back at me. He had a smile that glowed like the moon. As usual, the photo was always there with the other items. There were no other pictures inside the drawer. Not of family or anyone else. How strange. As I became older, I often wondered about that soldier, imagining that women surely swooned over him.

He wasn't my Dad. Who was he? Once I was able to read, I pondered the message on the back of the photo.

To, Louvenia
Love, Art

Tucked forever within the recesses of my mind lay this recurring childhood experience, along with the mysterious soldier in the photo. There was something vaguely familiar about the soldier, although I couldn't put my finger on it.

Years and years went by. Sometimes I forgot about the mysterious man, as my cares gave way to childhood indifference. If I decided, however, to peek into the drawer for a piece of chewing gum, my forgotten curiosity would pique once again. I would stumble upon the obscure picture, tucked deep in the bottom of the drawer. The fact that it was always there nagged me from time to time.

Deep within my soul, I knew not to question my mom. She had a quiet, calm indignation about her—aloofness and all. I recognized it in her even as a child, especially when the subject was something she didn't want to talk about. The fact that the picture was buried beneath other articles in the drawer certainly contained the hidden message: "Don't ask." My questioning would be useless.

I knew that she wouldn't reveal the stranger's secret identity to me. After all, I was a child who had long ago received the message not to question adults about "adult business." Somehow, I knew that this was one of those forbidden topics.

Year after year, I peeped into the drawer, got my gum, and put the identity of the handsome soldier out of my mind.

Out of my mind—until now, as I reflect on Bishop's counsel, "Don't get ahead of the Holy Spirit." Like Sherlock Holmes, the Holy Spirit has decoded mysteries and illusions I couldn't explain. He led me down the trail of my childhood, and to my father's boyhood home. Then the Holy Spirit awakened my suspicions, and revealed Gator's paternity through forensic evidence.

I watch my mom, still seated across the room, as the memory of the green gum beckons me. It's luring me onto another path with morsels of clues. A new understanding came from the previous route I'd traveled. But once again, I find myself picking up breadcrumbs.

ACKNOWLEDGMENTS

It took a village for this project to materialize. I'm extremely grateful to all of the individuals who allowed their energy to be woven into *Picking Up Breadcrumbs*.

To Pastor Tammy, All I knew was that I was meant to write. But, it was you who pointed me towards the redwood forest where this project officially began. Thank you for being a gentle reminder for me to stay the course.

Tommy Mouton, Your mantra, "Just let the story carry *you*," echoed until I was ready to surrender. I appreciate your coaching and for being in my ear.

Joanne Newberry, I'm always amazed by your perspective. Your ability to imagine the unimaginable is remarkable. Thank you for seeing what I could not.

Rev. Donna Edward, Thanks for being an example of "pushing through" and holding me accountable to that weekly word count. Your consistency is exceeded only by your gracious heart.

Becky, Christine & Tanya, All of those evenings in the coffee shop showed me what was possible for this story's existence.

Asya Blue, The artistic narrative on the book's cover takes my breath away. You took hold of the vision and designed elements that nearly leap from the page. It was a pleasure to hand you the reins.

Rosanna Chiofalo Aponte, Your insightfulness strengthened the narrative. I appreciate your talents and the editorial assessment which added more structure to the story.

To the folks at Milele Press, Your guidance and kindness is beyond what I'm able to express. Thank you for showing up at all the right times.

Mitch, Debby, Chris B. Giovanni, Chris, Ben, and the entire San Jose Writer's Group, I'm grateful for the time each of you took to critique my work. You pushed me until I hit my stride.

Mandy, Aunt Willa, Sheila, Sheryl, Anita, Karen, Brittney, Stephanie, Tanya, Erica, Lauren, You are spectacular beta readers. Your feedback helped me breathe through the final push. What a team of midwives!

Prayer Warriors 4Life, GGN & Morning Glory, Your prayers soared through the heavens, enabling this book to be birthed. Thank you.

Dear Pastor Long, Thank you for helping me grow.

Deborah, Julie, Glenda, Anita, Tanya, Renea, Your laughter, and sharpening is everything. Thanks for being family and for growing with me through life's bumps and bruises.

My cousin, Errol, Thanks for filling in the gaps for which I had little understanding.

Victor, you're the quintessential big brother that any little sister could only imagine. Thanks for being my biggest cheerleader.

To my family, My beloved Sid, always a steady and reassuring hand and my quiet inspirations, Darren & Melissa. Sometimes I wonder why God has blessed me so much. I love you beyond eternity.

And to you, the reader, thank you for being drawn to this novel, and for trusting me with what I hope is a captivating story.

*If you enjoyed this novel, please consider
leaving an online review.*